FINAL THESIS

FINAL THESIS

A NICK TOLAND MYSTERY

WILLIAM L. STORY

ST. MARTIN'S PRESS
NEW YORK

Design by Richard Oriolo

Library of Congress Cataloging-in-Publication Data

Story, William L.
    Final thesis.
    I. Title.
PS3569.T6554F5   1989   813'.54   88–29875
ISBN 0–312–02576–9

First Edition
10 9 8 7 6 5 4 3 2 1

FOR MARIE, SUZANNE,
AND DAVID

Special thanks to Chuck Taylor for giving me encourage-
ment and advice and to Jerry Tully for giving Nick Toland
added dimension. Dominick Abel and Charlie Spicer, of
course, I can't thank enough for seeing the manuscript
through and offering their counsel on where to add, but,
more importantly and much more difficult for an author
to see, where to cut.

FINAL THESIS

CHAPTER 1

It's not my style to say no to a pretty girl, especially one like Darlene Abbott, who, to tell you the truth, went a long way beyond mere pretty. I'm as big a sucker as there is for fluttering eyelashes and a breaking voice, not that Darlene deliberately turned on the histrionics, but, as I say, she was one fine-looking woman. Still, I found myself saying no, regretting it, not realizing I would regret it much more that night as I watched the ten o'clock news account of Darlene's murder.

We were sitting in the department office, where I'd been

correcting papers for my Freshman Comp I course. Actually, I had been doing more daydreaming than correcting, bathing myself in the sweet breeze blowing in the window. It was warm for late April and I longed to be outside, maybe sitting in the sun drinking beer or running on a beach, à la the opening scene in *Chariots of Fire*.

And then Darlene, whom I'd never seen before, had flounced in, all feminine and young and pretty, spring dress swirling around gorgeous legs as in a hosiery ad. Even old Tom Henshaw, who taught British literature and seemed neutered by age and too many years bent over sacred tomes, peeked over his half glasses, looking like Ben Franklin. He glanced embarrassedly away when he saw that I saw.

"Professor Toland?" she said, looking from Tom to me, her voice as sweet and beguiling as the breeze blowing in the window.

I've never been comfortable with the word *professor*. For me, it conjures stuffiness, pretention, and a tad of charlatanism.

I smiled, said yes, and tried to look pleasant. A fleeting image of running a beach with this lovely thing crossed my mind.

"My name is Darlene Abbott. Dr. Eigner suggested I talk with you."

"Oh. What about?" Norm Eigner was in the English department and was a friend. "Are you a student of his?"

"No. I'm not a student here at all. It's about a friend of mine who is Dr. Eigner's student. I . . ."

She seemed uncertain about something, so I pulled out the chrome and plastic chair from Jerry Buford's carrel next to mine and asked if she'd like to sit down.

She did, crossing those shapely legs. After a moment's

pause, she said, "Actually, would you mind if we talked somewhere else?"

I didn't. I was glad to get away from the compositions.

I asked if she'd like a cup of coffee. The cafeteria was just downstairs.

"No, thank you, but perhaps we could go outside?"

The English office is on the first floor near the exit to the quadrangle. Darlene stopped at the water fountain by the door, pushed the button, and took a drink. It was obvious she was nervous or agitated, and I was becoming curious. The refrigeration unit kicked in. She grimaced a little and said, "This water is terrible. It tastes . . . metallic."

"Kind of like drinking a nickel," I said.

Outside, students sprawled on the paths and grass.

We strolled and Darlene said, "I hope this isn't an imposition. I can't afford to pay anything, but Dr. Eigner said you might be interested in this sort of thing."

"Wait a minute. You've lost me. Pay for what sort of thing?"

"Well, I don't know who else to turn to. The regular police are no help at all and I can't afford a private investigator, but where you teach here and all and Kristin Williams is a student here, we—Dr. Eigner and I— thought you might, you know . . ."

"No, I don't know. I have no idea what you're talking about."

"Kristin Williams, Dr. Eigner's student, has disappeared and I'm really worried. I mean, she's just up and disappeared and no one knows where. Her parents, her boyfriend, the police even don't know where she is. It's been a week."

"Look, Miss Abbott, I don't want to appear rude or

dense or unsympathetic, but what has any of this to do with me?"

She looked puzzled. "Dr. Eigner said you were a kind of policeman or were a private investigator at one time. I . . ."

I laughed humorlessly. What the hell was Norm Eigner thinking? Wait till I saw him. "Miss Abbott, I'm a military policeman in the Army Reserve. A long time ago I thought about becoming a private investigator, but I'm afraid I can't be of any help to you."

"He said once you solved a case of a missing person."

"That was when I was in active service. It wasn't like this."

It had been a case with some twists and turns, going beyond a routine AWOL, while I was stationed in Germany, and had been written up as part of my profile in the faculty handbook. It was the sort of thing that amused academic minds, and some of the faculty jokingly referred to me as Mr. Keene, tracer of lost persons.

I said, "Mostly now, in the Reserves, I shuffle paper and supervise road traffic on the way to summer camp training." That wasn't at all true, but I didn't want to go into what I really did. "Besides, I have no jurisdiction."

"Oh." She seemed deflated. I studied her a little more carefully than I had. She looked about college freshman or sophomore age, maybe a bit older. As I say, she was exceptionally pretty, blond, fair-skinned, lightly made up. She could easily steal a college boy's heart or even a college professor's, especially one in midlife, ripe for a crisis.

"Look, tell me about it anyway. It wouldn't hurt."

She had stopped walking. "No. I'm sorry to have bothered you. I didn't understand."

"Really, please. Maybe I could offer some advice at least."

4

"Well . . ." She hesitated.

I nodded toward a nearby bench. "Come on. Let's sit."

She seemed to consider a moment and then said, "All right."

We went to the bench and sat. No one was near us, and it struck me that we might look like lovers. I wondered about my motivation for insisting on listening to her. If she were male or not so pretty I probably wouldn't be interested. Still, I had become a bit intrigued, although I expected not much more than a sordid little tale of pregnancy or abortion, not unusual on today's college campuses.

Colton College, where I taught, is a small, private college in suburban Boston with good roots. It's fairly well endowed and would probably be prestigious except for being overshadowed by Harvard, MIT, Tufts, and the like. I'd been there three years since getting my doctorate and leaving one of the state colleges. At Colton, Ph.D.'s teach their own courses and do time in the trenches with things like Comp I. But I felt it was worth it: the proximity to Boston, a quaint intimate campus all brick and ivy.

Darlene pushed some hair from her eyes and raised her face to the sun momentarily before beginning. She said, "Kris was doing a term paper for Dr. Eigner on illegal adoptions and was really into it with original research, interviews, the whole bit. I think her disappearance has something to do with her research. In fact, I'm convinced of it."

"A paper on illegal adoptions? That doesn't sound like the sort of thing you'd do for a literature course."

"It was a joint paper that she was also doing for a journalism course. Dr. Eigner allowed it. Anyway, in her in-

5

terviews she had contacted some pretty seedy people. I mean in the Combat Zone."

"The Combat Zone?"

Darlene nodded. "I guess the angle was that runaways and prostitutes often sell their babies to an adoption black market."

"Wouldn't they just abort if they didn't want the child?"

"I suppose most do, but some, especially runaways, think they want to keep the baby until they hear an offer they can't refuse."

I plucked a blade of grass—a leaf of grass—that was growing tall in a clump near the leg of the bench. "You said you 'guessed' that was the angle. Is that all? Just a guess?"

"No. I know that *is* an angle she was exploring. Kris is such a decent person, Dr. Toland. I mean, she really cares. I'd hate to think anything . . . Oh, God, I'm really worried." Darlene Abbott looked at me imploringly. She was gorgeous. Beautiful teeth. I'm sort of a tooth man, among other things.

And that's when, to my regret, I found myself saying no, not actually using the word but it translated to that. I smiled a smile I hoped she'd see as comforting and not paternal and said, "I hope this doesn't sound condescending, but I think it's likely you're jumping to conclusions. There could be lots of explanations other than sinister ones. As a matter of fact, that's likely. Most adults disappear of their own volition. We might quibble with the reason for taking off, but it's *their* reason."

"I know what you're saying. Someone gets fed up with it all, goes out for the proverbial loaf of bread and never returns. But that wasn't Kris. Just taking off is totally out of character."

She looked at me for a moment and then stood abruptly. "I appreciate your listening. Maybe I am jumping to conclusions. But I have this feeling. I suppose that sounds stupid or silly, like feminine intuition." She paused as if searching for something else to say, some further argument. "Well, thank you for your time."

"Wait," I said, also standing. "I don't know what I can do but I *am* interested." I took a pad from my pocket and wrote on it. "Here's my office extension number and the hours you can likely get me. When Kris shows up, it'd make me feel good if you let me know."

"Sure." Just a trace of cynicism. She had me figured wrong, but I felt a bit foolish anyway.

She took the slip of paper and I watched her walk away, thinking there was nothing stupid or silly about her at all.

My office hours were over and I had no more classes, so I gathered my stack of compositions and left for the day. I drove to my digs, three rooms on the top floor of a three-family on a quiet side street in a nice residential section of a North Shore town. I shared the rooms with no one except my cat Boxer, an alley rogue with double paws. Occasionally, Dr. Moira O'Shaughnessy, specialty Celtic literature, would drop by and we'd stimulate one another intellectually for a while before hitting the sack. It was a pretty good relationship. We gave each other plenty of space, which I really needed since coming off a hard divorce and all the trauma therewith. I saw my former wife as little as possible. I saw my fourteen-year-old son every weekend.

It was about four now. After feeding Boxer, I changed into a T-shirt and running shorts and shoes, and set out for my five miles, which included a couple of loops around a reservoir. As I ran, I savored the recollection of Darlene

Abbott. I have never as an instructor or professor had any dalliance with a student, not that Darlene was a student, but life is filled with first times.

I also thought of her story of Kristin Williams, but couldn't attach anything macabre to her failure to show up for a few days. I had enough police experience to know these things usually resolved themselves.

After my run, I toweled down and drove to the gym, where I worked on the free weights for a while. I'm glad to say that I'm not a yuppie Johnny-come-lately to the health scene. I've been running and lifting for over twenty years and am passable at each. Since the divorce, they mean a lot more than they used to.

Back home, I put a frozen lasagna in the oven, made a salad, and opened my first Bud. It was Bud this week, the old blue-collar standby. This Bud's for you, for all you do. I try lots of beers. Beer has also come to mean a lot more than it used to.

I got through a few compositions until the stove timer buzzed. I put my lasagna on a rack to cool and ate my salad. I put a small piece of lasagna aside for Boxer. For a cat, his tastes are eclectic.

I opened another Bud and attacked the stack of compositions again until I felt my eyes begin to cross.

I put on a Zamfir tape, and when that ran out it was time for the ten o'clock news, if I could stay awake through it. I didn't know, though, that I wouldn't get a lot of sleep that night.

The feature story on the news was of the brutal stabbing of a pretty young woman near the Combat Zone. The trench-coated reporter, live in front of an alley beside a restaurant in Chinatown, related the grim details.

And then the room tilted a bit when the photograph of a smiling, lovely Darlene Abbott, the murder victim, flashed across the screen.

CHAPTER

2

If I hadn't bumped into Norm Eigner in the department office the next day, I certainly would have looked him up. As it was, I nearly phoned him that night after I watched the news. After all, in a way, I owed him the loss of a night's sleep.

Norm Eigner is about my age, early forties, a bit pear-shaped, male-pattern baldness rather well advanced, thoroughly unglamorous, thoroughly rumpled in clothing and grooming, and thoroughly likable. He has a penchant for telling poor jokes poorly and indulging in what he sees as a mischievous sense of humor. He's the kind of guy who might leave plastic vomit on the table. But in him, it's droll.

He was reading Thomas Mann's *Death in Venice*. He teaches a course on the novella. I sat beside him and watched him underline his book and nod to himself.

After a few moments, he said, "Think they'll appreciate Mann's use of leitmotif, Nick?"

I murmured a sound to the rhetorical question.

"I doubt they will," he said, providing his own answer. "Matter of fact, I know they won't. Students, even at Colton, don't much go beyond being groin or dollar-sign motivated."

He put his hands behind his head and leaned back. He was dressed in an old herringbone sport jacket (elbow patches, naturally), corduroy trousers that hadn't seen an iron for some time, blue button-down shirt open at the collar as a concession to the balmy temperature, and dirty white tennis sneakers. In someone else, the tennis sneakers would have been an affectation.

"Course, on the other hand, I can't say I blame them. At times I see myself as a purveyor of pure poppycock. Imagery, symbolism, motifs. I mean, what's the application? Ever feel that way, Nick?"

"Occasionally. Look, Norm, about that girl you sent to see me yesterday."

"I suppose it's art for art's sake. I hope Art likes it." He looked at me to see whether I appreciated the pun. I smiled.

"What girl?" He furrowed his brow. "Oh, yes. The one I sent to see Mr. Keene. Pretty thing. I thought you wouldn't mind."

"Did you watch the news last night or this morning,

Norm? Or read the paper?" I handed him my copy of today's *Globe* opened to page two. Darlene Abbott smiled up at him.

"Jesus." He skimmed the story.

"I caught it on the ten o'clock news last night. It knocked the wind out of me."

"My god, this is awful," Norm said. He looked at me. "I suppose this lends credence to the poor girl's concern for her friend. Or does it? What do you think?"

"I don't know."

"You're a cop, Nick. I mean, in a way."

"Look, Norm, I think maybe you should go to the police and tell them this girl came to see you and what about."

Norm took out a handkerchief and wiped his forehead. The handkerchief was monogrammed NHE. Probably from his wife.

"God, I feel awful," he said. "The poor girl came to me and I just dismissed her. Sent her to you."

"And I did nothing."

"Yeah, but what—"

"I could have done something. I don't have jurisdiction but I do know a lot of civilian cops. I know procedure. I just didn't take the whole thing seriously."

"Nor I." Norm slammed shut his *Death in Venice*. "We live in this academic fairyland and when something real comes along we don't recognize it. Images, symbols, leitmotifs. Bullshit." He stood as if to go somewhere and then sat again. "Of course, maybe there's no connection."

"Norm, she told me a little about this research paper Kristin Williams was doing for you. What else can you tell me?"

"Well, she wanted to know whether Kristin had indi-

11

cated any names to me, you know, on note cards or a preliminary outline."

"And?"

"And I told her that material was at home. I couldn't remember what Kristin had submitted. To tell you the truth, I couldn't even remember right away what Kristin's thesis was. She asked whether I'd check and could she get back to me. I said I would and she could, but not very enthusiastically, and I guess she recognized the evasion. That's when I suggested she see you."

"She told me she was doing the same paper for journalism."

"Yeah. Dan Ritchie. Maybe she contacted him too."

"Maybe." My mind was still cottony from not enough sleep last night. After the jolt of the newscast, I had finally drifted off but slept only fitfully. A shower and coffee had done little to revive me.

I said, "Instead of you going to the police, let me. But first I'd like to see Kristin Williams's note cards, outline, and whatever else she gave you."

"Ah, the detective in you cometh out, eh? That wouldn't be tampering with evidence or anything like that, would it?"

"When are you off? I could drop over to your place, if that would be easier, to see them before going to the cops."

"I'm done for the day at noon. Done here, that is. Elaine has shopping plans. She's been muttering about new curtains and wants me to drive her. I can't imagine anything duller unless it's digging through Thomas Mann looking for leitmotifs."

"Well, no, if Elaine—"

"Jesus, come. Maybe she'll go by herself. I don't know

why she feels she has to have my opinion on something like curtains."

"Don't knock it. Barbara never wanted my opinion on anything."

"Well, none of my business, but I'd say you've found a fine woman in Moira O'Shaughnessy. A kindred spirit. Guard her."

"Two purveyors of pure poppycock? I don't know, Norm. That might be a lethal combination."

Norm Eigner lived in Cambridge close to Somerville but also close enough to sniff Harvard. To me, that might be too much like living near Fenway Park but knowing you'd never crack the bigs.

I sat in the living room with Elaine Eigner while Norm changed out of his academic robes upstairs. We sipped diet Pepsi, the only thing cold that Elaine had. I hate the stuff but Elaine had insisted. "Of course you'll have some. It's hot out. Norm brings someone home without telling me ahead, what can I do? We never have beer in the house. Norm doesn't drink two beers all year. A hot summer's day, maybe we'll have a beer. It tastes nice then. But to just sit and drink beer isn't our cup of tea. But I know you like beer, Nick. I told Norm a hundred times we should keep a little beer in the house in case someone like you who enjoys a glass of beer now and then drops by. But he doesn't listen to me. I'm telling you, Nick, he's getting to be the typical absentminded professor."

She paused to sip. "So how are thing? We don't get to see you nearly enough. Whom do we get to see from Colton? Hardly anyone. President's reception, Christmas party. That's about it. Everything's getting too imper-

13

sonal. Norm says teaching is just a job now. 'I'm off to the factory,' he says every morning."

Norm came ponderously down the stairs in a sweatshirt and chinos, a transformation from professorial to janitorial.

"Norman, I was just telling Nick how we'd be glad to offer him a beer if we *had* any. But, of course, we never do."

Norm extracted a rumpled wallet from his rumpled chinos. "Hon, why don't you go out and get a six-pack. Get something good. Michelob maybe, or . . . what do you like, Nick?"

I shook my head. "No, please. No beer." I hefted the diet Pepsi. "This is great."

"Sure?"

"Positive."

"Norman, you're not going shopping in that sweatshirt."

"Hon, Nick and I have to go over some material in the den. It won't take long. Then we'll go shopping."

We escaped to the den, Norm's refuge, as cluttered and disheveled as I thought it would be. A desk, layered with students' papers and tests. A Quasar television, the obligatory bookcases. A recliner chair. One surprise: a caged parrot.

"That's Iago. The bird is evil, I swear. Diabolical. Keep your fingers clear of the cage. Swears like a sailor. Didn't get it from us. His previous owner was a student of mine. I think he fed the goddamn bird drugs."

Norm sat at his desk and I sat in the recliner.

"How did you get a parrot from a student?"

"The kid did a composition on parrots. We got talking about it, the paper, I mean, and he mentioned he had a parrot but had to get rid of it. His mother was allergic to it or something. Said I could have it. Told me he paid a thousand bucks for it. You believe that? You think he was pulling my chain? But, to tell you the truth, I kind of like the bird. Not like a dog that you've got to walk and pat. With Iago, I just give him some seed, clean his cage once in a while. No complications."

Iago's cage looked as though it hadn't been cleaned in some time. And I was waiting for him to say something, but he hadn't done anything more than stare flatly at Norm and me and raise his right foot from his perch and lean slightly to his left.

Norm shuffled through the morass on his desk for a moment and said, "Okay, here it is. This is what Kristin Williams gave me. Note cards, preliminary outline, and working bibliography."

He handed them to me. I looked at the preliminary outline first and read her provisional thesis: A substantial black market for adoptions is supplied by runaway girls and prostitutes.

Then I shuffled through her note cards, and then again more slowly. "Norm, do you have a piece of paper and a pen?"

I jotted down names of people Kristin had interviewed in her primary research. It wasn't difficult to determine that they were, as Darlene had said, runaways and whores. I counted sixteen. Sixteen women—or girls—apparently had babies that they sold to some type of adoption black market. The sixteen names had been unearthed by one college girl doing casual research. What lay beyond that? What kind of money was involved here?

I felt a chill of apprehension for Kristin Williams.

"What do you have?" Norm asked.

"Names. Lots of names."

"You know, Nick, when I sent that girl to see you, I certainly wasn't trying to involve you in anything serious."

"I know that, Norm." Norm was trying to make me feel better or maybe himself but it didn't help. True, I had looked into one or two matters unofficially, but never a homicide. Not that I could have predicted Darlene Abbott's death and not that we knew it was in any way connected to Kristin Williams's. I kept telling myself that.

I said, "This guy's name is on four cards. Gerald Mason. And this one, Ronald Simpson, is on three." I wrote them down.

"Who do you think they are?"

"Pimps?"

Without thinking, I took a sip of the diet Pepsi. "What's this?" Paper-clipped to the back of one of the cards was a small piece of lined paper. I unfolded it. "Lieutenant Brian Connolly?"

"Cop, huh?" Norm said.

"Hmmm. Probably. I don't recognize the name but the Boston PD isn't Cow Dung, Wyoming. It's big. Of course, he doesn't have to be a Boston cop or any cop, for that matter."

"But what else?" Norm said. "Military? Army or Navy?"

"He's gotta be a cop," I said. "But I'll check."

I put the paper with the names I had written in my wallet and stood to go. I considered finishing the diet Pepsi out of politeness but decided to hell with it.

"You know what we're doing, don't you, Nick? We both feel guilty and we're trying to make amends, belatedly to be sure."

"Norm, let's just say we have some information that might be useful to the police and let it go at that."

16

Norm nodded and also stood. Iago squawked a piercing, metallic screech that startled us both. "At least it's clean," I said.

Norm fingered his sweatshirt ruefully. "Curtains," he said. "I'd rather read Thomas Mann."

I used a pay phone in one of those drugstores that sell everything from motor oil to grass seed to call Joe Forgione, a staff sergeant in my unit who is a detective with the Boston Police, I don't know what grade. Joe works nights and I remembered that he said he sleeps till one o'clock at the latest.

He answered on the third ring.

"Joe, Nick Toland. Sorry to bother you at home."

There was a pause and Joe said, "Oh, yeah. Hi. What's up?"

I recognized his problem. I had referred to myself as "Nick" and he didn't know how to respond. I was a major and, although the Reserves are informal, the informality didn't extend to his calling me anything but Major or sir. Former students often had the same dilemma. A first name stuck in their throats.

"Joe, can you can help me? I'm trying to locate a Lieutenant Brian Connolly, maybe with the Boston PD. You know him by any chance?"

"Hmm. Brian Connolly, Brian Connolly, let me think."

There was a pause. I heard a young child's voice in the background, preschool. At the drug counter, an elderly woman peered myopically at the prescription the pharmacist who looked young enough to be her grandson handed her.

"Yeah, there's a Brian Connolly at Headquarters, I think. I'm not sure whether he's a lieutenant." Another pause. "You want me to call? I can find out for sure. It's no problem."

"No, no, Joe. That's fine. It's no big deal."

"You sure?"

"Thanks anyway." I could sense that Joe wanted to ask me why I wanted to know but didn't dare ask. I was grateful for the barrier of rank as I hung up.

I lucked out. Lieutenant Brian Connolly was in and I got to see him. He sat squarely behind his desk, a good-looking guy in a scrubbed Irish sort of way, probably late thirties, early forties. He wore a striped, button-down shirt and charcoal pants. His hair, neatly parted on the left, was just beginning to show flecks of gray.

His office, a cubicle actually, and desk were the antithesis of the TV or movie cop's lair with disheveled paperwork and overflowing ashtray. Everything was right angles with Brian Connolly. A place for everything, and . . . well, you know.

"Darlene Abbott came to see you yesterday? And you had never seen her before? You didn't know her?"

"That's correct."

"And she came because she was upset over her friend's alleged disappearance?"

"Yes."

"And so you came to me because Kristin Williams had attached my name to a, what did you say, a note card that she turned in to you?"

"Not to me. She had turned in the card to a friend. She was doing research on an adoption black market located in the Boston area. I assumed that she had contacted you or was going to. I thought it made sense to contact you."

Sunlight shafted in through a window behind Lieuten-

18

ant Connolly. He was taking notes on a yellow pad. I couldn't see his handwriting but I was sure it would be neat and precise enough to tack over an elementary school blackboard.

He said, "Miss Williams did contact me. About a week ago with pretty much the same story you have. I work vice and she must have gotten my name. She gave me some names too. Girls: runaways, prostitutes. Two or three pimps. Some rather unsavory characters with the potential for violence." He paused, seemed to consider something, and then added, "More than the potential. They have records. Not for murder, but for beatings."

Lieutenant Connolly looked at his note pad and then asked, "Where do you teach, Mr. Toland?"

"Colton."

He nodded thoughtfully as though that information needed assimilation. "I don't want to alarm you, but I'm concerned that perhaps the characters Kristin Williams contacted know that she gave your friend their names, assuming that, in fact, she has disappeared or worse and that they, in fact, have something to do with it. What's your friend's name?"

"Norman Eigner." I wanted to add "in fact."

"And he teaches with you at Colton?"

"Yes."

"And you're assuming that there's a connection between what happened to Darlene Abbott and Kristin Williams."

"It seems like a possibility. That's why I'm here."

"Right. I appreciate that. Now, what I'm wondering is why Darlene Abbott came to see you."

"Norm Eigner sent her."

"Why? Why to you?"

Cops are funny about other cops. They are inherently protective of their own turf and suspicious of other cops. On the other hand, there is a bond, almost fraternal. I didn't know how Brian Connolly would take me. Factor in that I outranked him, but he was full-time civilian cop and I was part-time military. But rank sometimes doesn't cut any ice. Once I saw a Metro Captain in uniform get chewed out by Cambridge patrolman for double parking.

"I'm with the MP Reserves. Once, I thought of getting a private license. I enjoy, uh, puzzles. They know that at school." Years ago as a crypto expert I had dealt with ciphers.

"I see. Who are you with, if I might ask."

"The Three-fortieth, ninety-fourth ARCOM. CID here in town."

"At the Wells Building?"

"Right."

"Well, then, you'll understand if I ask a question or two."

"Of course."

"Your full name is?"

"Nicholas Toland." My mother was Greek.

"Address?"

I gave it.

Lieutenant Connolly took his time writing. The pen was expensive, probably a Cross.

"Phone number."

I gave that.

"And you are a professor—that's correct, isn't it, a professor?—at Colton."

"Yes."

"What do you teach, Mr. Toland?"

"English. Composition and literature."

Lieutenant Connolly smiled. "I've been calling you *Mister* Toland. I hope I haven't been shortchanging you. It's not *Doctor* by any chance, is it?"

"It is. But 'Mister' is fine."

Lieutenant Connolly waved his hand. "No, no. That's terrific. I took some extension courses and I know how tough it is." He gave a little Ronald Reagan shake of his head to underline his point.

"So you are a Ph.D. in what, English?"

"Yes."

"Great."

Something was askew. Brian Connolly was treating me too politely, too much as though I were Mr. Citizen.

"What time did the Abbott girl come to see you, Doctor?"

"Approximately three-fifteen to three-thirty."

"And you talked, where, in your classroom?"

"We talked outside. She came to the department office but she suggested we talk outside. There was another person in the office."

"Hmmm."

There was a pause and I watched the dust motes swirl in the sunlight slanting over Lieutenant Connolly's left ear. Outside, the city hummed and buzzed.

"Uh, no offense, Dr. Toland, but could you account for your activities and whereabouts last evening? You understand the reason for the question?"

"Sure." It had to be asked. I would have asked it. "From about quarter to six to quarter to seven I worked out at Masterson's Gym."

"Where's that?"

"In Lynn. Then I drove home and—"

"How long a drive?"

21

I shrugged. "Twenty minutes."

"Then what?"

"Then I stayed in. Ate supper, corrected some papers, you know, the burdened English teacher, watched the ten o'clock news, which is when I learned of Darlene Abbott's murder."

"I suppose that you can verify you were home last night."

The questions were taking a twist I didn't like.

"Why should I have to? Look, Lieutenant, I came here out of a sense of civic concern. If you're working vice, obviously you aren't the investigating officer. Naturally, you'll relate what I've told you to whoever is. But at this point, there is no established connection, is there, between Darlene Abbott and Kristin Williams?"

Brian Connolly spread his hands in a gesture of dismissal. "Nothing I know of yet."

"But, the fact is I can't verify I was home. My only witness is my cat. Maybe my landlords, but that's doubtful. They're elderly and probably didn't notice one way or the other. The second-floor tenants were out. At least their car wasn't there."

"Sorry. I withdraw the question. I was out of bounds."

"Lieutenant, I imagine a probable time of death has been fixed?"

"It has. Somewhere between eight and nine."

Our eyes held for a moment as that statement hung, pregnant with implication, I imagined. Cops theorize, a lot of it almost subliminal when the evidence is scanty. But it was easy to see the angle here, a romantic one. How did it look? The college prof smitten by the lovely young thing who finally spurns him. He does her in and then concocts this tale to cover himself, tries to appear up-

22

front and civically responsible. But I was concerned with being connected with Darlene Abbott's death through innuendo and supposition. That could have long-lasting, damaging results.

Lieutenant Connolly put his pen down and leaned back. "So you're with CID? Could I ask your rank? No, scratch that. I know you CIDs guard that pretty carefully. You're not an EM. I'd guess Major." He smiled. "Hope I'm not shortchanging you again."

I smiled too.

"One other thing. Were there names besides mine on those cards?"

I handed him a slip of paper with the names I had copied. He studied them a moment, shrugged, and said, "Some of the girls here I recognize. Combat Zone prostitutes. Gerald Mason and Ronald Simpson are pimps. They could be trouble. Especially Gerald Mason. He's bad ass. Mind if I hang onto this?"

"That's why I came in."

Brian Connolly stood and extended his hand. "I do appreciate your coming in. I'll see that homicide gets this. All information is helpful, but I don't have to tell you that. Naturally, they may want to talk to you further and to your friend . . ." Brian Connolly looked at his note pad. ". . . Norman Eigner. A doctor too?"

"Yes."

When I let go of Lieutenant Connolly's hand, I noticed the gold on his wrist. He was too layered with gold for a cop, I thought. Gold on his wrist, on his fingers, around his neck. And for some reason, I thought it didn't go with his neatnik personality. It looked like good stuff, although I had no expertise there.

I left the police station with a feeling of disquiet, not at all sure that it had been a good idea going there at all.

23

CHAPTER

3

Two days later, Saturday, saw me running with my son, Nicky, on Lynn Beach, which is long, flat, and rather picturesque with its sea wall and roadway right above it.

Nicky is on the high school track team and we often run cross country together or go to the track where I time him.

The warm weather was holding, which may sound odd to say in late April, but in coastal New England, spring is often a hoax. Small birds, terns I guess, scampered along the slick, compacted sand like nervous children, while gulls stood or strolled, conscious of their dignity.

Kristin Williams's whereabouts was still a mystery and the news reported the police had no suspects in the Darlene Abbott murder. But the sky and the ocean had the look of summer, I was with my son, I had plans for tonight with Moira O'Shaughnessy, and, while all wasn't right with the world, my mood was good.

We were running at a pace that allowed talk and we'd covered school and the Red Sox, who had had a pretty good April but we both knew they were as fickle as the weather.

"Dad, I can't wait till I can drive a car," Nicky said. Like sex, this is a normal enough but potentially risky teenage urge.

"Well, you've only got about two more years," I said, trying not to let my tone show that I was grateful for the wait.

"Nah. I can drive now. Gary lets me drive his Porsche."

"He does?" Gary was my former wife's steady. He was a CPA and had the big bucks that went with that.

"Not on the road or anything, but once at the rear of the mall parking lot and once in a state park or something in Ipswich."

I felt a twinge of jealousy. More than a twinge. That should have been me in the state park with my son, not this yuppie who didn't know that curly perms had gone out. He looked like a car salesman. And my five-year-old Fairmont two-door sedan certainly couldn't compete with a Porsche.

"Gary's an okay guy," Nicky was saying. "He's cool."

"Yeah, he seems like a pretty nice guy," I said. "How's Mom?"

"She's good. She's taking night courses, you know."

"Really? Where?" I kicked a beer can half full of something.

25

"At the Community College. Courses on taxes and the stock market. Stuff like that."

Probably she had designs on sinking her hooks into Gary and investing his money. But a CPA should be on top of that already. I foresaw trouble ahead if Barbara got a little knowledge and her opinion collided with Gary's.

I said, "Well, that sort of thing is always useful to know."

"I guess, but it sounds pretty boring to me."

We finished our run and went back to my place to shower and change. Then, at Nicky's request, we went out for Chinese food, which was neck and neck with pizza as his favorite. I didn't mind either one, myself, to tell the truth.

After we ate, I briefly considered driving to some deserted road to let Nicky drive the Fairmont, but quickly rejected it. I wasn't about to play catch-up with Gary. Instead, we drove into Boston, meandered through Quincy Market, where we did some more "chowing," in Nicky's parlance, and then walked over to the waterfront and looked at the boats tied up at the condos.

"That's my pipe dream," I said, pointing to a sailboat worth an easy quarter mil. *Serenity* was lettered on her stern. Gary probably owned something like that.

"Loot at that one," Nicky said, indicating a predatory-looking thing about forty feet long, red and black. "It's a cigarette boat, I think. Bet it'll do about seventy-five."

It reminded me of a PT boat. I said, "It's nice."

We walked to the aquarium, skirting around on the ocean side of the Marriot hotel, designed to look nautical. I pointed that fact out to Nicky but he thought the architecture missed its mark.

At the aquarium, Nicky decided he didn't really want to go in.

"It's pretty boring," he said.

I convinced myself it was adolescence talking but felt kind of hollow anyway. Barbara and I had taken him here a couple of times when he was little and maybe I was trying to recapture some of that.

For a while, we watched the seals in the outside pool—their antics amused a rather large crowd. We killed a decent interval that way until it was time to eat again. Actually, for Nicky, no interval was necessary. Chinese food might have won at lunchtime but now came the trade-off. We strolled to the North End and had a pizza at the European. Of course, later, I'd be eating again with Moira. If I did this every day, I'd soon be sideshow material. But today Nicky and I were cramming a lot in because he was going back with his mother tonight instead of staying the usual two days with me.

We had our pizza, big enough for a family, topped with things deadly to the arteries. I limited myself to one beer and denied Nicky's request for one.

"Be patient," I told him. "Soon enough you'll be drinking beer and driving cars." For all I knew, he was already drinking beer. Hell, he had driven a Porsche at the back of a shopping mall, which was more than I had ever done.

It was five-thirty when we pulled up in front of the house that had once been my home. I could easily become maudlin if I sat too long in front of it or angry, right now, because of the Porsche 944 sitting in the driveway. I thought I saw the bedroom window curtain move aside and I wondered whether Barbara and Gary were in there.

"Dad, I wish I didn't have to go to Maine tomorrow," Nicky said. Barbara and Gary were going to look at a camp in Maine, and Barbara had requested that Nicky be allowed to go with them. I agreed, thinking that he'd probably like to go.

27

"Did you tell your mother that?"

"No. She wanted me to go. It seemed important to her."
He paused and then said, "I'd rather be with you."

I tapped his arm and then let my hand linger on his
shoulder. "You'll have fun. Think of what you'd like to do
next weekend. We'll hit a Sox game or even a night game
during the week." We exchanged little punches and I
ruffled his hair. "See ya."

I watched him walk in and was glad when he didn't
even glance at the Porsche.

Maybe Norm was right. Maybe I felt guilty in some way
about Darlene Abbott. Maybe I was now concerned for
Kristin Williams. Or maybe the cop in me was coming out
and wanting to set something right. Maybe the wanting to
set something right was a load of bullshit and, all the
maybes aside, the curious cop part of me sent me back to
Boston. I was due at Moira's at eight and I wanted to pull
a quick reconnoiter. In fact, the whole time I was with
Nicky I'd been itching to scoot to the Combat Zone to
where Darlene Abbott had died. But the Combat Zone is
no place for a father and his fourteen-year-old son. At
least not this father.

The newspapers said that Darlene Abbott's body was
found by a Chinese cook in an alley beside his restaurant
on a side street off Washington where Chinatown and the
Combat Zone intermingle.

With my car safely nestled under the Common, I
strolled outside through the predictable throngs of
Frisbee throwers, prancing, menacing Dobermans, and
old folks feeding pigeons and squirrels. Near Tremont
Street, the omnipresent fanatic was exhorting a detached
crowd about salvation or doom.

Although the sun was low now, the air was still warm and managed to smell of spring even in the city. The trees on the Common were fuzzy and almost ready to burst.

I crossed Tremont, walked down to Washington to the pedestrian mall, and turned right. Quickly, I was in the midst of sleaze.

The Combat Zone, small by most big-city standards and probably overrated, offers routine raunch. As a rutty lad, I had put in most of my ritual of passage at Scollay Square's Casino. Innocent stuff it offered, compared to this, with its lights dimming just as you thought you were going to learn something.

I made it through the Combat Zone into Chinatown without being approached. Maybe I had cop written on me. Or English professor. Either one could be a turnoff.

Lee Chen's restaurant was less than one hundred feet from Washington Street, and the alley beside it ran back perhaps thirty feet and dead-ended against brick. I suppose if you've seen one alley, you've seen them all. Except that cook had seen something in this one that probably cost him a night's sleep. I wished I could talk to him but that would really be overstepping my bounds.

What the hell had Darlene Abbott been doing that night? An obvious theory was she had been checking on her friend. Had she eaten in Lee Chen's?

I surveyed the area. Restaurants, a laundry, a Vietnamese shop, and the fringe of the Combat Zone: a porn shop and a strip joint. Had Darlene been asking questions and then come to Lee Chen's to eat? It wasn't hard to imagine the scenario.

I checked my watch. Time to head home.

I crossed Washington and skirted around a police van

parked half on the sidewalk in front of a multi-X theater. It didn't seem to be affecting commerce.

"Evening, Doctor."

I turned to face Lieutenant Brian Connolly coming from the theater. Our eyes locked.

Then he smiled and his gold glittered in the fading sunlight.

At home, I showered, fed Boxer, and then drove to Moira's. I had done a nice job of digesting the pizza and would be able to hold my own when Moira and I ate.

I'm about a half-hour's drive from Moira's. She lives in Marblehead, the old part, on a one-car-width street without sidewalks. Her home is old, charming, and quaint, but it takes some getting used to wondering whether the front end of a Mercedes is going to pop into your living room at any given moment.

I swung into her driveway, brick in sand, and parked beside her Volvo. I think Volvos are a residency requirement in Marblehead. She was at the doorway. Just looking at her made me stop wondering (which I had been doing as I drove) what Lieutenant Connolly thought about my being in the Combat Zone. I was glad he hadn't seen me standing by the alley where Darlene Abbott had been killed.

Moira O'Shaughnessy is an Irish beauty of the flawless white skin, dark hair, and classic green eyes variety. She's not a fragile thing, but a respectable five-foot-eight or nine, with healthy flesh in all the right places. In public, she turns heads, and I know her students have fantasies about her.

As I got out of my car, I entertained one myself, and the desire to fulfill it made me forget about food. I held her and we kissed longingly for a moment. Then she pulled back, cocked her head, and smiled. "My, we are amorous tonight, aren't we? Usually you don't like to demonstrate your tomcat qualities here on the street."

"Well, let's go right to bed then. We'll have the wine and dreamy music after and maybe do it again."

"Nick, I think it's your urbanity that I find so attractive."

"That's all?"

"One or two other things, but you're going to have to woo me before we take a tumble in the hay. Translation: I'm starved. Let's go eat and get liquored up first."

"Oh, if only your students could hear this. But that's why I like you, my lass. You're not just a great mind."

We took her Volvo and found ourselves at a table in the bar of a local restaurant where the wait for dinner is never too long even on a Saturday night. I had a Sam Adams and Moira a Bloody Mary the size of a milk shake, one of which on an empty stomach could put some people under the table. But it didn't seem to bother Moira particularly. Irish heritage probably.

". . . and I think I've got a pretty obvious case here of plagiarism, but it's the usual dilemma: How do I prove it? I mean, for the entire course this kid just hasn't shown any kind of flair at all and the writing here is smooth enough for the *New Yorker*."

I smiled rather blankly.

Moira sipped her Bloody Mary and looked at me archly. "Nick, have you heard a word I've said?"

"Of course."

"You have not. I was telling you about a research paper comparing and contrasting Frank O'Connor and Sean

O'Faolain that I *know* was plagiarized. It makes me so damn mad."

"Is it adequately documented? Often you can get them on that."

"Hell, yes. It's letter perfect. I'm sure he bought the damn thing. With these term paper mills available, it makes you wonder about the value of research."

"Speaking of research," I said, "do you know a student named Kristin Williams?"

"No."

I told her everything from Darlene Abbott's visit to me to this evening's excursion to the Combat Zone.

"I'm a little worried for Norm Eigner," I said when I finished.

"If he's at risk, then Dan Ritchie probably is too, don't you think?" Moira said.

"Probably."

"And, of course, that Boston cop knows that you're sniffing around. Seems to me you've told me a thousand times cops don't appreciate outsider cops messing in their territory."

"Aw, he wouldn't necessarily think I was nosing around," I said, aware of the defensive note in my voice.

"If I were you, I'd rather he thought that than that you were watching a peep show or something. Doesn't say much for me if someone thought the guy I go with is reduced to peep shows."

"See what you've driven me to with your repressed Irish Catholic attitudes."

"Ohhh, poor boy. Poor dear." Her voice was lilting, suggestive. Sexual. Anything but repressed Irish Catholic.

She took a deep swallow of her Bloody Mary. "Come on, Nick, let's drink up, and after we eat we'll go back to my place, where we'll soar to ecstatic heights."

I moaned theatrically. "I love it when you talk dirty but poetically. It makes me tumefacient."

"Yum. I assume that's like tumescent."

"Better."

"Yum, yum."

My name was called and we were escorted to a table in the dining room. We ordered another round of drinks and our dinners, seafood croissant for Moira and steak tips for me.

"Moira, do you ever wonder about the relevance of what we do? Teaching, I mean. Specifically, what we teach. Norm said he feels that he is a purveyor of pure poppycock. That's how he put it."

She smiled. "Nice alliteration. But you know Norm. He's cynical. Nice guy, but burned out."

"I don't know. Frank O'Connor and Sean O'Faolain. Who cares. No offense. I've done the same thing. Foist things on students of questionable merit at best."

"Come on, Nick, spare me the angst. I know you're a damn good college professor and probably a damn good military cop. But you're not a civilian cop so butt out where you don't belong, which if I read you right is what you're doing or thinking of doing, and justifying it on the basis that it's more meaningful."

The waiter came with our drinks.

"Are those things full strength?" I said when the waiter left.

"They sure are. Are you worried that I'll conk out on you?"

I took her hand. Norm said Moira and I were kindred spirits, something Barbara and I never were. We had been lovers, we had produced a son, and toward the end, much too often, we had been antagonists, until finally it seemed

33

that's all we were. But at no time would I have said that Barbara and I were kindred spirits.

Moira brushed her fingers over the back of my hand. Beautiful fingers. Long and slender. An artist's fingers.

"Nice drink, huh?" she said.

"I wasn't thinking of the drink. I was thinking of something else that Norm said."

"What did he say?"

"Oh, let's just say he's an admirer of yours. In a nice way. Not lecherous, although deep down probably lecherous too. Any normal guy would have to be lecherous of you."

"Hmmm. I take back anything I said about Norm."

"You said he was a nice guy but cynical and burned out."

"Well, I take back the cynical and burned out part."

"No, he's that but he is a nice guy. He said you and I are kindred spirits, that you're a fine woman and I should guard you."

"Guard me?"

"Guard having you. As a friend and as whatever else we are."

"That's very sweet. Norm is a very sweet person. And so are you. More than sweet. So, you be careful about what you are doing. Skulking about the Combat Zone isn't the most prudent behavior."

"Don't give it another thought. I don't know why I went in there. For all we know, there's no connection between Kristin Williams's disappearance and Darlene Abbott's murder. Kristin could turn up tomorrow having been off somewhere on a personal funk."

The waiter came with rolls and salads.

"I'm famished." Moira attacked her salad. She looked at me and smiled. "And I'm dying to find out what tumefacient means."

34

CHAPTER

4

On Monday morning, I had finished a discussion of Kafka's "The Metamorphosis" with my Intro to Lit class when I spotted Hy Berman, Dean of Faculty, hovering outside in the hallway. He beckoned to me, peering myopically through thick lenses that magnified his eyes and distorted the flesh around them.

"You have a visitor. In your office."

"Oh?"

"It's the police." Hy seemed to think there was some drama to the pronouncement—and I suppose there was—

and was going to milk it for what it was worth. "The *Boston* police."

Boston police, while falling short of state police or the FBI, I guess are more significant than suburban police. I don't know where Reserve MPs would fit in.

Standing by the office door when I got there was a thinish, slightly stooped, rather ascetic-looking individual who nonetheless had cop stamped all over him. I wondered whether I would have thought that if I didn't know ahead of time that he was one.

"Dr. Toland?"

I gestured toward the office. "Won't you come in, please."

He flashed a badge and said, "I'm Inspector Gallo, Boston PD. Could I have just a moment? Are we alone in here, sir?"

I nodded. "No one else has office hours at this time."

"First off, I want to thank you for the information that you gave to Lieutenant Connolly. He forwarded it to me."

"You must be homicide division, then."

"Yes, sir, that's correct." Inspector Gallo appeared tired and was dressed too warmly for the weather. He looked, talked, and acted as though he had seen too many Columbo movies.

"Dr. Toland, you told Lieutenant Connolly that the Abbott girl visited you here on the day she was murdered."

"She did."

"And you stated that you didn't know her prior to that time. That was the first time you had met her." Inspector Gallo was looking at a notebook.

"Yes, that's right."

Inspector Gallo nodded. "Dr. Toland, what's the central phone number here at the college and the extension here at this office?"

His eyes were on the notebook as I told him.

"Those numbers were found on the Abbott girl's body. How would she come by them, would you know?"

I felt a twinge of apprehension. I had forgotten that I gave her those numbers. "Yes. I gave them to her."

"Lieutenant Connolly tells me that you're with Military Police CID and that the Abbott girl came to you because she was upset over the disappearance of a friend, a . . ." Inspector Gallo consulted his notebook. ". . . a Kristin Williams. Did you tell her that you could help her?"

"No, I didn't. What I told her was that Kristin Williams's disappearance probably had an innocent explanation but that in any event I couldn't help her because I had no jurisdiction."

"I see. Then why did you give her your phone number?"

"Well, she was upset. She said her friend had been missing a week, that her parents, that her boyfriend thought it out of character for her to just take off with no explanations or good-byes. That the regular police—that's the term she used; I don't know whether she was referring to the Boston police—had no explanation. She couldn't afford a private investigator. I felt she needed a sympathetic ear so I told her I was confident Kristin would show and I'd like her to call and keep me informed."

"Hmmm. Darlene Abbott was a very beautiful girl. At least her pictures show her to be. I saw her dead. Not too many people look beautiful when they've been murdered. Stabbed. You saw her alive. Did you think she was beautiful, Dr. Toland?"

"She was very attractive."

We had been standing and I sat down. "Sit down, Inspector."

He sat at Jerry Buford's carrel where Darlene Abbott had sat briefly. He took in the scattering of papers on

Jerry's desk, some uncorrected exams and compositions, the row of textbooks.

"God, how do you do it? Get up in front of a bunch of people and have something to say. I mean every day. It was me, I'd get tongue-tied, and then probably shit my pants."

"It's what you train to do."

"Now, that's interesting. I mean you do this—" He gestured toward the row of anthologies. "—poetry, literature, stuff like that which I never *could* get through my squash in school, and you're a cop too. What were you, ROTC, you don't mind my asking?"

I nodded.

"I figured that's what it had to be." Inspector Gallo ran the palm of his hand over his hair, a full head of it, but turning silver. "Me, I was army, too. Not MPs. Artillery. One-oh-fives. I was FDC, fire direction. Thought I was a smart bastard being in FDC. That's what they told us. You guys are the brains of artillery, what a deal, not out there humping the guns. It was the closest I went to going to school, I mean beyond high school. All the college boys used to screw around and us poor dumb shits would cram and really get into it and get the good marks. Went to Fort Sill in Oklahoma. Hot as hell there in the summer. Highest I got was E-6, which isn't too bad, I guess. This was right after Korea so I missed that. You in 'Nam?"

"No. Right time but I was sent to Germany instead."

"Hmm." Inspector Gallo consulted his notebook again and thumbed a couple of pages as if looking for something. "Now, Dr. Toland, you say you gave the Abbott girl those phone numbers. How did you do that? I mean, did you *tell* her the numbers?"

"No. I wrote them out for her."

"On what?"

"I don't—let's see. Sure, just a slip of paper from a pad."

"I see. Did you write anything else on that paper?"

I knew enough about interrogation to know this was leading somewhere. "I wrote the hours she could catch me in."

Lieutenant Gallo palmed his hair again. "Okay, let's see if I have this right. Darlene Abbott came here and you and her—you and she—which is it, you and she; you and her?" He grinned. "Gotta watch myself in front of an English professor, huh?"

I went along with the act. "She."

"The girl came here and you and she talked here and you gave her those numbers here." He paused. "Here meaning this office?"

"No. For the most part we talked outside. There was another teacher in here and she wanted to talk alone so we went outside. And I gave her the numbers outside."

"Oh." Inspector Gallo assimilated that for a moment. "Did anyone see you give her the numbers?"

"I don't think so. There were people about but no one nearby or paying us any attention. Look, Inspector, what's the drift here? What's the point?"

"Dr. Toland, you know what crack is, I assume."

"Crack. You mean cocaine."

"Right. See, the thing is, those numbers were found in a prescription bottle containing crack."

"Probably she put them there. Really, Inspector, I don't—"

"Yes, but what it is, they were written on the back of the prescription label."

I felt another twinge.

"How do you account for that, Doctor."

"I don't know that I have to. Obviously she wrote them there."

"Now, why would she do that? Why would someone transfer numbers from one piece of paper to another like that?"

"I have no idea but I assure you, Inspector Gallo, that I didn't write them on the back of any prescription label." I smelled the proverbial rat and wondered whether I needed a lawyer.

I glanced at my watch and Inspector Gallo caught it.

"You've probably got another class coming up, Doctor, but do you have just another minute?"

I nodded.

"Yeah, no doubt you're right. She must have written those numbers there herself."

I wondered whether Inspector Gallo was going to tell me about his wife or beat-up car or do some other piece of Columbo acting.

"Now, just one other thing. I want to make sure I have this straight. The Williams girl was doing research on illegal adoptions of prostitutes' and runaways' babies and this is why Darlene Abbott was worried about her and that's why she came to you."

"That's what she told me."

"And you told her you thought the Williams girl was all right and would probably show up sooner or later of her own will."

"I was trying to be reassurring."

"Yeah, you didn't want her worrying any more than she was. I can understand that. I mean, what else could you do?"

I looked at my watch again.

"Well, obviously Darlene Abbott won't be worrying any-more. But Kristin Williams won't be showing up either." Inspector Gallo smiled sadly. "Her body's been found. Dead over a week. Broken neck. Funny. She had a bottle of crack, too, and guess what?"

I felt numb.

"It had your phone number in it."

When Inspector Gallo left, I considered phoning Roy Newhall. Roy handled my divorce and will and, although he wasn't a criminal lawyer, he could advise me at this stage, but as I thought about it I wasn't sure what he could advise me that I wasn't already aware of. I didn't need a lawyer so much as I needed a detective, and that was no further than the nearest mirror, except maybe the adage against a physician treating himself or his family applied here.

My mind was busy spinning theories, sorting ideas. The first obvious leap was that I was being framed. But by whom and why?

My phone number being in a bottle of crack in Darlene Abbott's possession was explainable, although as Inspector Gallo had wondered, why the hell would she bother to rewrite those numbers?

Kristin Williams having them was another matter.

Although there was no evidence that I had committed any crime, none of this looked good for me. Police theory: College prof is entangled with student and her friend in drugs and perhaps romantically. Not provable but highly probable. Keep an eye on him. Girls are found dead, one stabbed, the other with a broken neck. The English prof as an MP has had some training in weaponry and the martial arts, is no stranger to seamy things, and is very capable of those kinds of murder. Motive? Drugs and/or romance provide all kinds of motives. He says he was just providing a shoulder for Darlene Abbott to lean on. Filled with the milk of human kindness, he is. Why, he probably hardly even noticed Darlene Abbott was beautiful, so beneficent is he.

But would he be dumb enough to put his phone number in the bottle with the drugs? Why not? There have been bigger screwups in the world. Besides being a quasi cop, he's a teacher and probably absentminded and doesn't have a hold on common sense.

I had back-to-back classes coming up and my mental mix wasn't conducive to a discussion of rhetoric. But the show must go on.

I'm sure I muddled my presentation. I caught more than one puzzled glance but puzzlement, at least, is a reaction, which is more than I sometimes get. Was it Abbie Hoffman who said today's college students have designer brains?

When I left for the day, it was afternoon. I drove to Fenway Park to check the Red Sox schedule and get tickets. One of my rules is not to make idle promises to my son. I didn't like thinking of the effect on Nicky of my name linked, however tenuously, to murder or drugs. Accusations or innuendo always leave doubts. Scars on me would be scars on my son.

I picked up the tickets, and when I got home I perused the copies of the *Globe* and *Herald* I had picked up. I went to the *Herald* first because stories of broken bodies are its specialty.

The story was on page three along with what looked like Kristin Williams's high school yearbook picture. It showed her to be an intelligent-looking, reasonably attractive girl.

The story said that her partially nude body was discovered late yesterday in a wooded area not far from Colton College. Two young boys were attracted by the yelping of their pet dog and at first didn't recognize what they had stumbled upon. The warm weather had hastened decomposition but not enough to prevent identification. The article said that Kristin had been missing for almost two weeks and that police had no motives or suspects yet but were waiting for results of tests by the Medical Examiner. Cause of death was apparently a snapped neck.

Theoretically, I could kill that way. Body found in the woods near Colton where she had been quietly rotting, the pathetic but not uncommon little scenario of the brutalized coed, and I was a suspect. Things looked terrific.

Boxer jumped onto my lap and I scratched his ears for a moment as I tried to think clearly. Of course, *my* phone number was simply the college and department phone number. Could the number found on Kristin Williams been given to her by someone else in the department? By Norm Eigner, for instance? She had been his student. I'd have to ask Norm if he had given her the number. If he had, his purpose must have been innocent. It was too much of a leap to imagine Norm involved with a student or being capable emotionally or physically of doing her harm.

But that was his English teacher friend thinking that way. The cop in me knew that anything was possible. Actually, no one would have to give Kristin that number. She simply had to look it up.

Kristin Williams had also been doing her research for Dan Ritchie, associate professor of journalism. Maybe Kristin had told him something or had turned in information to him that could shed light. I made a note to talk with Dan Ritchie.

But for now it was time to run. On my last mile I formulated a starting course of action. I sure as hell wasn't about to stand around and let myself be engulfed by suspicion or innuendo.

Tomorrow night I'd be on duty and would sound out some of this on my partner, Swede Knudson.

CHAPTER

5

Being in a military reserve unit can produce some peculiar pecking order situations. Often, one's civilian and military status can be completely reversed. A bank teller or a letter carrier can put on a uniform that transforms them to the leader of men, to receiving salutes, to being called "sir." Years ago, when I finished active duty and first joined a reserve unit, we had a high school teacher making up a summer camp with us. He was an E-3 or E-4 and for some reason was put on KP. The sergeant in charge of him was his former student. Both were embarrassed.

I am a major and my partner, Swede Knudson, is a sergeant E-7. Although we have a first-name relationship even on duty, theoretically, and in some situations, actually, he has to call me "sir." That's an interesting psychology; it acknowledges my superiority. It makes me boss and it has the weight of a deeply ingrained training and a long-standing tradition.

On the outside, I am a college teacher, a position whose social status would get mixed reviews. But by perhaps the greatest barometer of status in American society—money—Swede Knudson outranks me hands down.

Swede is a self-made man, which is in itself an American ideal. He is a decorated war hero, sent home from Vietnam with a plate in his skull and half a stomach. When he recuperated, he started a martial arts school before that became faddish and did fairly well. In Vietnam, he had been with the Special Forces and took to hand-to-hand and that sort of thing like a Doberman in a pack of cats. But he lacked the temperament and patience to be a truly good instructor and after a couple of years his school folded.

His other great interest was cars and he started a little garage in Cambridge specializing in foreign car repairs. In Cambridge, foreign cars are ubiquitous, a requirement of the intelligentsia, and with a large market, a lot of smarts, and good work, Swede worked himself up to acquiring a BMW dealership on Mass Avenue in Cambridge. And that is how Swede outranks me financially. On that scale, he's a general and I'm a shave-tail second looey.

I didn't bump into Norm Eigner in school and decided to wait until later to ask him whether he had ever given Kristin Williams the office phone number. And Dan Ritchie was out with a spring cold, so after classes, on a whim, I phoned Swede to see whether he was too busy to see me. If it struck him as odd that I wanted to see him now when we'd be on drill together this evening, he didn't say anything. But this evening we'd have other things pre-occupying us, most of them mundane.

I parked right outside the showroom door. Inside were potted fronds, tasteful paneling and carpeting, and the BMWs. Maybe Swede would let me borrow one sometime so that I could pick Nicky up in it when Gary would be around to see. I am very capable of sophomoric behavior in the right circumstances.

A salesman greeted me, I thought, rather coolishly at the door. I think he spotted the Fairmont. He was dressed tastefully as befits one representing machinery that costs more than decent houses did not so long ago. He wore a three-piece suit, subdued like a banker's. No curly perms, shirts open to show chains and chest hair, or elevator boots here. Chamber music played softly.

"Sir, may I show you something?"

I smiled. "Mr. Knudson is expecting me."

"Mr. Knudson?"

"Yes. Mr. Knudson."

"Yes. Ah, just a moment, sir. Whom shall I say is calling?"

Calling? "Dr. Toland. And it's *who.*" Let him think he had an eccentric brain surgeon here who likes to drive junk.

I spent about a minute looking at a BMW 635CSi priced in the midforties. But it was loaded.

The sales representative returned with a respectful smile. "Quite a car, isn't it?"

I smiled. "It's okay. I traded one of these in for that Fairmont out there."

The humoring smile was pasted on now. "Mr. Knudson is through that door. Second office on your right."

Swede was behind a big old-fashioned mahogany desk. He, too, was dressed in a three-piece suit, but he didn't look like a banker. He looked like a dressed-up prize fighter or Mafia hit man, except Swede was blond. At six-one, he's about two inches over me, and I'd guess he weighs about one-ninety, one-ninety-five, none of it lard. Like me, he runs and works out and looks it. But a close examination reveals his strength isn't just add-on. He's big-boned, naturally big across the shoulders, through the forearms and wrists. Big hands with long, powerful fingers that rumor has it did horrific things to the enemy when Swede did some interrogating in Vietnam. He was the primitive mesomorph whose civilization is no thicker than the clothes he was wearing. When he left the regular army, he eventually joined the MP Reserves just to maintain a taste of the life. I'm glad he did because he was a hell of a partner. In addition to the physical, he had a lot of savvy.

When he saw me, he stood. "Nick, what the hell's up? Shopping for a Bimmer?" He was smoking a long, thin, very black cigar. He offered me one from a box on his desk and slid a lighter shaped like a BMW at me. The status warp struck me as I lit up.

"Jesus, Swede," I said, "don't you get a guilty conscience over the price tags on those things?"

He laughed. "Hell, no. I'm grateful the upwardly mobile think they need a machine that accelerates and handles like a demon just to go down to the local White Hen for a half gallon of milk."

"My ex's boyfriend has a Porsche. How would a Porsche stack up against a BMW?"

"Depends on the respective models and what you're talking about when you say 'stack up.'"

"He lets my son drive it occasionally when he's with him."

"Porsche's a very decent car." Swede took a long drag on his cigar and blew expensive smoke at the ceiling. If he was impatient for me to get to the point, he didn't show it.

"Swede, I'd like to go into town tonight."

He nodded.

"To the Combat Zone."

"Oh?"

I pulled the list of names from Kristin Williams's research from my pocket. "Actually, I'm thinking of stepping out of our jurisdiction a bit. You up for that?"

"Nick—sir—you are the boss. Mine not to reason why and all that bullshit." He snapped a little salute.

"Here's why." I recapped the events from Darlene Abbott's visit to me to Inspector Gallo's.

Swede sucked on his cigar again, seeming to consume about a half inch of it. I handed him the list. "Any of these ring a bell? Mason and Simpson are pimps and bad ass according to Lieutenant Brian Connolly, who strikes me as a little too tight, by the way."

"I don't know the names. So what's the plan?"

"I don't know. We're limited. Maybe we'll go in and shake the trees a little and see what falls on our heads."

We left the Wells Building at 7:25 dressed in civvies. In CID we almost never wear uniforms. Swede had on pre-washed Levis and a white pullover shirt. I looked like a waiter from a brick, beams, and hanging plants restaurant, in chino pants and blue button-down oxford shirt.

We each wore running shoes and a light jacket to cover the .45 automatics we carried.

"Let's take mine," Swede said, pointing to a CSi like the one I had admired this afternoon. Our official car was a gray Taurus.

Swede drove the way you'd expect. Fast, with authority and skill. He passed a car where I wouldn't have and I felt myself pressed into the leather at the burst of acceleration.

Leaning over, I glanced at the odometer. Six miles. "Swede, this thing isn't broken in yet."

"This is how you do it. Best thing in the world for it. Don't even let the cobwebs build up." With that, he downshifted, the tach redlined, the car surged, and I sunk back.

"Some flat-chested yuppie from Brookline will buy this and not do over forty for a thousand miles," I said.

Swede parked in Chinatown in a tow zone. "Don't worry. It's insured."

The night was cool and the smells of Chinatown hung like a permanent, beguiling perfume and, although I had recently eaten, I felt my stomach juices begin to stir.

Within minutes, we were in the dazzling lights of the Combat Zone, what was left of it. If the appeal of Chinatown was to the stomach, in the Combat Zone it was to the groin. Sex was in the air. Breasts and buttocks thrust at us from everywhere, real ones from the whores who could hide neither their boredom nor desperation and neon ones, mounds and curves of perfection, on marquees.

"Let's go in here and see what happens," I said. We entered a den named Snatch a View. Inside, the air was blue with smoke. Booths were on the far walls and in the center, surrounded by the bar, was a platform on which contorted two nude girls. Their faces were expressionless but probably not too many looked that far up. Sounds blared from huge speakers on either side of the platform. Intimate conversation between young lovers would be tough here. There were no seats or booths free so Swede and I stood in a crowd near the bar. I caught the bartender's eye and ordered two bottles of Bud but ignored the glasses that came with them.

Halfway through our second beer just when I was beginning to feel guilty about not tending to MP business, I spotted two couples getting ready to leave a booth and steered Swede over to take up strategic position nearby. As they left, we squeezed in.

"Neat group," Swede said, indicating a table strewn with bottles and slop. The ashtrays overflowed.

"They were caught up in one another," I said.

"The guys probably wanted to take the girls home to Mom."

A large, hovering presence pressed against the table. A young guy, tall but too heavy through the gut, leered down at us. He had on jeans and a Puma T-shirt that revealed he worked out but concentrated on his arms. Two companions were close by.

"We been waiting for this booth an hour."

We looked up blankly. Swede drank some beer.

"You guys deaf or just dumb?"

Swede looked at him. "You have reservations?"

"You have reservations?" the guy mimed. "Blondie here's a comedian, you guys. He's a real funny man."

Swede put down his bottle and I shot him a warning glance. We didn't need a confrontation. I was considering surrendering both dignity and the table when Swede said,

"Look, sonny, why don't you guys go find some girls and throw a flex at them."

Puma put both hands on the table and leaned in close. His friends edged forward. The background music made it impossible for anyone else to hear the antagonism. It probably looked as though we were all close friends.

"Hey, pal, I'm gonna say this just once. You get your asses out of here or me and my friends are gonna rearrange your faces."

"Oh, dear me," Swede said. "You've got all the lines. You go to the movies much?"

As Puma started to react, Swede grabbed his right forearm, twisted it, and slammed it onto the table. Puma slumped to his knees. I watched his friends but they made no move. Eyes from the booth next to us strayed our way and then back to the cavorting girls. The bouncer at the door, a burly lump, looked wary, as though waiting for an escalation before moving our way.

"Look, I don't want to embarrass you or anything," Swede said, "but if you don't agree to find someone else to bother when I let go, I'll have to break your wrist here and now. Now you think about that. That'll put a real cramp in your lifting for a while."

One of Swede's huge hands was locked like a clamp on Puma's forearm, the other had his hand and was bending it back. Tears of pain welled from Puma's eyes. He was helpless and humiliated.

"What'll it be?" Swede asked.

"Let go."

"Will you be a good boy?"

"Yeah, yeah. Jesus, let go."

"Say the magic word. Say, 'please.'"

Puma looked at Swede through tears of hate. I looked at the bouncer again. He looked even more wary.

Swede bent the hand a bit more.

"Please." The word was reluctant but desperate.

Swede released the hand and the arm and Puma stood. He rubbed his forearm, livid from Swede's grip. "You son of a bitch."

"You just used up all your comebacks. Now beat it."

The three left with some face-saving black looks and muttering.

Swede said, "Sorry about that."

I looked at the bouncer. He was still staring at the point where Puma had knelt in mortification and penance.

"Maybe we should try someplace else, Nick. Unless you got a particular reason for this joint. Hope I didn't screw things up."

I waved my hand in dismissal of what had happened. It could have turned out worse. Probably we should get the hell out of here. Because I couldn't conduct a legitimate investigation, I had no real plan. "Let's finish our beers anyway."

For a few minutes we watched the girls on the platform and I wondered where the lust that I once would have felt had gone.

Just as we were finishing our beer, two more appeared, carried by a bulky guy, probably fifty, dressed in the kind of suit you might see at Suffolk Downs. The guy slid in beside me. "On the house." He smiled at us. "Nice-looking girls, huh? Young. Nothing's drooping yet, know what I mean?"

I said, "Yeah, nineteen going on fifty."

He looked at the table and waved a signal to one of the bartenders. "Stevie, this table's a goddamn mess. Clean it up, huh."

It took Stevie two trips to clean the table.

"Bring a couple of clean glasses, Stevie," our benefactor

said. "Couldn't help notice the way you took care of those punks." He eyed Swede's hands and forearms. "Never seen you around before. You guys cops?"

"No, we're not cops," I said.

"John Desi," he said, extending his hand. "This is my place."

We murmured noises.

"Yeah, that kid you put down's a strong boy, I'll tell you, but you handled him like a baby. I was you, though, I'd be careful when I went outside. He's the kind might try to get you from behind."

"We'll be real careful," Swede said.

"Snatch a View," I said. "You think of the name?"

John Desi smiled, revealing obviously false teeth. "Yeah, I got the idea from a T-shirt I saw. On the front, it said, 'You can snatch a kiss.' You can probably guess what it said on the back."

"Let me think about it."

John Desi opened a pack of Pall Malls, offered us cigarettes, and lit one. His hands and wrists were heavily jeweled. For a few moments he worked on the Pall Mall and watched the girls. I was about ready to leave when he said, "So you guys here to watch or do you want some action?"

I said, "What kind of action?"

"You name it. Mainly, people come here, they want broads."

"That sounds good to me," I said. "You have some in mind?"

"Guys like you, sure. I know some special ones. You fussy about the color?"

"No. We're real liberal," Swede said.

"Yeah, it's not like you're gonna marry them." Desi got

up. "You guys stay here. Watch the show. I'll send someone over. I'll send over a couple more beers too."

We watched him push his way through to the bar, say something, and then disappear to a back room.

"Why is that guy so nice to us?" Swede asked.

"He seemed to take a shine to you. Liked the way you handled that kid. Maybe he wants your body. But you know what I really think? I think he thinks we might be cops."

"Why would he set us up with broads then?"

"I don't know. That's an interesting one."

Stevie brought us two more bottles of Bud and took the empties. Five minutes later, the two girls arrived. Swede and I stood and let them in past us. Gentlemen. Beneath their jaded exteriors probably beat the stereotyped hearts of gold. They'd be moved to tears by our chivalry, the first men to treat them like ladies.

"Either of you studs got a fuckin' joint?"

"Or coke," the other said. "Coke'll do too." They both laughed at that.

"Girls," Swede said, "how do you know we're not narcs?"

"Nah, you ain't narcs. John says you're clean. Besides, you don't look like narcs. Hey, my name's Jeannie," the one beside me said (with the light brown hair, I thought), "and that's Cheryl."

They were young, probably not over nineteen, but had a lot of obvious mileage, and nineteen, for what they did, was middle age. Still, they were attractive, in the steely way of whores. Jeannie was blond (not light brown of tress) and with a change of grooming, dress, and expression, could look wholesome. Cheryl was dark, maybe with

Spanish or black genes, and tall. Each was dressed in the high fashion of strumpetry: boots, high skirts.

"So you gonna tell us your names or is it a big secret?" Jeannie asked.

Swede looked at me.

"I'm Frank. That's Mike," I said.

"Great. Now we're friends. So what are we gonna do, bullshit all night or get this show on the road?"

"I'd at least like a drink," Cheryl said.

They wanted margaritas and I went to the bar to get them.

We spent twenty minutes talking crude inanities while they drank and I itched to ask them questions and get out of here. But some things can't be rushed and this booth wasn't the place. When they finished, Jeannie nudged me and said, "Okay, follow us to heaven."

They led us to a back door and up worn, wooden stairs to a long corridor. We walked past four doors on either side to the last door on the left. From below, the bass notes thumped through the floorboards. The girls led us into the room. It smelled of past intimacies. Two beds were separated by a dressing screen to ensure the privacy of the less kinky.

Jeannie took my hand. "Do you want to keep the screen up?"

I led her to the bed and sat down. "Girls, you may not believe this, but we just want to talk."

"Oh, Jesus," she said.

"I don't believe it," Cheryl said. "You want to save us or something?"

"Look," I said, "I'll pay you whatever you would have charged." I wished I had a client and an expense account.

"John said it was on the house," Jeannie said, "but I

ought to charge you anyway. I can't stand talkers. Something wrong with you two? I never would have guessed it. Goes to show you."

She took a long feminist cigarette from the little bag over her shoulder and lit it.

"Okay, so talk. What do you want to talk about, your mother? God? You gonna tell us it's not our fault we're whores?"

"No." I looked at the list I had taken from my pocket and read the names. "Do you know any of these girls?"

"No, I don't," Jeannie said, too quickly, I thought.

I looked at Cheryl, who seemed unable to decide whether to look casual or hard. "I don't either."

"Let me try it one more time."

"You guys *are* cops, ain'tcha? That goddamn John. Sometimes I wonder about him. C'mon, Cher, let's get our asses outa here."

I stood at the door. "Girls, we're not cops. God's truth. This is kind of important to me, that's all."

They hesitated, I suppose because I was in their way. This was a hell of a way to conduct an investigation but under the circumstances I didn't know what else to do. I decided to press. "How about Ronald Simpson or Gerald Mason? Do those names mean anything to you?"

I thought Jeannie reacted to the names but I couldn't be sure.

"Hey, look, Frankie boy, or whatever the hell your name is, I don't know who you two are or what you're up to. You want to screw, let's screw. You want to talk, find someone else. Talk to each other. I don't give a shit."

She looked at Cheryl who edged forward. "Now if you don't mind, let us by or I start yelling and then you've bought more goddamn trouble than you thought possible."

I backed off. "Okay, girls, no problem. Thanks anyway."

"Yeah," Swede said, "what we are, we're reporters. We're taking a survey, actually, for a magazine."

"What you are is you're full of shit," Cheryl said. "You expect us to believe that? Let us outa here and you better get yourselves outa here too."

I opened the door. They stomped down the hallway. At the head of the stairs, Jeannie swung around and gave us the finger.

"Swede, let's get the hell out of here."

"You know where they're going, don't you? Right down to our pal, John Desi. I mean, you could tell they knew at least some of those names. Probably half of them are in Desi's harem."

Outside, we walked through the neon glow back to the sweet-and-sour smells of Chinatown and to the BMW. As we approached, I was surprised to see it, apparently still intact.

"We've got trouble," Swede said.

"It looks okay to me," I said, thinking he meant the car.

"Behind us."

I glanced over my shoulder and saw five of them, maybe sixty feet back, Puma, his two buddies, and two reinforcements. I swore under my breath. "We can beat them to the car," I said.

"They'll be on it before I can start it and they'll trash it. C'mon, in here." Swede grabbed my arm and led me into an alley. I knew what he was up to but I was going to have no part of it.

The five figures stopped at the head of the alley and

then slowly, like a wolf pack confident of its trapped prey, moved toward us. They were all young and good-sized and while Swede might be supremely confident of his martial skills, I was in no mood to play karate with five souped-up, burly studs. Behind us was a sheer wall that could not be quickly climbed.

"Nice spot you picked. Where do you go from here, ass-holes?" Puma said.

Swede said, "We go out past you, honey. Way one, you listen to reason, which I doubt. Way two, you make us prove the point which should have been clear to you ear-lier. We came in here because we don't want the cops dragging us in for unfair assault."

"Hey, blondie, you got me by surprise earlier and I didn't want to create a disturbance 'cause Mr. Desi's an okay guy. But you ain't gonna get me by surprise now."

They started toward us and I drew the .45 from under my jacket. They froze at the sight of it.

"Face the wall and lean against it," I said. "Put your hands up high where I can see them."

They were dutiful and I was ecstatic at that because I sure as hell wouldn't have shot them.

"We're walking out of here and you're going to stay sup-porting that wall for five minutes."

Swede quickly fell in behind me. I think he sensed that my anger wasn't directed at just those five leaning figures.

We took the Mystic River Bridge and picked up Route One north. When Swede booted the BMW, I said, "Cool it. I don't feel like explaining anything to local cops."

"It's after nine-thirty now, Nick. We're gonna make the North Shore by ten?"

"I just want to put in a token appearance." We had

business at a North Shore armory. "There'll be someone there."

Our speed dropped to fifty-five.

"Maybe we can still salvage something out of the evening."

Swede put on an FM station that played soft music, almost classical sounding, an incongruity with his appearance.

"Shit, Nick, it's tough trying to conduct an investigation when you can't be open about it. You know, can't say you're a cop."

"Yeah, doing it on your own behest and for a dead girl isn't the way to go, I guess. You wouldn't think so, but it's tough."

Swede was right. It was a lot easier being a cop when you could say you were one, could say, Major Toland, CID. Not Frank. Frankie boy.

I rubbed my eyes. I felt the start of a headache and that's about all I felt. I sure as hell didn't feel like much of a cop.

CHAPTER

6

The next morning I woke with my headache having blossomed overnight and the feeling that I had royally botched the previous evening. I didn't know the day wasn't going to get much better.

I showered, made coffee, and read the *Globe*. Boxer crunched some multicolored pellets. Strange, I thought cats were color blind.

I wondered if I could lure Moira over here tonight. In my freezer were some frozen steaks among the usual packaged dinners that are the calling cards of those who live alone.

Steaks, a jug of burgundy, a couple of potatoes, and start the gas grill for the first time this year. High living.

I was feeling better now, but for insurance I swallowed four aspirin and headed for Colton. On my desk in the English office was a note from Norm Eigner. He wanted to see me at ten.

I went to class, handed back some corrected compositions, discussed them and the crying need for greater use of transitional expressions, and went back to the English office to meet Norm. He was at my carrel, thumbing through an anthology of British poetry.

He peered at me. "How goes it, Nick?"

"Norman."

"Re the singular events of Darlene Abbott and Kristin Williams, whose murder I read about Monday evening and I assume you did too. I meant to call you about that. By the way, a new wrinkle has developed. Well, maybe not a *wrinkle*, but let me tell you about it. I'm curious to see what you think."

He put the anthology down and ran his hand across his balding pate. "I'm just sick about this whole thing. Those two girls. The Williams girl. I mean students here at Colton aren't just a number. We're no factory. I can picture that girl in class. She had too much promise to be snuffed out like that."

Norm paused as though trying to remember what he had wanted to see me about. "Anyway, I wanted to tell you about Dan Ritchie. You remember, Kristin Williams was doing the same paper for him. Actually, the topic was more directed to his course than mine. It was an actual journalistic exposé.

"Yesterday morning I had a note on my desk to please contact Dan Ritchie. So I did and he wanted to get together. I went over to his office in the Madison Building. We went through the usual niceties. Then he said something about what a shame it was about the Williams girl. And then he got to his point, and this is what I think is strange. He wanted to know whether he could see whatever preliminary material Kristin had turned in to me."

"Why would he want that?" I said.

"Why indeed? You know what he said? He said the topic she was doing was one he was very interested in. That he had done some research into it himself. That he was surprised that Kristin or anyone else for that matter was onto it. Said he was planning to do an article on it and any additional leads would be helpful."

Norm leaned back. "What do you think? Kind of strange, huh?"

"I don't know. What was your feeling about his doing an article on the same topic? How did that come across to you? Sincere?"

Norm spread his hands. "Hard to say. I know he's published articles. It just seemed so coincidental."

"Did you give him the material?"

"No. It was at home. I brought it in today but I thought I'd talk to you first. I'm supposed to see him at noon."

"Whatever she turned in to you, she probably turned in to him."

"Not necessarily. In subjects other than English, often all the instructor requires is the finished product. They don't bother with the preliminary materials."

"Is that the case with Dan Ritchie?"

"Do you believe I didn't ask? I guess that's what he wants me to assume."

"Okay, so on one hand the guy is actually going to do an article on this very topic a student was researching and now will never get to see her paper. He is, therefore, interested in her preliminary research. On the other hand; on the other hand, what? A coincidence, or are you suggesting that he has some other reason, some sinister reason, for wanting to see what Kristin Williams had unearthed?"

Norm looked almost embarrassed. "Aw, there's probably nothing there. I'm letting my imagination work overtime. Still, it's interesting how he independently came across what Kristin Williams had stumbled onto."

"At least," I said, "it raises another interesting question. Just how did she stumble onto it?"

We left it that Norm would keep his appointment with Dan Ritchie and would call me later to tell me how it went.

After my next class, I met Moira and she agreed to come to my place for steak, wine, intelligent conversation, and physical rapture. The day had turned gray with a chill drizzle blown off the ocean. A cozy evening inside with Moira seemed very inviting.

When I got home about three, the day had become sullen with that raw east wind that sets spring back to February. The drizzle had become a steady rain. Even the birds and trees seemed betrayed.

As I was changing into my rain-proof running suit, Barbara called. Her voice still does things to me. It's a spontaneous reaction beyond my control and I'm sure she can detect it.

We went through the usual polite inquiries and small talk before she got to the point.

"Nick, are you in some kind of trouble?"

That caught me off guard, and my hesitation was probably transparent.

"No. What makes you ask anything like that?"

"Nick, you can level with me. We've had our problems and difficulties but basically I'm still on your side, you know."

I resisted a comment.

"A Boston policeman was here, Nick, asking some questions."

"Oh?"

There was a pause and then a rush of air confirming my guess that she had lit a cigarette. Barbara always smoked when she talked on the phone. I wondered which phone she was using, the kitchen or bedroom. I could picture her sitting on the edge of the bed, probably looking in the mirror on her dressing table as she talked. I wondered how she was dressed and whether her hair was pinned up or flowing long and loose. Both ways she looked great.

"Nick, he wanted to know about the divorce."

"What do you mean, he wanted to know about the divorce."

"General questions. I didn't know whether I had to tell him anything or not."

"You didn't even have to talk with him, Barbara. What kind of general questions?"

"Mainly, I guess you'd say he wanted to know, well, why we were divorced."

I swore. "Who was this guy? Was his name Gallo?"

"Yes. That was it. He came by around noon."

"Well, what did you tell him?"

"Oh, Nick, he was . . . disarming. I guess I told him things without realizing it."

I could easily picture Inspector Gallo doing his Columbo routine and Barbara thinking he was cute or charming or cuddly.

"Nick, are you angry with me?"

I hadn't been but could feel it begin to rise. She was being the coy, helpless female, a role she sometimes feigned.

"What did you tell him?"

There was another rush of air as she exhaled smoke.

"Well, it came out about Diane."

"It *came* out."

"Well, she *was* the cause." The coyness was gone now. "Infidelity is an ugly word, isn't it, Nick?"

There was no point rehashing this with her. We'd been through it. Of course, she'd never admit that anything about her was the cause of my involvement with Diane Atkins.

"So, why did he want to know, Nick?"

"It's nothing, Barbara." I didn't want to talk with her. Especially, I didn't want to talk with her about what happened, but I felt an abbreviated explanation might be in order, especially since I didn't know whether any of this might hit the local papers.

"Well, there *is* something."

I glossed over it as best I could, telling of the murders and how I supposed because I had had contact with one of the girls I was one of probably many people who were being checked. I didn't tell her about my phone number being in the bottles of crack. "That's all there is to it, Barbara, I assure you."

"Oh, Nick, that's awful. You must be frantic."

"Barbara, it's not as if there's a case against me. But I will admit that innuendo that could develop has me a little on edge."

She made a noise of concern, probably as much for the potential ramifications to her as anything else.

I changed the subject. "How's night school?"

There was a pause as she shifted topics.

"Nicky told you?"

"Yes."

"Oh, I enjoy it, Nick. It gives me such a sense of worth to be doing something that could lead to something really worthwhile."

Sense of worth. That was the kind of textbook phrase she was fond of flavoring her conversation with. I wondered whether I was fair in sensing a criticism of me when she talked that way. Had repression of her been another of my sins? Add that to infidelity. At least I had never tried to break her neck or stab her.

"And the place in Maine?"

"Oh, that. It's nice. It's near Bar Harbor. Gary wants to buy it. He sails, you know, and the shops are very nice nearby."

I knew she'd love the quaint artsy-craftsy shops. How many times had she dragged me into them from Newport to Boothbay? There was a dreary sameness to them all with their scented candles and phony flotsam and jetsam.

"Sounds good. Look, I picked up tickets to a Sox game for Nicky and me in a couple of weeks. No problem, huh?"

"Not on the weekend, you mean?"

"Right. On Monday the twelfth."

"No. That's fine."

"If he comes by again, or anyone else, you'll let me know?"

"Who?"

"Inspector Gallo. The police. By the way, did he remind you of Columbo?"

"Columbo?"

"The TV cop. We used to watch that show."

"Oh, yes. Peter Falk was in it. Yes, he did, Nick. I knew there was something about him but I couldn't put my finger on it."

There was a pause.

"Nick. You be careful. Take care of yourself."

"You know me, Barbara. That's one thing I do."

"Are you eating right?"

"Jean Mayer would approve."

"Not drinking?"

"Just beer." Maybe some red wine tonight.

Another pause. Then, "Nick, are you seeing anyone?"

"Just Moira. I told you about her. She teaches with me."

"I remember. Anything serious?"

"Very casual."

"Well, do take care." (Another book phrase. This time a novel.) "I'll be in touch if the police, if . . ." She laughed. ". . . if Peter Falk comes by again. Should I talk to him, Nick?"

"I suppose there's no harm, Barbara. I've nothing to hide. Maybe I'll talk to Roy Newhall to see whether he recommends anything. I'll let you know."

When I hung up, I suddenly didn't want to go running and I wrestled with that decision for a moment. I looked out the window. It was still raining hard. That settled it. I liked to run in the rain, a preference that had always annoyed Barbara, especially when I tracked in mud or drippings.

As I ran, I thought of Diane Atkins. I hadn't seen her in three years and didn't desire to. It was a short affair, less than six months, and not very intense. And Barbara *had* driven me to it. I suppose it was especially galling to her that Diane was a neighbor living some ten houses away.

It ended when Diane and her husband moved away but it would have ended anyway, which is not to say there wouldn't have been others.

How do such things come to pass? How does a sweet love become bitter and malevolent? How does spiting and hurting become perversely pleasurable? And why, when everything that had ever been between Barbara and me was dead, did I find myself almost choking when I heard her voice on the telephone or saw her framed in the doorway when I picked up my son? And why, when I looked at my son, did I see his mother so clearly when everyone said he looked like me? And, yes, why when we talked on the phone were we so civil, as if we could just go back and rearrange the pieces?

These questions were the stuff of poetry I couldn't write and could barely stand to read, and whether they were maudlin or profound I couldn't decide. Probably profound to me, maudlin to others.

I was on the lonely stretch of roadway that looped around the fenced-off reservoir. I checked my watch and confirmed what I felt, that I was running very fast. The rain was heavy now, beading the road and puddles, but the Gortex was up to its job of shedding the wet away from me. A car hadn't passed me in several minutes.

I thought of last night and felt a stab of guilt over wasting the evening. I resolved to put the Darlene Abbott/Kristin Williams matter on a back burner or take it off the stove altogether and concentrate on MP matters. I reviewed the list of cases I had to deal with. Most were routine and dull, like police work anywhere. Drugs were a common problem, but what else is new?

The road was narrow now with a steady, rather sharp curve as it went around the reservoir. Behind me, tires hissed and splashed through the rain and my concentration on my priorities, and I edged toward the shoulder. The muffler sound was throaty.

I glanced over my shoulder and then darted up the little embankment beside the road. The fool driving wasn't paying attention and was going to squeeze me.

He zipped past me and when he did a Hollywoodish sliding one-eighty, I knew he had seen me and that his intentions were not friendly. For a moment, his tires spun futilely on the wet road as he came back at me.

I dropped over the other side of the embankment out of his sight. I ran through sloppy, soaked ground. Low scrub pine and brambles clawed into the Gortex. I heard the engine beside me, no more than twenty feet away, separated only by the embankment. I could turn to my right and scale the chain-link fence that bound the reservoir. There was about five feet of flat sand that would allow fast running but if whoever it was was armed I'd be an easy target.

The car stopped. Before I flung myself over the embankment, I had seen that there were two in the car. Beyond that generality, I could attest to nothing, not even the color of their skin.

It was a good guess that one of them would be coming over the embankment. I looked at the fence and the reservoir and decided that was a trap.

I doubled back, not a sophisticated evasive move, but my choices were limited. It was raining even harder now and I counted on the noise of it and the idling, rumbling engine to cover me.

If I stayed behind the embankment for about fifty yards, I could get back onto the road beyond the point where they'd see me.

My feet caught a tree root and I slithered face first into pine needles and mud. Voices cursed behind me. From the sound, they seemed about seventy-five to one hundred feet back. I lay still, trying to determine their direction.

I heard the word "fence." They were trying to determine whether I had climbed it. Didn't they know enough to look for footprints in the sand on the other side?

The voices came no closer and I stayed pressed into the ground for two or three minutes. As I started to get up to move away, their voices stopped. After another minute, they killed the engine.

In a low crouch, I moved away for another seventy-five feet or so and then climbed up and over the embankment. They were around the curve and out of sight.

I broke into a steady, quick pace, listening for the car and resisting the urge to break into a reserve-depleting sprint.

At the first side street, I cut off the reservoir road and headed out toward the main drag and back to home. I did lots of checking over my shoulder for my attackers but arrived uneventfully.

Inside, I took off the torn, mud-soaked Gortex, showered, and fed Boxer. Then I sat down, waited for Moira, and wondered about what had happened.

It didn't take a great detective to figure that my involvement with Kristin Williams's research had just escalated.

Moira sipped red wine while I worked at the cutting board on a salad. The steaks sat on a plate ready for the grill outside, and the potatoes were washed and ready for the microwave. I had a bottle of Molson beer open from the two six-packs that Moira had brought. I can't find anything bad to say about Molson.

"And you couldn't get the license plate?" she said.

"I never saw the rear end of the car. Don't forget, in Massachusetts, there is no front plate."

At first I wasn't going to tell Moira what had happened when I had run this afternoon, but then decided to. She wouldn't panic or nag and she made a good sounding board.

"But you could recognize the car."

"Well, I'd recognize the type. There are a million of them around, unfortunately. It was a Trans Am. You know the kind. With the eagle on the hood. Wide tires, very macho."

"Very phallic. Very silly."

I resisted a comment on the sensibility of spending in excess of twenty thousand for a Volvo.

"Well, what about warning Dan Ritchie and Norman. Have you? Remember we spoke of that?"

I shook my head. "No, and I spoke with Norm just this morning." I told her what Dan Ritchie had said to Norm about the research papers Kristin Williams had been doing for the two of them.

"Hmmm. Are you making something of that?"

"No. Norm's just letting his imagination run away from him."

"You've heard the rumor, haven't you, about Dan being owner, part owner, silent partner or whatever in a sleaze joint in the Combat Zone."

"You're kidding me."

"No, I'm not kidding you. At least about the rumor. How true it is, who knows? But it was whispered about a few years back."

I put down the tomato I was quartering. "Jesus, Moira, this puts a new light on things. What was the name of the place?"

"Oh, God, Nick, I don't know. I don't know that I ever heard. But it's an interesting twist, isn't it? That coupled with Dan's wanting Kristin's research casts a sinister light, wouldn't you say?"

I smiled. "Does he drive a Trans Am, by any chance?"

She laughed. "No class, Nick. I think he drives a Jaguar. I will say this, Dan Ritchie lives pretty well for a college professor. Lives in Milton, very nice home, I've heard."

My stomach rolled with hunger. I pushed Dan Ritchie out of my mind for the moment and went to the microwave. I set the timer for eleven minutes and put the potatoes in.

"How do you like your steak?" I asked, grabbing the plate and an umbrella. The rain was still heavy.

"Medium rare."

"Ah, enlightened Irish, like me," I said. "You mean you don't want shoe leather through and through?"

"Are you making fun of the culinary creativity of the Irish?"

"Well, you have to admit there is a certain lack of imagination involved in boiling potatoes."

Moira came to me and mock punched me on the arm. "You're Irish. At least part Irish. What part of you is Irish I'm not exactly sure."

I hugged her. "The parts that make you happy, the basic, unpretentious parts. Come on, how about let's go and you can do an exploratory and find them."

She kissed me, a tender, lingering kiss that filled me and made me forget my hunger for food. "Sounds like fun," she said, "but how about let's first eat those steaks you tempted me here with."

"And then?"

"And then maybe I'll give you an Irish dish I guarantee you'll like."

I took the plate of steaks and my umbrella and went outside. Two minutes later I was back in. "How about pan-fried steak?"

The gas grill was empty.

CHAPTER

7

The next morning I woke early and lay for a few minutes staring at the cracks in my ceiling and trying to put my analytical mind to work. My bed companion now was Boxer. Moira had decided not to spend the night, for no particular reason. Sometimes she did, sometimes she didn't, and the same with me at her place. I guess that was part of the space we gave each other.

I got up, fed Boxer, put him out, and started my Mr. Coffee before I showered. Over coffee and the morning television newscast I resumed my analysis and decided on a few things I could do, feeling slightly guilty that being an Army Reserve MP was returning to the back burner while I concentrated on my own situation for at least a little while.

The first thing was to see Swede, and if I moved smartly I could swing into Cambridge and catch him before classes. At the dealership, the same sales representative gave me a nod of recognition. Maybe it was the Fairmont that commanded his respect.

"You want to see Mr. Knudson? Let's see, your name was?"

"Dr. Toland. And it still is."

Swede was pouring over some invoices and seemed pleased to see me. I was glad of that. He wasn't very good at dissemblance and I didn't want to make a pain in the ass of myself. Actually, I knew that he enjoyed the police work we did together. It was his outlet, his therapy. God knows it wasn't for the money.

I told him about the Trans Am.

"You're sure that's what it was?" he said.

"Yeah, I guess. Big eagle or something like that on the hood. I'd recognize it or one like it."

"Sounds like a Trans Am. Piece of shit. Your Spanish types and people of color, as they say, go for them. The young studs who can't afford a 'Vette like 'em too."

"What I'd like to do is go into the Combat Zone and see if I can find that car. I know it's a needle in a haystack," I said regretting the cliché, "but I could have Stan Janski trace the plate. Maybe it belongs to Simpson or Mason." Stan Janski was a former major in our unit who was a captain with the Metro police.

"Sounds good to me, Nick. It was me, I'd do the same thing. Someone's gunning for you, to me, the best defense is a good offense, like the saying goes. Hit the parking lots, the alleys, the garages, and look for that Trans Am."

"It had a sunroof. Not original equipment. You know, the kind that's put in after. The pop-up plastic kind."

"Shit, Nick, that narrows it a lot."

I couldn't tell whether Swede was being facetious. "Of course, I don't know whether that car will be in the Combat Zone area. It'd be pure luck if we spotted it and even if we did what's to say that it's the same one."

"No, but it's a logical place to start. What the hell else you gonna do, hang around and let them come at you when they please and on their terms, the sonofabitches? Some night you and Moira are in the sack—no offense— and you find some goon in there with you."

He wasn't being facetious. He was with me.

"When are you going in? I'll go with you."

"When's good for you?"

"Can you meet me back here at four?"

With that arranged, I drove to school. I spun through the three faculty lots and spotted a maroon Jag sedan behind the Madison Building where Dan Ritchie taught. If Moira was right that Dan drove a Jag, it must be his. I jotted the license number down and then drove to my parking spot behind the Hartnett Building and went to my office.

After ten minutes of trying, I got through to Stan Janski and he said he'd see what he could do to trace Dan Ritchie's connection to an establishment in the Combat Zone.

"Could be tough, Nick. If your pal has any smarts, he probably has his investment well hidden."

"I understand that, Stan. It's probably impossible. Don't kill yourself on it. Whatever you can find, if anything, I appreciate."

Next, I went to the central office, checked Dan Ritchie's schedule, and came back to prepare for my first class. I glanced over some notes on Hemingway and skimmed through "The Short Happy Life of Francis Macomber." I enjoyed Heminway: the Code, the importance of ritual.

I drew myself a cup of coffee from the large coffee maker department members took turns tending, finished skimming "Francis Macomber," and took out the list of names I had copied from Kristin Williams' note cards. Maybe I'd luck out and find Ronald Simpson or Gerald Mason owned that Trans Am and were associates of Dan Ritchie.

Suddenly, I felt tired. I swilled the coffee and got another. Moira had stayed late. We had our dinner, listened to music, and talked. I guess my performance after that was uninspired or distracted, although adequate. Moira took it as a reaction to my encounter with the Trans Am. I didn't tell her it may have been the aftermath of my talking with Barbara.

I picked up my phone and dialed an outside line and then dialed Michael Sandler's office. Michael Sandler was my therapist. I asked his receptionist when I'd be able to see him and she told me had a cancelation at one-thirty if I could make it. I could.

I was grateful. I needed to talk.

After class, two students, lovers I suspect, lingered to discuss whether Francis Macomber's wife murdered him or shot him accidentally, a discussion, pointless though it may be, I wouldn't ordinarily discourage. But I was due to see Dan Ritchie and I wanted to talk with Norm Eigner before that, and when my impatience didn't telegraph itself, I referred them to criticisms by Carlos Baker and Jackson Benson.

In the department office, I caught Norm Eigner just as he was leaving, grabbed his arm, and propelled him toward my carrel. He started to protest about being late for class but I shut him off.

"Just give me a minute, Norm," I said as we sat down. He looked rumpled and disarrayed, as he usually did, something of a stereotype, and fragile and vulnerable. Not vulnerable as a synonym for sensitive, a quality that women are supposed to admire in men. Vulnerable as in unworldly and weak. He would be easy prey and I wondered how much risk he was at.

He smiled. "Just give you a minute, when I have a class full of students biting their nails in anticipation of my lecture on Henry James? An irreplaceable minute. Gone forever. Do you believe they find Henry James dull, an opinion with which I concur. *The Aspern Papers*, a novel or a novella? This is the kind of titillating conundrum I deal in. An intellectual farce, the equivalent of how many angels on a pinhead."

"Norman, how did your meeting with Dan Ritchie go yesterday, when you gave him Kristin Williams's material?"

"Oh, that. I know I was supposed to call you but I didn't have a chance. No big deal. I gave it to him, he thanked me and took it. Maybe there's nothing to his wanting that material, but, do you know what I did? I photocopied everything I gave him, just in case."

"You gave him photocopies?"

"No. I gave him the originals and kept the photocopies."

That was one precaution I should have thought of. "Very good, Norman. You'd make a good cop. Where are they, at home?"

"No. They're here. Do you want them?"

"Yes. I'd like to look at them again. I'm going to see, or try to see, Dan Ritchie in a few minutes, and I'd like to go over that material to see whether there's anything I missed."

Norm cocked his head at me. "You're on the case, huh?"

"Let's just say I'm sniffing around a little. I, too, get bored with the academic life occasionally."

Something nudged my memory. "Norm, by any chance, did you give Kristin Williams the office extension number?"

He scrunched his face, thinking. "I don't think so. My office hours and phone number are on the door. No, I don't recall giving them to her specifically. Why?"

"The office extension was found on her body but, as you say, the number was readily available."

"Found on her body? How do you know that?"

"Look, Norman, we've got to get together soon over a couple of beers and talk. For now, let's just say there are some things going on about the killings of Kristin Williams and Darlene Abbott that are a little bit . . ." I groped for a word but Norman was looking at his watch and was obviously itchy about being late for class.

"Yeah, Nick, sure, let's get together. You can come to my place and I'll get Iago to go through his repertoire of the seven or whatever dirty words." Norm got up. "I'll get you those photocopies and then I've got to run or that class will have passed around the attendance sheet and skipped out on me. I can't let them go through life short-changed on Henry James."

We went to his carrel. He unlocked his file cabinet and gave me the photocopies in a manila folder.

I hesitated and then said, "Look, Norm, just one thing. I

don't want to alarm you, but apparently the information on these sheets is touchy stuff to somebody and whoever has seen it may be in some, uh . . ." Again I groped.

"Some what? Danger?"

"Possibly."

"You? Me?" He pointed a finger at me and then himself. "What about Dan Ritchie?"

"That's why I want to see him." I let it go at that.

"What kind of danger are we talking about, Nick?"

"Norm, frankly, I think it's mainly to me. Because I've been nosing around a little."

Norm regarded me almost paternally. "Then *you* be careful." He hesitated. "But I still want you over for those beers."

"Sounds good," I said.

Norm knuckled me a salute. "Gotta run."

I sat at my carrel and went through the contents of the manila folder more carefully than I had looked at the originals that day at Norm's home. I wasn't looking for anything specific other than something I might have missed the first time.

Norm had laid the four-by-six note cards side by side and each photocopy sheet had two cards. I read them through carefully but found nothing new.

Next, I went to the photocopies of the three-by-five bibliography cards, of which Kristin Williams had only four. Apparently, most of her research was original. One looked interesting because it was to a local source and wasn't really a bibliography card. It simply listed a Rick Le Brun, *Hub* magazine, but it wasn't a reference to a specific issue of *Hub* or to an article from it. Perhaps she had interviewed him. I'd check.

I read her thesis again: A substantial black market for adoptions is supplied by runaway girls and prostitutes.

I returned everything to the folder, locked it in my file cabinet, and walked to the Madison Building.

I found Dan Ritchie at his carrel in huddled conference with a female student. When he saw me, he handed her a paper, told her he'd speak with her again later, and beckoned me in.

Dan was a big guy, late thirties. The kind that, as soon as you saw him, you know would have been a big mover in the fraternity circles, a stud, and an all-around burner of the candle at both ends except that he did his undergrad work in the late sixties when that sort of thing was out.

He had on casual slacks and a crew sweater with sleeves pushed back over brawny forearms.

"Nick Toland, what's up?" His puzzlement at my being here was evident. We have no more than a nodding acquaintance and seldom bumped into one another except at faculty get-togethers. "Coffee?" He gestured at a brewer plugged into his carrel.

"No thanks."

"What brings a member of the English department over here, not that I don't wish we saw more of you people?" He sipped at a Styrofoam cup.

"Dan, I understand that you're doing some research for an article."

"Oh?" He leaned back in his chair and arched his eyebrows as though at a loss over what I was talking about.

"Yeah, Norm Figner tells me you're thinking of doing an article on the same topic that that murdered girl was researching for you and Norm."

"Oh, yeah, that?" He leaned forward again. "Yeah, yeah, I was. Like I was telling Norm, I was just surprised that someone else had come across the same thing I had."

"Yeah, that is kind of funny."

"Shame about the Williams girl."

"Yeah. I'm curious. How *did* you come across the adoption black market, Dan, if you don't mind my asking?"

"I don't. Thing is, though, it's still kind of confidential, I mean with my sources and all. You understand." Dan nodded at me.

"Sure." I nodded back.

"Uh . . ." Dan smiled. "Now I'm curious. Why are you into this, Nick, if you don't mind *my* asking?"

"Well, as I'm sure you know, I do some police work, and before Kris Williams's body was discovered a friend of hers came to Norm all worried about what Kris was into and where she was. Norm referred the friend to me and, well, to make a long story short, the reason I'm here . . ." I paused just a bit. I was watching Dan carefully for reaction without trying to look it. ". . . I have reason to think that anyone knowing of what Kris had uncovered—I mean especially specific names, you know, that were in her notes—may be in some danger themselves."

"Oh wow." Dan didn't look like an 'Oh, wow' guy. But, after all, it was an expression from his undergrad days. "So you're here to kind of warn me. I appreciate that, Nick."

"Yeah, well, Kristin Williams was poking around the Combat Zone, asking questions and—"

"So what you're saying is that there's a connection between her research and her death."

I shrugged. "I don't know. It's a reasonable hypothesis. A prudent one, I should think in your case. I mean the Combat Zone isn't exactly the sort of place pedagogues like us are at home in, Dan. You ever been in there? I don't mean just driving through, gawking the way a lot of people will do out of curiosity."

It struck me that I was playing Inspector Gallo and Dan Ritchie was me.

"Just a hypothesis, Nick? Hell, I'd hate to give up an article on the basis of a hypothesis. There could be any number of other reasons that that poor girl was killed."

"Yeah, it is a hypothesis, Dan, but I do have some reasons. I don't want to go into them now, but it's not just a gut feeling." I smiled. "Confidentiality."

Dan sipped at his coffee again, then drained it. He poured himself another cup. "Sure you don't want any?"

I shook my head no. "Thanks."

"You're, what, an MP, Nick?"

"Reserves."

"So you're not investigating Kristin Williams's murder."

"No." I tried to make the word heavy with implication.

Dan stirred powdered creamer and a sugar cube into his coffee. "I think I understand, Nick. What you're saying is that you don't have official jurisdiction but that, well, as a military cop you have connections with the civil cops." He tested his coffee and set the cup down. "Well, I appreciate your coming over. I really do and I'll take the caution under advisement."

I stood to go. "Any idea, Dan, how Kristin Williams stumbled onto this?"

Dan's eyes went wide with wonder. "No, I haven't, Nick. No idea at all."

I stopped at the faculty cafeteria and picked up a couple of plastic-wrapped tuna sandwiches and a salad for my lunch. I wondered if I could squeeze in Rick Le Brun, if he'd see me, between Michael Sandler and Swede. It could turn out to be a busy day.

Michael Sandler has been my therapist since the divorce and has moved up in the world since I first went to him. He now had an office in a nice suite in a new building near a shopping mall. I wondered how long it would be before I could no longer afford him.

He's an intelligent, young guy with a pleasant manner, an MSW, and an impressive list of references. Lots of people told me he was the guy to see. Talking to him helped, no question about it, but, you know, even though I'm not supposed to say it or think it, so did the booze, at least for a while. Maybe it's because I controlled it pretty well and never developed a taste for hard stuff. You have to drink a lot of beer to get a meaningful buzz.

We sat in comfortable stuffed chairs across from one another. The office was bright and cheerful. Michael was dressed in neatly pressed chino pants and a red striped button-down shirt. He looked very academic, competent, and caring. Which he was. All three. The impression was that Mike was a friend and that he had all the time in the world for you, just you. Sometimes the cynical part of me really got in the way. I knew the guy had a schedule and had to earn a living but often I couldn't let it go at that.

We reviewed things for a few minutes. It had been three months since I had last seen him. I told him about last night. How simply talking with Barbara on the telephone had been an intrusion into what I had with Moira.

"Were you impotent?"

"No." I resented the question but knew it had to be asked. "But she was there. Barbara, I mean. She still affects me. Just talking with her still affects me. I don't love her anymore. I wouldn't go back with her, not that she'd have me."

"Do you love Moira? How have those feelings developed? Last time we talked you weren't sure."

"I don't know." I just looked at Michael Sandler for a moment. He returned my gaze, thoughtful, waiting.

"I don't know," I said again. "Jesus, I'm not sixteen. I should know how I feel, shouldn't I?"

He smiled. "At sixteen, feelings are often deceivingly complete and total. You're convinced you know what love is and that you're in it. With maturity—and experience, some of it good, some not so good—you learn about the ambiguities and shades of gray, in yourself, in others, in your feelings."

The words were good, soothingly spoken, but I had the feeling I was listening to textbook talk.

"Don't try to force the feelings. Take it one day at a time. You've apparently got a good relationship with Moira. Take it for what it is. Enjoy it for what it is. If it changes, it changes."

I thought of what Norm had said about Moira.

We sat for a few moments saying nothing. Michael often did that. He let me digest thoughts.

Then he said, "How's your son? How are you doing with him?"

"Fine," I said. "I think my relationship with Nicky is good. Considering the circumstances. You know, seeing him mainly on weekends, but the time is quality time. We probably do things together that we wouldn't if we were together all the time."

Michael nodded. "That's the way it often seems to work. It's a compensation."

Another pause.

"There's something there, though, isn't there?" Michael asked.

"How do you mean?"

"Something with your son that isn't quite right with you."

"Why do you say that?"

Michael smiled. "Nick, I do this all the time. It's what I do. You're not exactly a mask."

I shrugged.

"Well?"

I thought of the red Porsche and Gary letting Nicky drive it in the parking lot of a mall and in the State Park in Ipswich.

"Are you trying too hard with your son?"

"How the hell can you try too hard with your kid?"

"Nick, sometimes you don't let things flow. You try to force them. Sometimes it's better to back off."

I felt an irritation I didn't usually feel talking with Michael Sandler. But there was a deeper irritation at the image of that red Porsche and Gary and Nicky, probably laughing, bonding, sharing what should be a father-and-son experience, an experience contemporary yet somehow elemental. The irritation threatened to bubble out of me but I checked it. It was shameful.

Michael allowed another pause. He watched me but didn't push. He nodded and smiled. "You're not being very communicative today, Nick. What else? Is there anything else?"

I had requested this purgation. This confessional. Articulation was, of course, essential to the process. But somehow the session seemed combative rather than therapeutic.

"Anything else you want to talk about, Nick?" A small prod, a nudge. Open up, Nick.

Somehow, my reasons for coming here now seemed

vaguely defined to me. Did they have to do with Barbara and Moira? With Nicky? I wasn't sure. With the killings of Kristin Williams and Darlene Abbott and my fears of entanglement there, of innuendo and how it might affect my son?

"Mike, it's me. Not you. The mood isn't there today. Why don't we call it a day?"

"Is that what you want to do?"

What I wanted to do was get on with the day. I wanted to get hold of Rick Le Brun. I wanted to go into the Combat Zone again with Swede to look for the black Trans Am. Barbara's intrusion now seemed remote and I chided myself for having to come here. I couldn't run to Michael Sandler every time the phone rang or Nicky told me he rode in Gary's Porsche.

"Actually, Mike, this has been helpful today. Don't measure your success by how much I pour out my heart."

"I don't. Measuring my success is something I haven't really learned how to do, Nick. What I do isn't like tuning a car. Probably a lot like teaching, I imagine. Sometimes it's awfully hard to tell whether you've made a connection and, if you have, whether anything resulted from it. So, I do what I can and hope for the best. And try to let it go at that."

He walked me to the door and we shook hands.

"That's a nice outlook, Mike. One could do a lot worse."

I stopped at a pay phone, called *Hub* magazine, and got through to Rick Le Brun. Yes, he could see me. Reporters are always curious, I guess.

Hub is located on Commonwealth Avenue and occupies the entire second floor of a nice brownstone. Like its cousin *Boston*, it's a slick regional, heavy with advertisements of pricey cars, clothing, and real estate. Its readership is upwardly mobile but concerned with the meaningful issues and appreciates droll or ironic humor.

Rick Le Brun ushered me into a cubicle whose size and location at the end of the row suggested he was low on the pecking order. He was tall, thin, and rather open looking. About thirty, I guessed.

Briefly, I explained that his name came up in connection with a paper that a student at Colton was doing on the illegal adoptions of the babies of prostitutes and runaways.

He asked me the name of the student and I told him. He had been slouching in his chair but now sat erect.

"The girl who was murdered? How did my name come up?"

I told him it was on a card that suggested he might have been an interview source.

"Yes. I did an article on the Combat Zone and its prostitutes when I was with *The Oracle*, but the article had nothing to do with adoptions." *The Oracle* was a counterculture rag that finally went mainstream and so was able to cling to life but showed much less vitality than it once had.

I was disappointed that the article had nothing to do with adoptions because finding how Kristin Williams fell upon the idea for her paper might be helpful.

I asked, "Do you know how she got your name?"

"Not really. *The Oracle* isn't indexed in the *Reader's Guide*. Perhaps someone told her of the article. Maybe she read it. That was only, let's see, a little over two years ago."

Two years ago, Kristin Williams was still in high school. I didn't think articles on social issues in bohemian publications would attract high school students but you never knew.

I took a plunge. "Mr. Le Brun, do you know Dan Ritchie? Does his name mean anything to you?"

Rick Le Brun unwrapped a stick of gum, bent it into a U and popped it into his mouth.

"I know Dan Ritchie," he said. "Well, let me say I know of him." He worked the gum for a few moments. "But why don't you tell me what this is all about first, Mr. Toland. When someone inquires about and connects me with a murdered person, I'm naturally intrigued. You said on the phone that you teach at Colton. It sounds to me like you're playing detective. I assume that Kris Williams was a student of yours?"

"As a matter of fact, she wasn't." I didn't want to disclose any more than I had to. "She was a student of Dan Ritchie's and of a friend of mine. I'm afraid I'm going to let it go at that."

Rick Le Brun nodded and half smiled. He had folded the silver gum foil into a spear and slid it back and forth between his fingers. "Dan Ritchie's free-lanced a few articles locally. Even did something for *The Atlantic* once, I believe. Sociopolitical stuff. Not bad but a bit heavy and pedantic, I thought.

"About him personally, I don't know a great deal. Perhaps less than you do. He is your colleague, after all."

Rick Le Brun regarded me thoughtfully and chewed. He threw the foil into his basket. He asked, "Is there a story in this for me?"

"I wouldn't know. Not at the moment anyway."

"You'd keep me in mind, though, wouldn't you?"

"I would."

"I'll tell you this. First, to reverse the rules, this is off the record?"

I nodded.

"Dan Ritchie, as I understand it, is one odd duck."

I waited.

"I mean for a guy who seems interested in social mores and customs, he has or had some strange ones of his own. Perhaps you've heard?"

"Not really."

"Well, Dr. Ritchie, it seems, was a frequent visitor to the Combat Zone and on friendly terms with its inhabitants."

That was what I was looking for. I fed an enticer. "Well, who hasn't paid an occasional visit to that kind of place?"

"Occasional, yes. But Dan Ritchie was a known frequenter and his choice of companions was strange, to say the least, for a wearer of academic robes."

"Oh?"

"Whores, pimps, and some general all-around deviates."

"Maybe he found faculty parties dull," I said. "To be truthful, it is rumored at school that he has holdings in a joint or two in the Combat Zone. Would you know anything about that?"

"I don't but it wouldn't surprise me. Not the sort of thing to sit well with the hierarchy at Colton, I'd think, though."

The picture being painted of Dan Ritchie was unbecoming and suggestive, but was it simply that? I looked through the glass to the next cubicle and watched a black guy work a word processor.

I said, "You say Dan Ritchie had odd habits. Hanging around the Combat Zone, is that what you're referring to?"

"This is becoming a gossip session, I'm afraid. What's all this germaine to?"

"I'm not sure. Maybe I'll know when I hear it," I said.

"I don't want to press you, Mr. Toland, but, as I say, it sure sounds like you're playing detective. Let me just say that Dan Ritchie was purported to be involved in some bizarre behavior, things that went beyond the kinky. Maybe they were just experiments of some sort. Who knows?"

"Experiments?"

"Yeah. Look, Mr. Toland, I really think I've said enough there. The guy hung around the Combat Zone. That's no crime. If someone gets their kicks in ways that shock middle America, what's the big deal? As far as I know, Dan Ritchie never did anything to hurt anyone. I want to make that clear."

I shifted. "What can you tell me about Kristin Williams? Did she interview you?"

"She came to sec me. About a month ago, I'd say. She asked some questions about prostitutes, where they lived, where they got medical service, their relationship to their pimp, that sort of thing. Some of the questions I could answer, some I couldn't."

"Did she reveal the angle she was working on at that time? I mean the illegal adoption market for babies of prostitutes."

"No."

It was likely at that point, then, that Kristin hadn't formulated her final thesis, that she had discovered the adoption black market in subsequent investigation.

"But she did say that she was onto something that I might use and that she would probably contact me again. She never did. I read of the discovery of her body and naturally wondered about a connection between her

91

death and what she said she was onto but actually you're the first person I've talked to about it."

"You didn't go to the police?" I said.

"With what?"

I shrugged.

"With what, Mr. Toland?"

He sounded defensive.

"No, I don't imagine there's anything there they could use." I wanted to appease him. I also wanted to know whether what Kristin Williams told him she was onto was simply the adoption angle or something else. Had she discovered who was behind it, who was profiting? One thing was sure, the prostitutes themselves, as usual, weren't the ones making the most from their services.

"One last thing, Mr. Le Brun. Are any of these names familiar to you?" I fed him the names from Kristin Williams's list.

He pondered and said he didn't know them. "Why do you ask?"

"Apparently, they're names of prostitutes and pimps. Kristin uncovered them."

He shrugged.

I looked at my watch. I was due to meet Swede in fifteen minutes. I thanked Rick Le Brun for his time and stood to leave. He seemed ill at ease.

"You're sure you don't want to tell me what this is all about, Mr. Toland?"

"It's a sad, serious business, isn't it?" I said. "A decent young girl with a lot of idealism loses her life uncovering some dirt that needs still to be uncovered. Maybe I'll be back to you, Mr. Le Brun, with some filth that you can air."

I gave him my phone number and asked if he'd get in touch if he thought of anything helpful.

As I walked back down to Commonwealth Avenue, I remembered that the last person I gave my phone number to had been murdered.

I had parked around the corner on Dartmouth Street and I sat in my car for a few minutes looking at the list of names and thinking. I wondered how forthright Rick Le Brun had been. I also wondered what he meant by Dan Ritchie's "experiments."

Something else had been nagging me all along. How likely was it for prostitutes to become pregnant or, if pregnant, to go full term? I had no statistical evidence, but that occupational hazard was so preventable as to be nonexistent. When I was on active duty in Stuttgart, we had much occasion to be in official contact with the local brothels and I couldn't recall knowing or hearing of a pregnant prostitute who went to full term.

I looked at the names again. What was the common denominator, if any? The list didn't read like the B-movie roster of ethnic diversity. Nothing Mediterranean. Nothing Hispanic. The names sounded Northern European or WASP. Or black. Names like Johnson or Moore could be black. What did that mean? Maybe I'd ask Stan Janski to run them through for me.

I put the list aside and drove to Cambridge.

Swede was dressed for action. Pressed Levis, running shoes, and a poplin windbreaker over a white sweatshirt. We took the same BMW and sped down Memorial Drive. Light rain misted the windshield and a low overcast amputated the tops of the Prudential and John Hancock buildings on the other side of the Charles.

We crossed the river at the Longfellow Bridge. Late afternoon traffic was thick and it took over twenty minutes for us to get to the Combat Zone. I told Swede that I just wanted to patrol the streets for a while and peruse the lots and alleys to see whether we could turn up the Trans Am.

We came down Tremont, turned left at Boylston, left on Washington, and then right. We came back up through Chinatown, peering into alleys, including the scene of our near tussle, checked parked cars, did it again, this time swinging wider through Chinatown, and saw one Trans Am, but older and bronze.

I wondered whether this was pointless.

We came back up Washington Street at a stop-and-go pace. Two ladies of the night—in this case, late afternoon—eyed us and threw a little body language our way. I smiled at them.

"Gol-lee," Swede said, "is them real, live whores, out to do evil things to the yokels like us?"

"'I have seen the painted women under the gas lamps luring the farm boys.'"

"How's that?"

"From 'Chicago.' Sandburg."

"Ah, you literary types. A quote for everything."

This time Swede went straight up Washington, out of the Zone to the pedestrian mall, turned left and came out on Tremont. We patrolled past the Common, crossed Boylston, went through the theater district and left again. He was making concentric circles, progressively larger.

"This was not one of my better ideas," I said. "At the risk of lapsing into cliché, it is the proverbial search in the haystack."

"No it's not. The odds are nowhere near as good." Swede grinned. "But what else is new about police work?"

My stomach was sending signals and I suggested we eat.

"Sounds good to me," Swede said. "Want to just grab a sub or go to a Chinese place?"

That was no decision. I suggested Lee Chen's, next to the alley where Darlene Abbott's body was found.

When I told Swede *sotto voce* about the alley, he said, "Don't you think it's a little dicey coming back to the scene of the crime, as they say?"

He was working on a combination of rice and something from the sea. Some guys had problems with Oriental food after Vietnam but Swede certainly didn't. He was a man without hangups.

"Adds spice to the meal," I said.

Lee Chen's was a small restaurant and this was apparently not its busy hour. Besides us, two banking or insurance types in State Street uniforms and a young couple were the only patrons.

We concentrated on the meal for a few minutes. I had chicken smothered in mushroom and pepper sauce. We each had a bottle of Bud. I decided I wanted to talk with the cook who had found the body. It sure would be a lot easier if I could flash a shield.

I caught our waiter's eye, held up my bottle of Bud and two fingers. Sign language. When he brought the two beers, I said, "Is Mr. Chen in, by any chance?"

He smiled and nodded and so did I.

A minute later a man in the kind of shiny black suit that so many Chinese seem to favor came to our booth. "Gentlemen. Is there a problem?"

I smiled, slid over, and gestured him to sit. "No, no. The

food is terrific. You have to come into Chinatown for the best Chinese food. No question."

He smiled but didn't take my offer to sit. "Thank you."

I beckoned him close and he bent down. "Look, we understand you had some trouble in the alley a few days ago."

"Police?"

I shook my head. "No. I knew the girl, though. Awful thing."

There was a nodding of heads over that.

"Can we buy you something to drink?" Swede asked.

"No thank you."

Swede proferred the bowl of iced pineapple. The host gestured a polite refusal.

I said, "Terrible thing, stabbed like that. Did you see her?"

"I didn't discover the body but I saw it. It wasn't a pretty sight," Lee Chen said. The English had no trace of pidgin.

"Really hacked up, I understand," I said.

Lee Chen nodded, tight lipped. "Multiple wounds. A mess."

"Probably a crazy got her by surprise, dragged her into the alley, and knifed her in the back," I said.

"I'm not sure about that," Lee Chen said. "From what I could see, it appeared that she was stabbed from the front. She was lying face down and there was no blood on her back. And there was no sign of a struggle. No barrels knocked over or anything."

Swede and I sat quietly for a moment. Lee Chen stood patiently. Rain ran in crooked rivulets down the window beside me.

"Had she eaten in here?" I asked.

"No. No one here ever saw her before."

Lee Chen eyed us carefully, probably absorbing detail so that he could describe us to the police. He'd likely be on the phone as soon as we left. What the hell.

"She was your, uh, girlfriend?" he asked.

"Nothing like that," I said. "Just a friend."

Lee Chen smiled. "Tommy Wong, one of the cooks, went out to the alley to throw away some cartons and found her. Sometimes bums will sleep out there. He didn't know what it was at first till he got up close and saw the blood all over the place. He came in and got me real fast. I took one look, and called the police. It's too bad. Her pictures in the paper show she was a real pretty girl."

"She was." I thought of how she looked that day in my office.

"No offense to you gentlemen or to your friend, but this kind of thing gives Chinatown a bad name. I mean what spills over from the Combat Zone. Pornography, prostitutes, and drugs is a combination that adds up to trouble. And a murder outside your restaurant isn't good for business."

"She wasn't a prostitute," I said.

"No? If you say not." He smiled. "Enjoy the rest of your meal and be sure to come back."

We paid two bucks and drove the BMW from the small parking lot. There were still a few lots we hadn't checked and we drove around and did that. At one, we did a double take but the look-alike turned out to be a black Z-28.

"Two to go," I said.

"Whichever we do first, it'll be in the second," Swede said.

But we lucked out. On our way I saw it in a small lot

that we had already passed at least twice. It must have just come in.

Swede stopped on the narrow street and I got out to get the license number. A kid sitting in the attendant's booth reading a skin magazine eyed me as I copied the plate number.

"Looks the same. Has a sunroof," I told Swede when I got back in the car. "But how many dark-blue Trans Ams are there?"

"Want to stake out?" Swede asked.

"Why not? We'll try it for a while and if they don't come out, I'll give Stan Janski the number." That's probably all I should have done but I was curious.

Swede had pulled around the corner and he circled back, but the closest we could park was about forty yards from the lot. The rain was now a heavy mist and every couple of minutes Swede flicked the windshield wipers on.

"You know something?" he said. "Having no official capacity has its advantages. These guys come out to the Trans Am, we follow them, grab them, and use some friendly persuasion to find out what's going on. What'd they try to run you over for? We're official, we can't do that."

I smiled grimly and thought of the things I'd heard about Swede when he was in Vietnam. He had been in the Third Corps, Special Forces, Tay Ninh Province, near the Cambodian border. He had been a master sergeant and had done two tours, two years, in Nam with thirty days at home in between. Two tours. A regular tourist.

From what I'd heard, in addition to his martial arts skills, his specialty had been interrogation. Supposedly, he'd put the Gestapo to shame, could get a sphinx to talk, and he didn't need pliers, pins, or electric prods. He didn't need anyone tied to a chair or held by someone else. Those big hands and ice blue eyes were more than adequate.

I knew he'd love to get his hands on whoever owned that Trans Am. But he'd likely act first and not let any presumption of innocence interfere. I didn't need that.

It was nine-thirty when the Trans Am pulled out of the lot and we followed. It meandered about the maze of one-way streets and finally headed up Washington and then swung out toward the Common. On Tremont, two cars got between us but we caught up on Boylston and followed it as it turned onto Charles. The darkness and the rain-dotted windows obscured whoever was driving or how many were in the car. It turned left on Beacon and when we were past the Public Gardens, Swede made his move.

He downshifted and tromped the accelerator.

"What the hell are you doing?" I said.

We were almost up to the Trans Am.

"Back off, Swede."

He did and I leaned involuntarily toward the dashboard. He looked at me and I said, "Just follow them."

"It's your show, Nick. We could lose them."

But we didn't.

I was disappointed when the Trans Am didn't lead us to a place in Milton that would turn out to be Dan Ritchie's. Instead it ended up on the Jamaicaway and finally pulled into a driveway that looked more accustomed to Benzes than fast American iron.

And the girl who got out, from what we could determine in the dark, looked a far cry from what I expected.

CHAPTER

8

Friday morning, I met Norm Eigner on his way to class and asked whether he knew any students that Kris Williams had been friendly with. He did. She was in this very class.

"Let me talk with her for just a minute, Norm."

"Not too long, huh, Nick. We'll be reviewing Hopkins's use of sprung rhythm and we wouldn't want her short-changed in that."

From the girl, I got the name of Kris Williams's boy-friend. It was Kenny Dobson. She eyed me a little suspiciously, but students generally don't question a professor's reasons. Maybe if Kristin had found anything startling in her research she had divulged it, and she would be more likely to do that with a boyfriend than with her parents. Besides, confronting a distraught mother and father was something I had little stomach for, not to mention the jurisdictional thin ice I was walking on that they would be more likely to question.

When my classes were done for the day, I ran a fast five miles, staying on the main drags, keeping an eye out for hostile Trans Ams and wondering whether they'd be dumb enough to use it again. Earlier, I had called Stan Janski and he'd said he'd get back to me when he had traced the number of the car. The woman driving the Trans Am hadn't looked like anyone who made her living in the Combat Zone but the car didn't look like Jamaica Plain either. An intriguing puzzle but my gut feeling was that it would lead to nothing.

After I showered, I had a can of sardines between two slices of whole wheat, a dill spear, and a bottle of Molson left over from what Moira had brought. Then I called Kenny Dobson. He lived with his mother, which by today's standards, I guess, means he is either an innocent or parsimonious.

He agreed to talk with me when I told him why. He seemed curious and wary and I assumed the police had been hounding him. Boyfriends are automatic suspects. I lied a little and told him I wasn't a cop but that I might have something that could lead to finding Kristin's killer, which perhaps he could add to.

He lived in Somerville and we arranged to meet at seven-thirty at a Dunkin' Donuts place he gave me directions to. We could conspire over munchkins and coffee. This kid wasn't living in the fast lane.

I opened another bottle of Molson and looked at the list of names again that Kristin had compiled even though I practically had them memorized. No new insights revealed themselves as I knew they wouldn't. It was a week and two days since Darlene Abbott was killed and four days since Inspector Gallo told me Kristin Williams's body was found. If you don't find the killer in the first few days, the odds are you'll never find him.

At five-to-seven as I was getting ready to leave, Stan Janski called. "Nick, your car's registered to a Joanne Lewis, Beacon Street, Brookline."

"Brookline?" Brookline is a posh suburb.

"Yeah. By the way, I haven't forgotten about that— what was his name?—Ritchie guy you wanted checked out."

"Yeah, any connection to a joint in the Combat Zone."

"Right. I'll get back to you."

"Stan, got a minute?" I read him the names from the list and told him who I thought they were. "You familiar with them?"

"No. I don't do that stuff, Nick, thank Christ. Let the Boston cops deal with it."

"Hmm. Look, if you can find anything on this Joanne Lewis, I'd appreciate that too. Also, anything on this address." I gave him the Jamaicaway address.

"What the hell you into, Nick?"

"Deep shit, maybe. You know the Colton girl whose body was discovered and the girl stabbed in Chinatown little over a week ago? Has to do with them."

"Talk to me, Nick. What's it got to do with you? Doesn't sound like anything the three-fortieth ought to be involved with."

"It isn't. We'll have a beer some night. I'll tell you all about it."

"Let's do that, Nick. I sure wouldn't want to read about it."

The Dunkin' Donuts place was in a minimall and Kenny Dobson got out of his car when I pulled in. I had described the Fairmont and he'd told me he'd be in a Honda.

We shook hands and I said, "Want to talk in my car?" I didn't really want to go into the doughnut stand, for that would require ordering coffee and/or doughnuts, strictly morning fare to me.

That was fine with him. I asked a few questions and found he knew about Kristin's research. I told him I thought it was likely someone involved in the illegalities she was uncovering had killed her. Then I leveled with him. I told him how I knew about Kris's research, that I was an MP reserve officer. "All of this. Your talking with me. My probing about. It's all unofficial. But I'll tell you this. Someone's uncomfortable with the fact that I know what Kris had uncovered." I wondered about Kenny's own danger.

"So that's why I'm here. Maybe you can give me some piece of information that'll help to indicate who might have killed Kris."

Kenny Dobson nodded. He studied me for a moment and then said, "I told Kris that she was messing around with stuff that she shouldn't be. Going into the Combat Zone like that is nothing a girl should do, but that's the way Kris was. She got a hold of something, she wouldn't let go."

Kenny Dobson was a clean-cut-looking kid. No earrings.

No punk hair. That observation, by the way, is just a statement of fact and doesn't reveal a bias.

"Do you know how she found out about the illegal adoptions?"

"A runaway kid she interviewed told her."

"Do you know the kid's name?"

"I'm not sure. She told me but I don't remember."

Slowly, I fed him the names from the list. When I finished, he shook his head. "Sorry. I can't say."

"How'd she find out about the prostitutes? I just can't see them talking about that sort of thing to someone like Kristin."

"The kid told her."

"Yeah, but how'd she get the names?"

"I don't know."

I had seen and done enough interrogating to know an evasion when I heard it. Kenny Dobson was holding back.

"The cops been talking to you?" I said.

"A couple of times."

"You knew Darlene Abbott?"

He nodded and his eyes started to fill.

Then I said, "You sure you don't want to tell me how Kris got those prostitutes' names?"

He looked at me and then out the window to his right. "What the hell am I talking to you for? You're not a real cop. An MP reserve. What the hell's that?"

"It's all you've got if you want to help find out who killed Kris. I'll tell you something. The cops do the best they can but they're overworked and understaffed. They'll scratch around but the odds are they won't find who killed either Kristin or Darlene. Sad but true. And the longer it goes on the slimmer the chance gets."

"So who the hell are you, Sherlock Holmes?"

"No. I'm no brighter than the Boston cops. The difference is I have a personal interest and I don't have a caseload like theirs. But I do have access pretty much to what they have on an informal basis."

I studied Kenny Dobson's profile for a moment. He was frightened. "So, come on, why don't you level with me?"

"What makes you think I'm not?"

"Just a feeling. I think there's something you know that you didn't tell the police. You've got to tell someone."

Kenny Dobson chewed his lower lip for a few moments. I prodded. "Come on, Kenny. What is it?"

He chewed his lip some more and I thought he might cry.

"Okay, there is something. Kris was passing herself off as a prostitute." He looked out his window, then at me. "Do you believe that? And pregnant. I guess that opened things up for her."

I scratched my chin. "How the hell do you do that, I wonder. I mean prostitution isn't free-lance, at least in the Combat Zone, I don't think. You'd have to operate through a pimp."

Then it hit me and I shut up. I looked at Kenny Dobson. "Satisfied?" His eyes were watery.

"She'd go that far?" I said.

His voice cracked. "I don't know. She might. That's why I didn't say anything. Because of her parents."

Another realization hit me. This gave Kenny Dobson motivation to kill his girlfriend. But why would he tell me?

"Was she pregnant?"

"I don't think so." He looked straight out the window, avoiding my eyes. A couple of early-teen boys rode up on chopper bicycles, nearly sideswiped my car, clattered them against the side of the building, and swaggered inside.

"You want a coffee or to go someplace and get a beer?" I said.

He shook his head. "No."

He took a handkerchief from his pocket and blew his nose. "She said that some of the—the whores—that some of the whores said it was really worth their while to get pregnant. More money in selling their babies than in being a whore."

I thought about that, about how much they'd have to be paid to make more money than prostitution paid. When would a girl start to show her pregnancy? How long would she be out of work?

"She also told me a kid of hers would be a good candidate for the adoption market."

"Why?"

"Because she was white and blond. Her baby, if blond, would command more dough. Nice commentary, huh?"

We were quiet for a few moments. The more I heard, the more this mess deepened. If Kristin Williams was passing herself off as a prostitute, then who knew she was doing a paper and that I had access to what she had uncovered? My hypothesis to this point had been that she had mentioned she was doing research to someone she had interviewed. Of course, I still had no explanation for the attempts to frame me or run me down.

"Does the name Joanne Lewis mean anything to you?" I said.

"No."

"Did Kris ever say anything about Dr. Ritchie? She was doing the same research for him."

"She might have mentioned his name in connection with the paper. Is that what you mean?"

106

"No. Other than that."

"No."

"Okay, so what we have here is a girl who found out about an illegal adoption market and got killed for finding out. At least, that's how I see it." I watched him for reaction as I spoke.

He shook his head. "She was onto more than that," he said. "She told me she had found more than that and that it would blow things open. But she wouldn't tell me what."

"Wait a minute," I said. "Her last thesis was that a black market for adopting children of runaways and prostitutes exists in the Boston area. You're saying she found something beyond that?"

"Yes. Something she'd probably have to give to the newspapers."

"When was this?" I said.

"Just before she disappeared. She said she had found the final thesis for her paper."

On my way home, I stopped at a phone and called Moira. Was she busy and did she want any company? I asked, which she probably took as an ill-disguised way of my saying I was in rut. But that wasn't the case. She was correcting a set of exams but said she'd welcome a break. Next, I stopped at a package store for some beer.

In Revere, I took the shore road where the amusement park once was and headed for Marblehead. As I drove, I mulled over just what Kristin's final thesis might have been. The obvious theory was she had homed in on who was behind the black market. She found someone or something and would "blow things open." And they knew she had found out. Someone who was trying to frame me and/or kill me.

Several times I checked my rearview mirror for trailing cars, and was especially watchful when I got onto roads that were lonely and not brightly lit. But things looked clear and I pulled up to Moira's without escort.

Moira lives in a circa Revolutionary War house that has been done over into four apartments with modern baths and kitchenettes but which retains the low ceilings, fireplaces, and general ambience of the Minuteman period. I've occasionally tried to get her to dress as a colonial kitchen wench and serve me tankards of ale before we warmed the bed but she tells me my kinkiness is sick.

I let myself in and chided her for not locking the door. Even in Marblehead, violence and thievery lurk. She was correcting her tests at her kitchenette table. I opened a couple of beers, pushed one her way, and started on my own.

"Want to help?" she asked, indicating the pile of exams.

I watched her sip her beer and my stomach did its usual little flip when I just looked at her. I was a lucky guy. Sometimes I thought of solidifying our relationship and protecting my claim but I was still marriage shy. Besides that, two things held me back. One, I didn't know how Moira would react to a proposal since I had never asked. Two, my stomach also still did a little flip when I looked at or talked to Barbara.

"Moira," I said, "what kind of money do you think a Combat Zone prostitute turns?"

She looked quizzical and then smiled. "I have no idea. What's the matter, do you feel denied? Want to borrow some money?"

"I'm not talking about exclusive, independent suburban 'escorts' you occasionally read about. The ones who get a few hundred bucks for all-nighters with businessmen."

She went to the cabinet over her sink for two pilsner glasses. "These are more civilized." She poured her beer into one and set the other in front of me.

"Okay, I'll bite. What are you up to? Why do you want to know the going rate for trollops?"

"I'm trying to figure how much a prostitute would earn, let's say, in four months."

She nodded. "Go on."

"There's a further wrinkle in the murder of Kristin Williams."

I told her of my conversation with Kenny Dobson.

"If it was worth the whore's while to have a baby just to sell it, she'd have to give up wages for the time her pregnancy showed. You know, her marketability would be definitely affected by a protruding abdomen. And that would be what, four months?"

"Easily, I'd say. Don't forget, she's out of commission for a time afterward, too."

"How long?" I said, trying to remember the length of the hiatus after Nicky was born.

"Depends on the girl. Besides getting her figure back, she's got to be careful of infection. A month. Maybe six weeks."

I poured the rest of my bottle into the pilsner. "So she could be losing five, maybe six months' wages? What would that be?"

"There's one way to find out. Go in town and get a girl. See what she charges you." Moira's eyes had that elfin, teasing glint. "Get the different rates for the, uh, different services. For the quickie, for the all-nighter. You can figure it from that."

"Ah, I don't want to do that."

"You don't have to consummate the deal. Just get the

prices and then back off. Say you're not interested. Walk away."

I made a gesture of dismissal but the suggestion had merit.

I picked up Moira's pen and took a napkin from the holder. "Let's say she earns a hundred bucks a day. Does that seem right?"

Moira gave me a "beats me" expression.

"Five days a week," I continued. "Five bills a week. Twenty-five a year, give or take a little."

"No vacation time?" Moira asked. The elfin glint was still in her eye. It was easy to see she found this amusing.

"Oh, sure. Probably a trip to Lourdes or St. Peter's Square. Does that seem right, twenty-five thousand a year?"

"I suppose. But it's tax free, don't forget."

"Okay, so she loses, let's say, half of it. Would they pay her ten to fifteen thousand for a baby?"

"Dunno. Even if they paid her less, it's probably easier than her usual work. If she doesn't get morning sickness."

"But she could earn more than twenty-five thousand. I think the figure's conservative. She might earn double, triple that, in which case she has to be paid even more for the baby for it to be worth her while to quit work."

"Uh huh."

"How much would people pay for a child?"

"From what you've said, you're talking about a very affluent consumer, someone with the bucks who wants to do away with the red tape and the waiting period. The laws of supply and demand work here as well as anywhere else. Let's face it, as educators we're small time on financial matters. I can see people for whom a hundred thousand plus for something they really want would be no problem. Hell, look at the price of cars, real estate, art."

"Yeah," I said, "there sure are a lot of Benzes out there."

We sipped our beers quietly for a moment. Then I killed mine and went to the refrigerator. "Ready for another?"

"Not yet. I want to finish these papers tonight."

"Kris's boyfriend told me the big demand is for the blond-haired, blue-eyed child," I said, sitting down.

Moira nodded. "The Aryan. Hitler lives."

"The names on Kristin's list all sounded Anglo or Northern European. I wondered about that."

Moira shook her head. "This is all so sick."

"It is that," I agreed. "Deliberately using prostitutes for breeding. The prenatal care must be terrific."

Moira shuddered.

On the napkin I wrote the names Dan Ritchie and Kenny Dobson. Moira arched a quizzical eyebrow.

"Suspects," I said. "Kenny Dobson had motivation to kill Kristin Williams. He may have been jealous or enraged about her turning tricks if she was. But that doesn't explain Darlene Abbott. Why would he kill her unless she suspected him? That could be. She could have suspected him."

"But that's not why she came to you."

"Right, and why would he try to kill me? Besides, his being in cahoots with hit persons who drive Trans Ams doesn't add up. Also, I can't see him as the type who would break someone's neck."

I crossed out Kenny Dobson's name.

"I'm watching a trained police investigator in action."

"Right. This is how we do it. Impressive, huh?" I said.

"Very scientific. Napkins. Flair pens. Impeccable logic."

I underlined Dan Ritchie's name. "Our colleague had or has the Combat Zone connection, we *think*. He says he was doing the same story that Kristin Williams was. But he didn't know of my involvement until yesterday—I think. So, again, how do we account for the attempts to frame me—'implicate me' might be a more accurate expression—and run me down?"

"He might have known about Darlene Abbott, though, if she was asking questions around the Combat Zone," Moira said.

"Why do you say she may have been asking questions around the Combat Zone?"

"Well, that's where she was killed. Logical assumption is she was in there inquiring about her friend. Ergo, they, whoever 'they' is, killed her. Further assumption is that Dan Ritchie got wind of her inquiries."

I put question marks around Dan Ritchie's name. "We'll put Dr. Ritchie on hold."

I wrote another name. Moira turned the napkin to read it.

"Brian Connolly. Who's he?"

"The Boston cop I spoke with the day after Darlene Abbott was killed. You remember. I told you about him. His name was on one of Kristin's note cards."

"In what connection?"

"I assumed," I said, "that she was going to see him about what she had uncovered. He's a vice cop."

I turned the napkin around and underlined his name.

"He'd certainly have connections with the prostitutes," Moira said, "but wouldn't it be an adversary relationship?"

"Officially it would. And to begin with it would. He'd have contact with the whole Combat Zone infrastructure."

"'Infrastructure'? Dear me, Doctor, such jargon. But what's his connection with adoption outlets?"

"I don't know. But he knew Darlene Abbott had come to me and he knew I knew what Kristin was probing into because I told him. That could explain the Trans Am trying to run me down, but I still don't understand the phone numbers in the bottles of crack."

"What phone numbers in what bottles of crack? What are you talking about?"

I told her.

"I don't like this, Nick. I think you should see a lawyer."

"I've got it in mind. Just yet, though, things are okay."

"You be careful. This is messier than I thought."

I smiled at her. "I'm careful. But I can't just walk away from this. For a number of reasons."

"Yes. I understand that and I suppose it's admirable and I further suppose there's no way I can dissuade you from what you're doing." She took my hand. "But for now, what say we put all this stuff aside. Exams, names of suspects, estimates of whores' wages."

"And?"

She came around and sat on my lap. "And I attack you."

She pressed her mouth on mine. We kissed for a long moment. The smell and feel of her made me giddy and as randy as a seventeen-year-old. My hands explored, my fingers unbuttoned and unhooked.

She murmured little sounds and her own hands became busy. "I know you have kinky fantasies, but what say we try the bedroom?" she said, her voice a husky whisper. "I'm just an old-fashioned girl but I can promise you more than lights-out missionary."

I didn't have to be asked twice. But first I gave a quick look outside and locked her front door.

CHAPTER
9

The next morning I got up early (for a Saturday) and before picking up Nicky I drove to the college.

At the Colton College library is a section of publications in trade books and periodicals by members of the faculty. This doesn't include the products of the publish-or-perish syndrome, the stuff found in the wasteland of the professional journals.

There were seven novels (none mine) split among three members of the English department; nineteen nonfiction titles, five in the pure sciences, six in the social sciences, two on linguistics, three on foreign languages, three on art; and several periodicals, each tagged with the faculty member's name. My ego suffered a bit as I took in the list.

I pulled four by Dan Ritchie, including the three-year-old *Atlantic*, which I looked at first. The article was entitled "Whither the Proper Bostonian?" Skimming it revealed it to be about the change in attitude in Boston toward things sexual or prurient. The style was correct and, while not stilted, perhaps a bit pedantic as Rick Le Brun had said. It traced the "banned in Boston" mentality of a previous time, discussed Scollay Square (now plowed under and reincarnated as a clean, modern government center) with its Old Howard and other dens of various types, and finally examined the Combat Zone. Naturally, at that, my pulse did a little jig and I bore down. I read it through once and then again. But Dan said nothing self-incriminating or even suggestive that he wrote from a first-hand familiarity with the place, its denizens, or its establishments. I was disappointed.

I looked at the next, a Sunday tabloid delivered free of charge in the Boston area that earns its keep by carrying a lot of advertising. The article was about a mid-nineteenth-century religious cult whose fanatical leader tried to convert prostitutes to the path of righteousness. Apparently he played the role of the Holy Spirit and through his flock of fallen women bred descendants of them and him who would enjoy salvation. Keeping his harem with children must have been a full-time occupation. The good minister sired thirty-two. Eventually, the cult threatened to fall apart through lack of members willing to work to support their communal structure. But the minister, a practical man, ordered his women to work at their former profession. However, strong traces of puritanism still lingered in the good people of the central Massachusetts village on whose outskirts the cult had been flourishing. They drove the tarts and their whoremaster/spiritual leader clean out of the state to a destination unknown.

The article said the minister indulged in strange sexual practices with his ladies, scourging them to make them pure receptors for his sacred seed. For their penance, he made them perform self-degrading sexual acts. I wondered if Dan Ritchie's alleged bizarre practices were in any way derived from these.

An article in *Yankee* on school life in eighteenth-century New England proved innocuous, as did the last, in the *Boston Globe* Sunday magazine, a comparison/contrast of the industries of Massachusetts in the past and present. Dan Ritchie had some respectable publications to his credit.

I sat for a moment with the works of Dan Ritchie on the table in front of me and wondered about the man. I had been doing a lot of that lately. Did he know Joanne Lewis, the driver of the Trans Am that Swede and I had followed to the Jamaicaway? Did he know Lieutenant Brian Connolly? Did they all know each other?

I was tiring of this conundrum and wanted to sweep it aside, except for its implications to me. And, for now at least, I would.

I drove to pick up Nicky and my spirits lifted.

Outside my former home, I tooted a couple of crisp notes and eyed Gary's Porsche while I waited. The damn thing was attractive, sexual actually. Fire-engine red, a car for boys of all ages.

It had rained last night and the morning sun, now completely broken through the clouds, was raising steam from the puddles and the sheet metal of the Porsche.

I thought I might take Nicky to a batting cage and then, after lunch when things dried out a little, maybe we'd do nine holes at a nearby public course. We both liked to golf and, to tell the truth, Nicky was now better than I was.

I turned on the radio to find a station that I thought would be suitable to us both, a compromise that seldom worked. I knew I would end up letting him pick his own station. The compromise that would finally be worked out would be that he'd keep the volume within limits that wouldn't shatter the windows or my eardrums.

I drummed my fingers on the steering wheel in time to something I wasn't familiar with but which I was sure Nicky would like. That would be a good way to start the day; for him to get in the car while a tune he liked was playing. I wished the car had stereo. No doubt the Porsche did, probably even a cassette.

I blipped the horn again and Barbara came out, dodging the puddles. She had a bathrobe tugged around her, which I think I gave her, and slippers. Her hair was tousled. I checked my watch and knew I had woken her. God, she looked great.

I turned down the radio and rolled down my window. As she leaned her face close to mine, my stomach did its little flip.

"Nick, I'm sorry," she said. "I tried to call you last night but I guess you were out. There was no answer. Nicky's gone for the day with his friends to some school affair."

She smiled a sympathetic smile. "You're not mad, are you?"

"Of course not."

It was an arrangement that if anything came up Nicky could pass on our Saturday together. I knew as he got older that would happen more and more often. I wanted to be there in his life but didn't want to encroach on the other things that are part of adolescence.

She hesitated and then said, "Can you come in for a coffee?"

The lingering perfume of her and the morning huskiness of her voice insinuated themselves through my senses. I wanted her and I wanted my son, in different ways, of course. I was beginning to feel sorry for myself.

As I looked at her, the inevitable comparisons with Moira forced themselves on me. The way they looked: That was a draw. They didn't look alike, but each was a knockout. The way they made love: another draw. The way they were to live with? I would never go back to that with Barbara. Moira was an unknown there.

The flap to Barbara's bathrobe was open at her throat and hung loose, exposing the curve of her breast, but I maintained firm eye contact as I said, "I'd love a coffee, Barbara, but I've really got to run. Got a million things to do. Thanks anyway."

Of course, that made no sense and I knew she knew. If I had had time for Nicky, I had time for coffee, but she didn't press it.

"How's it going? You know, what you were telling me about on the phone the other day."

"Nothing new there. I expect things will just fizzle."

She didn't seem to want to leave. My peripheral vision saw the flap to her robe open a bit more and something inside me moaned a little note of anguish.

I know some couples occasionally make love after a divorce but we hadn't. The act would be ecstasy; it always was with her. But the aftermath would probably do a number on my head. Merely to entertain the thought was to venture into dangerous emotional territory. Not that the choice was necessarily mine to make. When she asked me in for coffee, that was likely just what she had in mind, for the two of us and Gary to sit over coffee and get chummy.

I'd pass on that.

She said, "Nick, I had a strange phone call last night. A man asked for you and when I told him you didn't live here anymore, he asked if I ever saw you. I said I did and he said to give you a message. He said, 'Mind your own business or someone's going to get hurt.' What's he talking about, Nick? What did he mean?"

"I don't know."

"Has it something to do with those girls who were murdered?"

"Jesus, Barbara," I said, exasperated, "it's just some nut. Maybe a student. I don't know."

"I didn't like his tone. It frightened me."

"What did he sound like?"

"What do you mean?" She looked puzzled. The flap was still open, exposing the soft flesh where my head had often lain.

"Did he sound young? Old? Did he have an accent?"

"He sounded ordinary. A fairly deep voice. Not a kid. By that I mean not a college-age student."

Dan Ritchie's voice was fairly deep. As was Lieutenant Brian Connolly's. As were millions of other male voices. But Dan Ritchie and Lieutenant Connolly knew I didn't live with Barbara. Whoever had called got the number from an older directory.

"Nick, you're being careful, aren't you?"

"Barbara, this is nothing. Don't worry about it." My tone was harsher than I wanted it to be. I softened it as I

119

said, "There really is nothing to worry about. But if—and it's very unlikely—*if* he should call again, you'll let me know?"

She put her hand on my shoulder. "Don't let anything happen to you. Nicky needs his father."

I resisted the impulse to put my hand on hers. "I'll be careful, Barbara. I'm always careful."

Our eyes locked for a moment. Then I broke my gaze and said, "Tell Nicky to keep Monday night open for the Sox game. I'll pick him up about six so we can watch batting practice."

"I'll tell him."

I drove home with that peculiarly empty feeling that is akin to a sense of loss. I tried to focus on tonight and what Moira and I had planned but I got all the way home and I was still thinking of my son and my former wife.

Thinking of them and wondering who had made the phone call.

I decided I needed a long run and wondered whether Swede would be interested. I called him at the dealership and it took a bit of persuasion to get through the receptionist to the boss himself. But rhetoric and persuasion are part of what I teach and together with my wit and charm they broke the receptionist's steely reserve.

"I've already run, Nick," he said at my inquiry. "Besides, I'm really tied up here today."

This might be the day for me to seek solace in poetry of alienation. Either that or I could buy a dog.

We hung up and just as I was ready to leave, thinking of the loneliness of command, divorce, and the long-distance runner, the phone rang. It was Stan Janski. Good old Stan. A man to count on.

"Nick, on that Jamaicaway address. The house belongs to one Eric Lohnes, M.D. That's L-o-h-n-e-s. He's an ob-gyn man at Beacon General. Big practice, well respected. Haven't had a chance to get anything on the Lewis broad yet. You've got me intrigued, Nick. When we going out for that beer?"

"I'll be in touch, Stan. Thanks."

"This Eric Lohnes mean anything?"

"Don't know. There are some pieces to be put together." I was wondering what the hell a chick driving from the Combat Zone had to do with a respected physician. Could be anything, though. The parking lot was also near Chinatown and shopping areas.

"I'll know more if you can dig up anything on Joanne Lewis."

"Do my best."

At that point I would have bet my money that Joanne Lewis and her Trans Am and Eric Lohnes were dead ends as far as I was concerned. Yes, I would have indeed bet on it. I didn't realize it then, but time, of course, would prove me wrong and a bit obtuse. I should have more quickly seen a gynecologist as a natural in a baby-selling ring. I like to tell myself that maybe it was too easy and that's why I was thrown.

I ran ten miles and, after I showered, drove to a nearby ice cream place and bought a banana split, two scoops of chocolate and one of vanilla drenched with crushed pineapple, strawberries, hot fudge, nuts, and real whipped cream. I felt a lot better as I ate it. Nicky and I would have had one after the batting cage, but, what the hell, I'd have one alone.

I spooned hot fudge from the plastic bowl shaped like a little boat and wondered what to do with myself until I picked up Moira. Maybe I should drive to the Jamaicaway and check out Dr. Lohnes's home again. But what for? Or maybe I should do nothing, let things run their course. That sounded good.

I leaned against my car and tilted my head to the sun. Except for a few gauzy clouds, the sky was brilliant blue. For a moment, I watched the clouds and sky and let the sun tingle my skin.

I scooped more hot fudge from the bowl. A scattering of flitty, quick sparrows and a couple of ponderous pigeons, their necks iridescent in the sun, cleaned the hot top around the trash barrel. A large yellow mongrel sat nearby and regarded me hopefully. From his girth, he looked as though he was a frequent opportunist at the barrel and dined regularly on ice cream handouts. His sad brown eyes probably did him well. A regular canine Dickens character.

Suddenly, I felt lethargic. Maybe I'd go home, lie in the sun or shade in the backyard and nap, something I rarely did, but the thought now seemed appealing.

I clicked my tongue to the dog and put the plastic bowl on the hot top. With my foot, I secured it as he licked it clean. When he finished, I reached down to pat his head and he walked away. I picked up the bowl, threw it in the trash, and drove home.

A plain dark-blue Ford sedan was parked across from my place when I pulled up. This Ford was so ordinary as to be extraordinary. Of course, it had to be an unmarked police car.

Inspector Gallo got out and rambled toward me with his disarming shuffle and rumpled, hangdog Columbo act.

"Dr. Toland," he said. "Or should I say, Major Toland?"

He snapped me a little salute and smiled. "Still get a little nervous around officers. Even after all these years. Funny, huh?"

"There must be a development in the case, Inspector, to get you out here. Like to go inside?"

"Well, it'll be just a minute, but, sure, why not?"

We sat in the front room. Boxer was lying on the rug in a shaft of sunlight. I figure he gets about twenty-two hours' sleep a day, with breaks for chow and an occasional jaunt outside. I guess when you're a eunuch there's not much else but food and sleep.

I offered Inspector Gallo coffee or a beer, which he declined. "Both of 'em make me piss like a racehorse. But thanks."

We sat through a minipause and I said, "What can I do for you, Inspector? I understand you've talked with my former wife."

"Oh, that. Yeah, well, you know how it is. Gotta cover all angles. Christ, I don't have to explain that to you. You're a cop and from what I understand, a damn good one." He smiled at me. "You're a well-respected investigator, Dr. Toland. Conscientious, thorough. Everybody had nice things to say." An image flitted through my head of Inspector Gallo talking with my associates and superiors at the Wells Building. Great.

"You haven't come up with any idea on how your phone number was in those bottles of crack, have you, Dr. Toland?"

"No."

"That's a funny one, all right."

"Inspector Gallo, that phone number is just to the college and the department extension. Anyone could easily get that."

"Oh, sure. I understand that. It's just one of those things."

"Well, anyway, I'm sure you didn't come out here just to go over that again."

Inspector Gallo smiled and reached down to pat Boxer. The cat rolled onto his back and tilted his head. He liked his chin to be scratched. "Look at the paws on this guy. Good fighter, I bet."

"He's a cupcake," I said.

Inspector Gallo ran a finger back and forth under Boxer's chin and the cat began to purr. Inspector Gallo was having better luck than I had with the dog.

"Dr. Toland, tell me about James Atkins."

So that was it. "What about him?"

"Oh, come on now. You nearly killed the man." Inspector Gallo continued to scratch Boxer's chin. "Oh, you like that, don't you kitty? Yeah, you do."

Jim Atkins was Diane Atkins's husband. "That's not true. That's—" I bit the words off. I knew I should stop talking and I knew what Inspector Gallo was up to. He was trying to rattle me. The bastard was clever and devious. A good Columbo.

"A man is cuckolded, you've got to expect he'll react, Dr. Toland. You would, I'm sure. Vicious display of temper you showed, I'm told. I mean, how's the man to react finding out such a thing?"

"Look, Inspector Gallo, I think—"

"Witnesses say you nearly killed him. Nearly broke his neck."

"That's bullshit and you know it. I doubt they said that because it's just not true."

Inspector Gallo was still leaning over Boxer but had stopped scratching. The cat nudged him with his head. Fickle bastard.

124

"You were trained in self-defense, the martial arts, right, Dr. Toland? I mean, you had to be."

"I'm no black belt or anything like that. Not even close."

"Maybe not. Still, compared with the average guy you could probably handle yourself. Am I right?" He resumed scratching.

"He attacked me. I defended myself. I came nowhere near killing him. I wouldn't be capable of that if I tried. I'm not that good. As a matter of fact, I came nowhere near hurting him."

"You had him on the ground."

I stood. I felt like saying, get your goddamn hands off my cat. "It was a quick scuffle. It was embarrassing. But anyone who said I nearly killed Jim Atkins doesn't know what they're talking about, is exaggerating, or is easily impressed."

"I thought it was 'he.'"

"Huh?"

"Shouldn't you have said, doesn't know what *he*'s talking about?"

"You're cute, Inspector Gallo, you know that?"

"Just doing the job, Major Toland. Just doing the job. You know what it's like."

He gave Boxer a final scratch and pat and stood. "Nice cat. I like him."

"Well, I'll tell you this much, Inspector Gallo. You do your job right and you'll find you're wasting a lot of time nosing around my affairs." I regretted the word "affairs" as soon as I said it and made a clumsy attempt to recoup. "I assure you I had nothing to do with either Kristin Williams or Darlene Abbott, if that's what you're thinking."

Inspector Gallo turned at the door and smiled. "Now Major Toland, what on earth would give you that idea?

Really, sir, for a hotshot cop you seem to be pretty jumpy about all this. Hey, I'm just a dumb guinea who has to peck and scratch to get results. Your conscience is clear, you got nothing to worry about from me."

I watched him walk to his car. Behind me, Boxer mewed and stretched beguilingly to have his chin scratched.

CHAPTER

10

Sunday morning was sunny, warm, and windless. I brewed coffee and took myself to the backyard with a steamy cup and the *Globe*.

I began with the funnies, went to the glossy ads, and then skimmed the magazines. My procedure never varies. After the funnies, magazines, and ads, I first look at the automotive section. Cars mildly interest me and lately I'd been thinking of a replacement for the Fairmont. Something more sporty probably. Something that would whip the ass off a red Porsche for under ten thousand. Maybe a used Corvette. Was that my image?

I skipped the help wanted and skimmed the real estate and financial sections. I give these cursory attention because I feel I should, but, to tell the truth, reading about Ginnie Maes, IRAs, and interest rates is to me a soporific.

Finally, I start at page one and read everything else in order. I check the Megabucks number to see whether I'm now a millionaire and can retire from teaching and the MPs and maybe buy a tropical island someplace and live like Marlon Brando. And, lately, I'd been paying close attention to news of sleaze and lowlife.

When I finished, I sat and let the sun bathe me. Boxer rolled in the grass beside my chair and I scratched his belly. Then I picked everything up and went in and called Kenny Dobson.

Kristin Williams's mother and father sat on the sofa opposite me. They looked anguished and I could easily relate to that. If anything ever happened to Nicky. . . . Behind them was the dining room and the table still had the detritus of a Sunday dinner. The house smelled of roast. Life must go on, I suppose. There were motions to go through.

At my request, Kenny Dobson had set up my meeting with them. I had been straightforward with them, as far as it seemed necessary to be. I wanted to see whatever additional notes on her research paper Kris might have left at home in her desk, especially anything that related to her final thesis.

It took a bit of explanation to make it clear that I thought there was a clue to her killer in those notes. Her mother especially seemed unable to concentrate on what I was saying. Kris's parents weren't much older than I, although they looked grief weary. They sat close together as if to draw strength from each other. Kris smiled from a picture on an end table beside them.

They offered me coffee, which I took because I sensed they wanted me to. They seemed to want to talk.

Kristin's father asked the unanswerable question. "You're an educated man, Dr. Toland. How do you make sense out of something like this? A young girl, her whole life ahead of her, an idealistic kid . . ." His voice trailed.

What good were all the philosophy courses now?

"I'm sorry. I can't make sense out of it, Mr. Williams."

Did priests tire of the words they said or did the faith remain strong?

"I didn't mean that I thought you could," he said. "It's just that that's all we've been thinking of. I've been having such thoughts, when I work, when I eat." He looked at his hands, large, working hands. "I don't sleep much."

After some further stumbling, painful conversation, I was led by Kris's father to her room, where her desk and school-related things were kept. "You'll have to go through it yourself," he said. "I wouldn't know what to look for and I don't think I could . . ."

I wanted to get this intrusion over with. I said, "I understand. I'll be just as fast as I can."

Kris's desk was a hollow, urethaned door set on two file cabinets, probably made by her father. I sifted through the contents of the drawers and notebooks and within five minutes located the skeleton of her paper. There were no notecards. Presumably, she had turned them all in to Norm Eigner. I skimmed the handwritten rough draft, eight pages that revealed nothing different from what the notecards had said.

I sat up and looked around. Kris's room faced south and was sun-filled. Stuffed animals sat on her bed. An unframed print of something in pointillism was tacked to one wall. Her high school tassel was slung over her bedpost. A bookcase traced her biography from girlhood to womanhood. The bottom shelves were lined with Bobbsey Twins and Nancy Drews, all in order, while the top shelves held some contemporary novels and her college texts. I fingered them and lifted the handbook that she used in Norm's course.

There were several folded sheets of composition paper, filled with scribblings and doodles, tucked into the binding. Most of the notations were random and had nothing to do with what I was looking for. I returned the book to its place.

As a last try, I looked through the drawers again, and this time in the bottom right drawer uncovered a small memo book. Feeling a bit like a voyeur, I thumbed through it. Near the last page, I found a nugget: a Jamaicaway address and the name Dr. Eric Lohnes.

It was dated just shortly before the time that Kristin was probably killed.

Moira was sunning herself on an old lounge. Most of the yellow and white webbing was frayed and torn and her delightful derriere nearly touched the ground. Her yard is typical old-town Marblehead, which is to say that it's not quite a postage stamp. There's a splash of grass and a little terraced garden which her trowel and empty flats gave evidence she had been working on. A copy of Lee Iacocca's biography lay open on the grass. The yard is sheltered from sea breezes and it was actually hot in the midafternoon sun.

"I'm back," I said. "Can't seem to get enough of you."

She wasn't expecting me. I had said nothing about visiting today when I left her last night.

She was wearing loose jeans rolled to the knees and a light blouse open at the throat. Little beads of perspiration dotted her upper lip and I kissed them off.

"You should be wearing a bathing suit," I said. "You must be roasting in those jeans."

She smiled. "You know, something tells me you aren't really concerned about my comfort. I bet you just want to ogle me."

"Oh, there's no question about that. I thought I'd dress it up a bit but you saw right through my ploy."

"There's an old guy next door and I think I spotted him a couple of times in the upstairs window peeking. I wouldn't want him to fall out. He'd land right on me."

I laughed. To understand what next door really means you have to see old Marblehead. Houses are so close an extramarital affair could be held with neither party leaving their own bedroom.

"Besides," she said, "Irish skin and the sun have to meet judiciously."

She sat up. "Would you like a beer?"

That question's like asking an eight-year-old if he wants an ice cream. "Of course."

We went inside to her kitchen, which in contrast to the sunlight seemed doubly dark with its stained pine. Moira got two bottles of beer and we sat at the table.

"When's the last time you saw a gynecologist?" I said.

She smiled. "That's a clever new line. Let's see, you could add it to an old standby. Are you new at the lodge and, if you need to see a gynecologist, I'm one."

"I need to find out about a Boston gynecologist, one Eric Lohnes, and I had the bright idea you could help." I told her what Stan Janski had come up with and about Kristin Williams's memo book.

"So what am I supposed to do, put my feet in the stirrups and check him out while he checks me out?"

I drank some beer. "I guess I'm groping."

"Why don't you let this go, Nick?" She regarded me

131

carefully a moment. "Do you feel pushed? That's it, isn't it? You feel pushed, threatened by this."

"Let's just say I don't feel comfortable sitting still and letting things run their course."

"Well, I don't know what you want to know about Dr. Lohnes or why you need to know it but I do know him by reputation, an excellent one, by the way. Several friends of mine go to him."

With her fingernail, Moira worked at the label on her bottle.

"I can tell you this much. Apparently he devotes less time to his practice than he once did."

"Oh?"

"I've heard he's cutting his work load. His associates do more and more of his work."

"Hmmm."

"But I guess that's normal for a guy of his stature and experience. Or do you read something else into it?"

"Would I do that?"

"Of course you would. And are. Just be careful, please."

Moira leaned back and looked at me archly. "Are you up, pardon the expression, for some afternoon delight?"

"Huh?"

"All this talk about gynecologists has heated me up."

"A-ha. Suspicions confirmed. So that's why more women go to male gynecologists than to female ones."

"It might have something to do with the fact that there are more male gynecologists. Besides, any female doctor who'd want to . . . Oh, never mind. Come with me."

She took my hand and led me to her bedroom.

On my way home, I stopped by the used car section of a Chevy dealer. Sunday is the best time to browse car lots because there are no salesmen.

A white Corvette had caught my eye. A sign inside the windshield told me it was a '77 and that the price was $10,500. The sign also told me the car was very clean with low, one-owner miles.

I cupped my eyes and checked the odometer, which read fifty-one thousand and change. Meaningless.

Very clean. Meaningless.

One owner. Meaningless.

I liked the car. It had a luggage rack and wide tires with gobs of tread left. Ten-five. Probably a bit less after negotiating. I could afford it.

I pictured Nicky and me in it. He'd definitely approve.

I pictured Moira and me. She wouldn't.

I could return tomorrow and the car would be mine. Meaningless.

That evening I read a *Car and Driver* I bought on my way home. It had a picture of a Porsche on the cover. Know thine enemy. Predictably, the magazine glowed about the Porsche but I tried not to let that depress me. I perused its performance figures, practical things for the common man having to do with drag coefficient, skidpad g's, and quarter-mile acceleration. They didn't mean much to me but I knew they'd make the Fairmont look anemic. How would a one-owner '77 'Vette with low miles stack up?

After I read the editorial columns, which were surprisingly well written, I made a couple of thick ham and cheese sandwiches on pumpernickel, opened a bag of chips, extracted two dill slices from a jar, and poured some beer into a frozen mug. With little effort, I could make my life revolve around food and drink.

While I ate and drank, I thumbed the *Car and Driver* absently, then put it down to watch some Sunday evening "Masterpiece Theatre." From lowbrow to highbrow. After about ten minutes, the combination of beer and low-key British accents began to cross my eyes.

The phone rang and when I answered, after a moment's pause, the muffled male voice said, "You're a nosy bastard. You know what happens to nosy bastards?"

I said nothing.

After another pause, the voice said, "They get hurt real bad." Pause for effect. "Real bad. Or they get snuffed out."

I was trying to make out the voice.

"Are you listening to me, asshole?"

I didn't want him to hang up so I said, "I'm listening."

"Or maybe their kids get hurt. That's a nice kid you got there. For his sake, get the point, huh?"

The line went dead. Jesus, they wouldn't touch Nicky. But, of course, they would.

I dialed Barbara. The phone rang seven times before she answered. I didn't want to alarm her but I got right to the point. "Barbara, is Nicky home?"

She was sensitive to nuances and the edge to my voice startled her.

"He's out. What's wrong, Nick?"

"Nothing. I just want to know where he is. Where is he?"

"I'm not sure. He's out with friends." She sounded defensive.

"You don't know where he is? At this hour?"

"At this hour? It's only nine-thirty. He's *fourteen*." After a pause, she repeated, "Are you going to tell me what's the matter?"

"Barbara, I'm coming over. I'll be there in a few minutes."

*   *   *

We sat in the living room, Barbara, Gary, and I. I hadn't been in the living room since the divorce. The furniture had been rearranged some, a change that was no improvement, I thought. The wallpaper was the same. I had put it up, a damn good job.

Barbara was quickly becoming distraught. She and Gary sat side by side on the sofa. He alternated between holding her hand comfortingly and putting his arm around her shoulder.

She had just finished calling the homes of friends Nicky might be with. Three of the friends were home and hadn't seen him all day and four of the others were themselves out.

"I think we should call the police," she said.

I shook my head. "What time could he be out to?"

"Ten-thirty."

I looked at my watch. "That's just over a half hour. Let's give him that at least."

"Goddamn, your son is in danger, probably kidnapped or . . ." She groped for a word, couldn't find it, and said, "You act pretty nonchalant, I must say."

She lit a cigarette, her third since I arrived.

I said, "Whoever it was seemed to indicate some future time, not tonight." I hadn't wanted to tell her what prompted my coming over but obviously had to.

She shook her head. "Then what the hell did you come over here for, scaring me half to death if you think Nicky's in no danger?"

Gary clucked sympathetically and patted her hand. The curly perm gave him a bland, cherubic look, and in general he looked rather washed out and bordered on being amorphous. Was he the best she could do? Did a fat wallet go that far?

Gary had offered me a beer when I came in which I didn't take. Somehow it didn't seem appropriate.

In the kitchen, a replica schoolhouse clock with a quartz movement chimed ten. We had bought it just before the divorce. I was surprised Barbara would remember to replace the battery. At the time, I wanted to buy a thirty-one-day wind clock with brass works but Barbara insisted on this one. That's me, Mr. Genuine.

When the ten chimes finished, Barbara fidgeted as though they were a signal for some kind of action we should be taking. She dragged deeply on her cigarette. I'd bet Gary smoked a pipe.

I sensed an awkward pause developing. I wished I had taken Gary's offer of a beer. When the pause extended to almost a minute, I said, "Gary, I'll have that beer now, if you don't mind."

He seemed relieved to do something. Obviously, this was awkward for him, being with Barbara and me in a potential crisis that involved the product of our loins.

On impulse, I went to the kitchen with him while he fetched a couple of beers from the fridge. My refrigerator, his beer. I was surprised he drank beer. I would have suspected him a martini, Manhattan, or mixed drink of some sort man. Probably wrong about the pipe too. Maybe I was even wrong about him. Probably one helluva guy. Christ, I could hardly be objective.

We each drank from the bottle, a couple of hard guys swilling down our Heinekens. Somehow Heinekens didn't fit the hard guy image and didn't seem to be made to swill from the bottle.

Gary said, "Nicky's a real nice kid. You must be proud."

"I am."

"I'm sure everything's okay with him but I can understand why you came over. Barbara rattles easily sometimes."

He paused and then took a quick swig of beer, sensing the awkwardness of explaining to me about Barbara's qualities.

But by now I agreed with him that Nicky was okay. I was the one who had rattled. I wished I hadn't come here.

I eyed the quartz clock.

"Nicky tells me you've taken him driving. Damn nice of you."

Gary smiled. "He gets a kick out of the car."

"I can see why. It's a beauty." I recalled a *Car and Driver* figure. It was inane but, hell, I had to say something. "Do about ninety in the quarter?" Master of small talk.

Gary smiled again. "I wouldn't have the slightest idea. It's got plenty of pep but that's all I can tell you. I never push it."

Nicholas Toland. Ph.D. Educator. Officer and Gentleman with the Military Police. Adolescent.

Maybe I should buy the Corvette and come by sometime and challenge old Gar to a drag race in front of the whole neighborhood. That would put him in his place and impress everyone. Or some time, I could flip him around in front of Nicky. Make him squirm. Maybe I could make fun of the perm.

Where the hell was Nicky? I wished he'd get home. I was sure he was all right but I had to see him. I wondered whether we could send him away some place until this mess was over. But how long would that be? Besides, school had a bit longer to go and his exams would be coming up.

I could stop being a nosy bastard and sit back and let someone frame me or kill me.

A nosy bastard.

Who knew I was a nosy bastard?

Barbara had gotten her call Friday night. I had met Kenny Dobson Friday evening. I had talked with Rick Le Brun on Thursday. Swede and I had trailed the Trans Am to the Jamaicaway on Thursday.

Who knew about those things. Or going to Lee Chen's. Or about anything that I did?

Gary finished his beer. Rather quickly. Another surprise. He went to the fridge.

"Ready for another?"

I swilled down the rest of mine.

"Sure." We'd see who'd drink whom under the table.

We were halfway through the second bottle, making spiritless small talk, when Barbara joined us. It was ten-twenty.

At ten-twenty-six, Nicky came in with a crash and clamor of doors that used to annoy me. Now I didn't mind at all.

He came to the kitchen in his never-ending quest for sustenance. When he saw me, he beamed and my heart soared. "Hey, Dad, what are you doing here?"

I ruffled his head. "Just dropped by for a chat with Gary and your mom. And to remind you to keep Monday open for a Sox game."

For a moment, I thought Barbara was going to blow it, but she composed herself and put on normal airs. I could tell she was bubbling with emotion, though.

"Who we playing?"

I liked that. He always said "we." His identification with the Sox was intense, like mine.

"Tigers."

"We'll kill 'em."

He went to the refrigerator and came out with the makings of a healthy sandwich.

"Dad, sorry I missed you yesterday."

"Me too. But that's okay. You had a good day, huh?"

"Yeah, sure did." He told me about his day with his friends. As he talked, I noticed Barbara smiling. She was glad he was okay, that was the main thing, but I knew she was genuinely happy that Nicky and I related so well. Give her that.

Even Gary seemed damned happy and I felt a bit of a chump. Maybe I'd grow to like the guy. Might even become buddies. Couple of hard-drinking, fast-car-driving studs.

I stayed through Nicky's snack, the sandwich, two glasses of milk, four Oreo double stuff cookies, and an orange. Probably just enough to make it through the night.

Thank God he was into sports and food rather than, as far as I knew, drugs. There had never been any evidence of that. No sign of pot. Or crack.

When I went out to my car, I eyed the Porsche. For some reason, it and Corvettes didn't seem to matter an awful lot anymore.

I had a hard time falling asleep. At one-fifteen, I went to my kitchen and opened the fridge. Maybe some beer would help. Maybe two six-packs. Instead I put a glass of milk in the microwave for thirty seconds. Not exactly the way Grandma would have done it.

139

Boxer rubbed against my legs as I drank my milk and I gave him half a can of something called Southern Style for cats. I watched him enviously. It must be nice to have such an uncomplicated life. He didn't have insomnia. Never saw a cat that did.

I watched TV for a few minutes, an old movie about terrorists.

At two o'clock, I hoped enough time had passed for the milk and movie to do their work. But when I hit the pillow, I could tell it was going to be a while yet. I should have gone with the beer.

The Trans Am trying to run me down and the phone numbers in the bottles of crack were bad enough but the threat to Nicky really set me off. My mind was revving, indulging in the sweet things I'd like to do to the person who phoned me. After some time at that, I reviewed what had happened since Darlene Abbott had come to my office.

The last time I squinted at my clock it was three-forty. I fell asleep after that and dreamed about a voice calling me a nosy bastard and saying, "That's a nice kid you've got there."

And then Nicky, a strong boy, but at fourteen still innocent and vulnerable, and in many ways, the best and most important thing in my life, was talking animatedly to me about the Red Sox.

And finally, Gary was telling me what a nice kid Nicky was and how proud I must be.

CHAPTER

11

When I woke, shortchanged of sleep, to the dentist office music my radio was set to, my mind and body tingled like exposed nerves. I was still angry and I thought about what made me that way for a few minutes. I knew I had to do something to secure Nicky's safety.

Before classes, I phoned Swede and then I phoned Barbara and drove out to see her. What I had in mind about Nicky took some convincing but in the end she agreed. She wanted to inform the police about the threats to Nicky and rely on them to protect him.

"They aren't going to post guards about him, Barbara. The best bet is to get him away from you and me. Someplace, when he's not in school, he can't easily be found. It won't be for long."

The plan was that I'd pick Nicky up after school, tell him that he'd be staying with Swede, and bring him home to do whatever packing he had to. How much I'd tell Nicky about why this was necessary I wasn't sure yet.

When I left Barbara, I still had plenty of time before my late-morning class so, for no particular reason, I drove to Beacon General. Boston does two things very well: colleges and hospitals. Beacon General is one of its better hospitals, which means it's one of the best in the world. It lies between Beacon Street and Storrow Drive and is fairly close to Mass General. Either one is the place to go to for a bypass or a transplant.

Rush traffic was over and it was a pleasant drive. I had the windows down and soft music on. I approached the hospital from its front side, the Beacon Street side. The original hospital, built sometime after the Civil War, is four stories of brick. Today, modern appendages of steel and glass sprawl and tower from it.

From behind me, a siren whooped and an ambulance sped past and then turned in by the emergency entrance.

I pulled over and stared at the hospital. Would a respected physician earning big money involve himself in something grimy? I knew it was entirely possible. On the scale of unlikely, shocking scenarios, it would be nothing unusual at all.

Beacon General and I stared at one another placidly for a few moments. When no revelations were forthcoming, I drove up Beacon Street, turned left, and then left again on Commonwealth. At the Public Gardens when I saw an empty parking space, I pulled into it.

I took my lit textbook from my briefcase, locked the car, and went to sit at a bench in the sun and read James Joyce's "Araby," reviewing my notations and underlinings.

When I finished that, I leaned back and let the sun massage me. A squirrel came close, checked me for handouts, and then went his way in the fluid, slow-motion manner of squirrels.

Nearby, a couple on the footbridge leaned over and watched the water in the swanboat lagoon. They held hands and talked earnestly and intimately. I felt a touch of nostalgia, thinking of Barbara and me and the times we had brought Nicky in to ride the boats when he was a little boy.

I didn't like putting it on Swede but he readily assented to letting Nicky spend his afternoons at the dealership and evenings at his place. Swede was quite a ladies' man, and wryly I wondered whether Nicky would get a lesson or two or whether his presence would put Swede out of commission temporarily. In any event, the arrangement wouldn't last long. If need be, when school was out, Nicky could visit my sister in Colorado.

I felt like spending the day on this bench, absorbing the sun, watching lovers, and feeding squirrels, kind of a cross between an urban Thoreau and a voyeur. But duty and a lit class called and I forced myself to my car and Colton.

In the English office, I checked my mailbox, half expecting a menacing message, but there were just the usual notes and memos.

When I went to my carrel, Tom Henshaw peered up from something he was reading and said grimly, "You've heard, I assume. Quite a blow to old Colton."

I looked blankly at him.

"Did you know Dan Ritchie in the Journalism department?"

I felt my head rush.

"Awful thing. He was murdered last night."

I sat for a few minutes to recover from the jolt and afterward, as I went to my class and walked past other faculty members, I thought they looked at me strangely. Maybe it was paranoia but certainly by now wagging and whispering tongues were linking me with at least some of what had happened. First a student murdered, then her friend, and now a faculty member. Tragic but juicy. Almost fascinating enough to wish that summer break wasn't coming.

If I thought I was going to breathe life into Joyce's "Araby," I settled now for simply making it through the class. Without any—I hoped—discernible stumblings.

After class, when I went back to the department office, I really wasn't surprised at all to see Inspector Gallo waiting for me. My Columbo was becoming my Javert.

"Inspector Gallo, I presume." He didn't seem amused.

"Hi, Doctor."

"I don't suppose you came here to discuss teaching methodology or techniques of detection."

"No, I didn't."

"Well, then."

"Doctor, I imagine you know your colleague, Dr. Ritchie, was found dead last night. It's a definite homicide."

"I found out about an hour ago."

Inspector Gallo had on a rather natty outfit for today. Lightweight tan suit, blue shirt, brown and blue striped tie, and lightweight Rockport shoes. He wasn't at all rumpled or hangdog or Columbo-ish looking. Maybe things were getting really serious. As he shifted his weight, his jacket fell back, exposing a small holstered snubnose .38 on the back of his left hip.

"Let me ask you straight out, Doctor. Where were you last night?"

"Oh, my. This is getting serious, isn't it? At what time?"

"Can you account for the entire evening?"

"Gee, Inspector, I guess I could surmise from this that I'm a suspect. Is that right? Am I a suspect?"

Inspector Gallo looked patient. "Last night, Doctor?"

"I was at my wife's home. Former wife."

"All evening?"

"No. Just a short time, actually. Probably ten minutes to ten to about ten-thirty, ten-thirty-five."

"Before that?"

"Home. Alone. Sorry, the only witness to that was my cat. I read, ate, watched some TV. Sounds pretty lame, huh?"

Inspector Gallo said nothing. He was writing in his notebook.

Curiosity pricked me. "Inspector, how was Dan Ritchie killed?"

"Now that's the interesting thing, Doctor. Broken neck. Same as the Williams girl."

"Hello. We can make a lot out of that, can't we? Did he have a bottle of crack with my phone number in it, by any chance?"

"Dr. Ritchie was a rugged guy. It would take someone pretty good to snap his neck cleanly without much of a struggle."

"No struggle, huh?"

"That seems to be what the evidence suggests."

Dan Ritchie *was*—had been—a rugged guy. The inspector was right. It would take a very capable man to break his neck. I doubted I'd be capable of it without a struggle or even with one. Swede perhaps could. It's not easy to snap a man's neck.

"Dr. Toland, what was your relationship with Daniel Ritchie?"

"I barely knew him. Beyond a very casual nodding acquaintance with a person I worked with, I never had anything to do with him."

"You met with him in his office last Thursday."

I nodded, wondering how he knew. A student had been with Dan when we met. Norm Eigner knew but I couldn't imagine how the hell that would have come out if he had talked with Inspector Gallo.

"You mind telling me what that was about?"

I laughed what I intended to be a light laugh of innocence but it sounded hollow. "I don't even remember. Nothing important."

"You tell me you never have anything to do with the guy and yet you can't remember why you went to see him just last Thursday?"

"It was an interdepartmental matter," I said, thinking quickly how I could elaborate if I had to. I certainly didn't want to tell him that I was nosing around.

"You've also been sniffing around the Combat Zone, I understand." Inspector Gallo was good. Excellent footwork. Kept you off balance.

"Is going to the Combat Zone a crime?"

Inspector Gallo smiled. "Let's not play games, huh, Dr. Toland. Whyn't we just put our cards on the table. You've been to the Combat Zone and asking questions. You know what I think you're doing? I think you're playing detec-

146

tive, which I realize is what you are, but this isn't your jurisdiction. You're out of bounds."

I thought of John Desi and Lee Chen. Suddenly I felt very tired. Hearing about Dan Ritchie had jolted away my fatigue, but that had worn away and my weariness seemed bone deep.

"Well, which is it, Inspector Gallo? Am I a suspect or am I playing cop? Don't the two seem contradictory?"

"I don't know."

"For chrissake, Inspector, if you know that I've been nosing around the Combat Zone, you must know a little more than that. You must know what I've been asking about. Would someone kill people and then go inquire about them?"

The office window was open and outside the maintenance crew was cutting the lawn. Lawn mowers and line trimmers hummed and snarled. It was pleasant if cacophonous sound, suggestive of sun and summer. The scent of freshly cut grass sifted in. It struck me as strange that I should be aware of these externals at this time.

"Dammit, Inspector, do you know why I was at my wife's last night? I just had a phone call threatening my son because I'd been asking questions. I've had incriminating evidence planted on both Kristin Williams's and Darlene Abbott's bodies, I've been nearly run over, and had my son threatened."

Inspector Gallo looked at me steadily. He scratched his head and then rubbed his eye. I was sure he was thinking that I was part of something sinister or illicit and that my cohorts were trying to shut me up or cut me out.

"Look, Inspector, I have work to do. You say let's stop playing games. Let's do just that. I know nothing of Dan Ritchie's death, nor Kristin Williams's nor Darlene Abbott's beyond what I've told you. But, apparently someone else besides you thinks I do."

Inspector Gallo got up, went to the open window, and looked out for several seconds. Then he turned back to me. "This seems so peaceful. This place and teaching. I know there must be stresses but your job must be just great. Rewarding, prestigious. Unhurried."

"So why should I screw things up? That what you're thinking?"

"Don't put words in my mouth." Inspector Gallo took a package of mints from his pocket and popped one in his mouth. "If things are as you say, Doctor, you'd best be very careful. And be sure to contact me about any more threats to you or your son. Don't try to be your own cop. That usually doesn't work. You know that."

He handed me a card with a number on it. "You probably won't want to answer this," I said. "Do you have any other suspects?"

Inspector Gallo smiled. "Dr. Toland, I'm sorry to say that we have more dead people than suspects."

I parked across from the high school. It was a few minutes to dismissal time and a row of Yellow Birds was queued up behind and in front of the school, a pre-World War Two structure of bricks and high windows, the kind that require window poles. A modern wing of steel and glass jutted from one side. Groups of students stood about or sat and smoked cigarettes on a low cement wall they no doubt thought was built for that purpose. And for grafitti. LEE AND JODI 4-EVA. SCHOOL SUCKS. VAN HALEN.

A police cruiser pulled up and a cop got out to direct traffic. One group of kids looked at him nervously and then moved away. A few minutes later a school administrator came out, shooed the kids off the wall, and then talked with the cop.

About two minutes after that a bell rang, and out they came, all sizes, shapes, and colors, scattering to the buses or waiting cars. I looked to see whether any boys carried girls' books. I saw none. The price of liberation had trickled down.

Four hard guys in denim and leather posed for a few minutes, dragging on cigarettes and leering at the girls, and then strutted off in a slightly bandy-legged swagger, probably headed for the malt shop to meet the gang and discuss homework.

Nicky was with three other boys headed for a bus. I tooted. He saw me and came over, curiosity on his face. Last night and now today. I told him we weren't going home and so couldn't give a lift to his friends. He waved them a signal and got in.

As we drove to pick up his things, he said, "I thought you said we weren't going home."

"I had to talk with you alone." I started to explain. At first I tried to weave a cover-up but then leveled with him and told him everything.

He stared straight ahead through my narrative and I wondered whether he thought I might be guilty. When I finished, he said nothing for a few moments.

"Nicky, this is just a precaution. You'll be fine. But I'd just rather have you someplace other than around me or your mother." I wondered about next Monday's baseball game. Should I take him?

He turned to me, his eyes moist. "Oh, Jesus, Dad, I'm not worried. It's you. What about you? Are you gonna be okay?"

I wanted to stop the car and hug my son. It was a long

time since I had. Too long. His concern filled me. It made my day.

I said lightly, trying to keep the feeling from my voice, "I'm going to be just great. This is a mess but it's temporary." I laughed. "After all, I'm on the side of the angels."

I hoped I wouldn't soon be with them.

After Nicky packed, I dropped him at Swede's new condo in a woodsy section of Belmont. It spoke eloquently of Swede's material success. And of his bachelor's life. I would have suspected Swede to be of contemporary design taste but his place was bricks and beams, traditional fireplace, board floors with expensive braid rugs. Sailing ships in black frames adorned the walls.

I settled Nicky and stayed with him for a half hour. I told him I'd call but probably wouldn't be by very often. Swede would drive him to school and pick him up. Short of the Secret Service, I couldn't ask for much better security than that. I owed Swede.

When I left, I drove home, got on my running shoes and shorts, and then drove to a quarter-mile track behind what used to be a high school and was now housing for the elderly. Hardly anyone used the track anymore and weeds grew out of the cinders.

I did some stretching and then an eight-minute mile followed by two more at six minutes each. Next I did a slow quarter mile and then opened up and did one in sixty-two seconds. I walked two laps and then fell to the ground and did fifty push-ups.

At one end of the track was a tree with a strong horizontal branch about eight feet up. I jumped to it and did a repertoire of chin-ups, twenty-five conventional, and ten reverse handed, arms spread wide. The branch was rough and when I finished my hands were scuffed and scratched.

Then I drove home, showered, and wondered about Dan Ritchie.

Dan Ritchie's funeral was Thursday. Moira and I, along with much of the faculty and administration and many students, attended. The morning was appropriately overcast. The service was in an Episcopal church. Dan's family—his mother, brother, and two sisters—huddled solemnly in the front pew. The brother's arm was wrapped protectively around his mother's shoulder and occasionally he whispered to her.

After the church service, we drove to the cemetery. A light mist frosted my windshield and the wipers scuffed and clacked a dirge.

At graveside, we gathered and listened to the words that laid Dan Ritchie to rest. The wind slanted the mist under the canvas and rustled the plastic turf draped around the coffin. When the minister finished his text, he announced that friends were invited back to the Ritchie home. Moira and I would forgo that. I guess we didn't really fit into the friend category. Besides, the postfuneral ritual of food and coffee was too inappropriately festive for my taste.

As we headed back to my car, I scanned the scattering crowd. I did a double take at John Desi ducking into a Lincoln Towncar. I couldn't be sure but I thought he had been talking with Dr. Lloyd Markham, Colton's president. I was about to nudge Moira when I saw Inspector Gallo, three cars behind Desi's, start the engine to his unmarked Ford. I wished I knew whether they had been together.

We lay on Moira's bed with a sheet protecting us from the cool Marblehead wind blowing past her window curtains. My stomach was full of salad, boiled lobster, and beer. It was the poetic time for a cigarette, if I smoked, flat on my back, staring at her ceiling, watching the shadows cast from the streetlight, my stomach full, my love requited. Soft music played from the stereo in Moira's living room. I had told her about my puzzlement over John Desi's and Inspector Gallo's presence at the funeral. We batted it around and came to some obvious conclusions. Dan's interests and holdings in the Combat Zone were probably his connection to Desi. Inspector Gallo was simply on the scent but, goddammit, the man was devoting a lot of time to all of this. As for Desi talking with Lloyd Markham, I had no doubt been mistaken. Collusion between them was too unlikely.

"I want another beer." I slipped from under the sheet. "You?"

"Please."

I came back with two bottles of Sam Adams, good stuff if you like your beer full bodied and heavy, like a Rubens woman. We lay back and sipped. Actually, I guzzled the first half of the bottle. Something slow and lilting by Elton John was now playing.

We lay quietly for a few moments. We drank and I did some more shadow watching.

Moira said, "You seem pensive."

"I'd like to say that I was into some deep thoughts but I was just drinking this beer and watching the shadows on your ceiling."

"I thought you might be brooding."

"It's a facade I try to project of a brooding thinker."

"You weren't still thinking of Dan Ritchie and the rest of *l'affaire?*"

"I suppose it was at the back of my mind."

"I should think so."

"You mean philosophical considerations of life and death, their condition and meaning?"

"I was thinking more of the immediate impact upon you."

"Yes, that. A nagging thing, isn't it." I drained my bottle and set it gently beside the bed. I wanted another but decided to wait.

Moira said, "Sunday, you were asking about Dr. Lohnes. I gather you're interested in finding out whether he's involved in this adoption black market."

"Uh huh."

"I have an idea."

I watched shadows as I waited for her to explain. She gave it a dramatic pause of a good thirty seconds and I nearly said, "well?" when she said, "He deals with prostitutes, you think. What if one went to him tired of her life-style, worried about herpes and AIDS, and wanted a checkup. Then she let it be known she wanted out of whoring but needed an income. That would be the bait."

"Fine, but where do we get such a person?"

"Me. I'd do it."

"Absolutely not."

"Why not?"

"It's out of the question. Thank you but forget it."

"I'd be a free-lance suburban prostitute who had heard of Dr. Lohnes's fine reputation and who didn't want to go to a local gynecologist. If he's involved, it would be the perfect bait."

"Stop it. Just stop it. There's no way in hell I'd let you do something like that."

"*Let* me? My, my, a bit of an anachronistic viewpoint, wouldn't you say?"

"You don't look like a whore. You have no sleaze factor."

"What's a whore look like? You—"

I interrupted her. "C'mon, there must be certain telltale signs—no pun intended. A wear and tear factor he'd detect."

"Stop it."

"Really."

"I could carry it off. What's to lose? What's the risk? I wouldn't use my own name. If he doesn't go for it, we're no worse off than we are now. If he bites, then you know what you want to know."

"Then what?"

"That's your game, Major Toland. But one step at a time, huh?"

"It's ridiculous. Forget it."

"I think it might be kind of a lark. Come on, say yes."

"Ridiculous."

"You said it was fine before you knew I'd be the one to go."

I made a noise of derision.

"It's settled. I'll do it. Now I'm curious."

I rolled toward her. "I know what you're doing. You're trying to make it easier for me. You think that deep down I want you to do this but that I have to protest it. That's not the case. I *don't* want you to do this."

"Fine, but my mind's made up, so let's not hear another word."

She pulled the sheet from us. "Now, let's work some more on that wear and tear factor you spoke of."

Friday afternoon at 1:43 I was ushered into Dr. Lloyd Markham's office. He stood from behind his desk, large, old, and mahogany, that I guess was supposed to connote all sorts of positive things about Lloyd Markham and the office he held.

His greeting was effusive. "Nick, Nick, sit down. Here, sit down." Repetition can sometimes take the place of substance. "How goes it? How are you?"

"Fine thanks, Lloyd. How are you?"

I was here in response to a memo in my mailbox this morning. Actually, it wasn't a memo, the official Colton envelope and letterhead elevating it above that status. "Dr. Toland" was typed on the envelope. No postage. The salutation on the typed note said "Nick." Chummy. The body of the note read, "Could you be in my office at 1:30 today?"

The signature "Lloyd" was penned in a neat hand above the typed "Lloyd Markham." First name basis with my president. Heady stuff.

"We don't get to see one another much around here, do we? I mean administration, faculty."

"No," I said. Lloyd Markham was medium height, medium build, midfifties, graying, thinning hair combed straight back. Half glasses, hanging from a cord, jiggled on his chest. He had on a banker's suit, bluish gray with a muted stripe. He was so medium and average that he was damned near invisible.

"Except at Christmas parties and semester meetings," he said.

I cocked my head inquisitively and politely as I adjusted myself in a big chair across from his desk. The chair was leather with brass studs. I tried a smile instead of a verbal response as I wondered what he wanted.

"And at wakes and funerals." His face was serious now as he sat behind his desk and leaned back.

Ah, yes. Now we get to the point.

"Sad, sad thing about Dan Ritchie. Terribly sad thing. Awful thing. What a world we live in . . ."

His voice trailed and he fixed a gaze at me filled with sorrow over the human condition. Oh, the futility of words.

"I saw you at Dan's funeral. I didn't know you were friends."

"We weren't."

He arched an eyebrow.

"Just a casual, nodding acquaintance is what we had." But any man's death diminishes me, because I am involved in mankind.

"Oh, I thought you and he were cronies."

"No, not really. Not at all, actually. Why would you think that, if you don't mind my asking?" I was more than curious about this line of conversation. I guess suspicious was the word.

"Just an impression."

I wanted to ask, from what? How on earth would you possibly know anything about the kind of relationship between Dan Ritchie and me?

Lloyd Markham and I had no mutual places of association and I knew he had never seen Dan Ritchie and me rubbing elbows at faculty parties.

"But that's not important," Lloyd Markham said. "That's not what I wanted to talk to you about."

The hell it isn't, I thought.

Lloyd Markham got up and came around and rested one buttock on the edge of his desk in front of me, a pose like something from a TV ad, informal but projecting sincerity and knowledge. Then he flashed a smile that radiated as much candor as a used car salesman's.

"I noticed your name on the list for next fall's lecturer exchange program."

I smiled and perked up. He referred to an exchange of classes, residences, cars—everything but wives—between Colton professors and those in participating European universities.

"Rarely does anyone under five years seniority get selected." He wiggled a design in the rug with his right toe. "For that matter, I don't recall that ever happening."

He smiled again. "But it could."

What the hell was he driving at?

His expression became serious. "God knows, as president, I'm not without influence in seeing who gets the nod. I notice you put in for a transfer to England."

"Yes. There are two exchanges there that look attractive. Germany would be nice too."

"Marvelous opportunity. It's definitely the way to see and get to know other places and cultures. You've been to Europe?"

"During the service. But it's been a while."

Lloyd Markham went back behind his desk and sat for a moment without speaking. I became conscious of the functional noises of the office, the inexplicable creaks and ticks.

"How would an early start appeal to you?"

"An early start?"

"Yes. This summer. Right after exams. One of the British chaps has indicated he'd like to come and teach a summer course or two and stay on through the year."

"Really?"

"It's quite a plum. We just got word on it. I don't think Peg Simpson has tossed it out yet to those who might be interested."

Peg Simpson was English chairperson.

"I could arrange it," he said.

I said nothing. Ordinarily, I would have jumped but there was an assessment to be made of Lloyd Markham's motivation. Obviously, he wanted me out of the way for a year. But why?"

"That is, if you're interested."

"Lloyd," I said, "why me? Why go out of your way to set up this deal for me? As you say, I have no seniority. You'll antagonize a lot of people in the department who'll be drooling over this."

"Not that many. The notice is short. You're single and have fewer commitments and arrangements than most anyone else."

"Why *me*? Why *you*?" I was probing him, but what the hell.

He ignored my question. "What do you say? Interested?"

"Do I have to tell you right now?"

"That would be nice. Go ahead. Say 'yes.' Be spontaneous. What an opportunity. You'll kick yourself later if you say 'no.'"

Jesus, I ought to. It was a deal and a half, something I'd love to do. Why not just cover my ears and eyes and go? What did I care what his motivation was or whether he was tied up in any of this mess or how it turned out? I could get time off from the Reserves. There was no problem there. I could probably finagle to take Nicky with me.

Nicky and I safe in England. What an experience for him.

"No."

Lloyd Markham was leaning back in his chair. For a moment, he said nothing. Then, "I didn't hear you."

"I said, 'no.'"

"Why?"

"I don't like being pushed."

"Who's pushing?"

"I don't know. You tell me."

"What are you talking about?"

Briefly, I thought that maybe he *didn't* know, that possibly this was a guileless offer, that he recognized me as an excellent teacher who deserved a reward, that he would intercede on my behalf at the risk of alienating the English department and its chairperson.

I stood. "Thanks, Lloyd, but no thanks. Pardon the expression, but this sucks. I've been threatened, framed, and nearly run over. Now I'll be cajoled. How high does this go?"

"I don't know what you're talking about."

"The hell you don't."

"I don't like your tone."

"Live with it," I said and turned away. When I was at the door, he said, "Nick, wait a minute."

I turned to him and paused.

He smiled and it didn't seem insincere now. It seemed desperate.

"Sleep on it," he said.

CHAPTER

12

I picked up Nicky at Swede's at six o'clock. I parked in a garage near Kenmore Square and we were in the ball park in time to catch batting practice. We began our multicourse meal of Fenway's best, beginning with a couple of dogs each, some peanuts and ice cream bars. Nicky had his first coke and I had my first beer.

We oohed and aahed at batting practice, at balls that screamed over and into the net off the left field wall. Far fewer were hit out of the park to right field. It's a good poke. How did Ted Williams manage 521 home runs, especially with those years lost to two wars?

Being in the ball park with my boy was doing a good job of driving the events of recent days from my mind. Over the weekend, I had told Moira of my meeting with Lloyd Markham.

"Strange," she said. "This is strange." She had brooded about it and even urged me to consider Lloyd's offer seriously. "I really think you need to get away. England's as good a place as any."

But she accepted that I wouldn't and we didn't wrangle over it. She also told me that she was able to get an appointment to see Dr. Lohnes on Tuesday, tomorrow, because of a cancelation. We didn't wrangle over that either. Foolishness matched foolishness.

By the time we stood to honor America by singing the National Anthem, I was on my second beer and slightly abuzz with the diversion of the national pastime. Ah, baseball and beer.

The first four innings were scoreless but in the top of the fifth, the Tigers got three runs on a walk, a single, and a screamer over the net by the Detroit center fielder.

The Sox came back with one on a double followed by a single. But a double play and a foul pop-up to the catcher ended the minirally.

In the top of the sixth, we nearly snagged a souvenir foul ball but it bounced away and was snapped up by someone two rows behind us.

In the last of the sixth, the Red Sox got one more back on a solo homer by Ramon Mendes, the first baseman. At the end of the inning, Nicky went to the men's room. Three cokes will do that. Barbara wouldn't approve and once I wouldn't have. I guess being divorced and not seeing your kids all the time makes you like an indulgent grandparent.

The first two Tigers reached on an error and a single to

center in the top of the seventh. A conference on the mound followed that, filled with vigorous nodding, and concluded with an encouraging pat on the pitcher's buttock by the catcher.

But the grand strategy of the conference didn't work. The first pitch was wild and both runners advanced. An intentional walk loaded the bases and the Sox manager, Duke Perotta, walked gravely to the mound. A left-handed batter was due up and the Sox had a lefty in the bull pen who had started to warm up just before the intentional pass.

The predictable conference to stall for time was finally broken up by the umpire and the call went to the pen.

The lefty ambled in, a junk specialist and reputed sandpaper artist who could get batters to hit the ball on the ground, for which talent he was paid close to a million dollars a year. Almost enough to make you believe in communism.

He didn't earn his money. The Tiger lefty stroked a two-two count to the left field corner, scoring two. We now had a five-two game with two still on and no one out. A righty and lefty threw in the pen and Duke Perotta came back out to the mound.

He wanted the righty. The junk specialist gave up the ball and shuffled off to whatever penance million-dollar failed relievers do.

The righty struck out the first batter, gave up a single for another run, and got the next two on a pop-up and a fly to right.

Six to two going into the last of the seventh. Not hopeless in Fenway. Time to stand and stretch.

Where the hell was Nicky?

I scanned the steps and walkway he had taken. How

long since he left? I wasn't sure. Probably stopped for more food.

Jesus, they wouldn't try anything here.

The crowd sat. I checked my watch. I'd give him five minutes. I tried to concentrate on the game, on the first Sox batter readying himself at the plate. A called strike, a ball, and two fouls later I was on my feet and headed to find Nicky.

At the walkway, an usher pressed a note into my hand. "I was told to give this to you, sir."

"Jesus. Who?" I tried to quell morbid thoughts.

The usher shrugged. "I dunno. A guy."

I walked down a rampway to below the grandstand. I scanned the note quickly. The anger would hit me later. I sprinted to the closest men's room. Nicky wasn't there but a guy against the wall near the exit beckoned to me and nodded for me to follow him outside.

He stopped about ten feet from a souvenir stand. He was slightly shorter than I and younger, probably mid- to late-twenties. He was swarthy and very compact. I guessed he made his living breaking limbs and, where that didn't work, taking more extreme steps. He looked as though he was good at what he did and as though he might enjoy it.

"You're an asshole, you know that?" he said. Subtle.

"Where's my son?"

"You've had more chances than you deserve. It was up to me, I'd put you in a dumpster somewhere. Right now. With your kid."

Strangely, the words were a comfort for they indicated that Nicky was probably unhurt.

"And I still might," he said.

"Where's my son?"

163

He put a thick forefinger against my chest and pushed. "I ask the questions, shithead."

I backed away from the finger. "So ask. Stop playing games."

"You want to see your son? Sure you do. You back off, you stay out of what don't concern you. Just teach your goddamn poetry. You want to play cop, stick to harrassing soldier boys."

We held a brief staring contest. He complemented his steely stare with an appropriately contemptuous sneer and slight head quiver.

"Where's my son?"

"I'm gonna spell it out. Any more messing around and you get it or your son gets it or you both get it. Get it? He's on the bridge over the Mass Pike. He didn't go there on his own, either. Let me tell you, it would have been nothing for an accident to happen."

The finger was back in my chest. "You get the point?"

But I was past him and out of the ball park and around the corner to the bridge over the Massachusetts Turnpike.

"He told me to wait here for you."

Nicky stood by the railing. Traffic gushed below. He recounted what had happened, of the goon outside the men's room who told him to come with him and be quiet or his father and mother were history. A heavy load for a kid, but his shoulders were square, his head high.

"I didn't know what to do, Dad."

"You did just fine." This was a strong boy, my son.

"I mean, he didn't look like the type who'd be kidding around."

"He probably wasn't."

"It's about what you told me, huh?"

"Yes."

"You gonna be okay?"

"Yeah. So are you and Mom."

From the ball park, a prolonged roar sounded from over thirty thousand sets of lungs.

"Sounds like a home run," I said. "Want to go back?"

"Can we?"

"Why not? We still have our stubs. And we're not going to let a couple of creeps keep us away and ruin our night, are we?"

Nicky grinned. "No way."

"Come on then. Back to the game."

I looked back down many feet below to the Mass Pike and the headlights of the crushing traffic.

The Sox had tied it when we got back to our seats and then won it in the last of the ninth. It could have been a golden moment for my son and me, a night together of Americana and innocence, but it had been marred by Nicky's having to glimpse the threat of savagery and, I feared, wondering just what his father was really into. It was almost the worst possible scenario, one which could be eclipsed only by anything actually happening to Nicky.

We made light of it, however, and stopped at a deli for a pastrami sandwich and milk shake for Nicky and a coffee for me. We talked of the game, of the ninth inning home run by Nicky's favorite player. We promised to come in again over the summer and I thought of Lloyd Markham's offer and Moira and the goon who told me how easy it would be for an accident to happen. I thought of the traffic on the Mass Pike and of flattened animals mauled by cars' wheels.

As I drove Nicky back to Swede's, I checked the rearview mirror repeatedly but wondered whether that wasn't futile.

To my surprise, Swede was reading a book. Nicky told him about the game. I was proud of my son for his sensitivity at not mentioning the incident.

The three of us talked for a few minutes, I said good night to Nicky, and Swede walked me to my car. I told him what had happened and then said, "What can I borrow that's light and easily concealed? The .45's too damn big and heavy." Swede collected handguns.

"Want it now?"

"No. Bring it with you tomorrow night."

I got in my car. For the first time in many years, I wanted a cigarette. Instead, I rolled down the window and breathed in deeply.

"Goddamn," I said as I pulled out and headed home.

The next night I was on the phone in the Wells Building talking with a friend who was a cop in a North Shore city when Swede came into my office.

"Everything's copacetic, Nick. He's studying for a test. Don't know how he does it with my stereo on just about full blast listening to his cassettes." Swede laughed. "It wasn't on loud while I was there but as I was pulling out he really revved it up."

"Hey, Swede, don't let him—"

"Nick, I'm not complaining. You give me that restrictive shit, and I won't give you reports. He's my guest." Swede grinned. "Sir."

"Thanks, Swede. You're a brick."

"Yeah, sure. Here, try this for lightness and concealability." He handed me a small automatic.

"Looks like a water pistol," I said.

"It's a Beretta .25 auto. For its size you won't beat it."

"Swede, when this is all done I'm going to rob a bank and buy a BMW from you. It's the least I can do."

After I fired a few rounds through the Beretta, I stayed at my desk going through various cases: payroll fraud, impersonation of an officer, unauthorized use of a three-quarter-ton vehicle by parties unknown that resulted in damage to civilian property.

I felt my eyes beginning to cross and called Moira. "I'm coming up to the North Shore. You up for some company?"

"Sure," she said. It wasn't exactly a breathless or breathy answer but it would do.

I cheated. Theoretically, I was still on duty, but I went straight to Moira's. But I was working on cases, I told myself, because I was thinking about them.

Moira hadn't eaten and had one of her frequent urges for lobster. She knew a place in Salem that had lobster at reasonable rates. We took her Volvo and drove out of Marblehead to Salem, past the State College to the downtown, which has been quaintly urban-renewed.

Moira ordered a boiled lobster and I went for a lobster roll and another beer. We sipped beer and wine, made small talk, and enjoyed the ambience for a few minutes while we waited for our lobster.

My intent had been not to tell Moira of what happened at Fenway but somehow it leaked into the small talk.

"I have a problem connecting Lloyd Markham with leg breakers. I can't see him issuing them orders," I said.

"Maybe that's not his connection. Maybe our president and the gorillas work for the same person or persons."

"Which means this whole thing escalates a notch."

"And," Moira said, "I'm sorry to say that I can't add anything to point to Dr. Lohnes any further." She sipped some wine. "I saw him today. Fed him my spiel about being a disgruntled hooker looking for some other lucrative livelihood but got no reaction."

"What did it cost you?"

"Forget it."

"Come on. You did this for me. What did he charge?"

"Cut it out. I was due for a checkup anyway."

Our waitress came with our dinner, tied a paper bib around Moira's neck, and told us to enjoy.

For a few minutes we ate. Moira cracked and probed. My lobster roll was large and delicious, complemented by thick, tasty fries.

After we ate, we strolled to a combination of marina and small shops. We stopped at a restaurant deck right on the water and stayed for a nightcap. Quarter-million-dollar sailboats bobbed just feet away, their gear slapping against aluminum masts.

We sat in the midst of spike-haired singles, most of whom were drinking frosty concoctions like margaritas or sunrises or sunsets of various types. There were a few genuine sorts like me drinking beer.

We had our drinks, watched and listened to the harbor, and then sauntered back to the Volvo. We drove to Marblehead and I stayed the night with Moira.

CHAPTER

13

I got two breaks on Wednesday. The first was around one o'clock. Stan Janski let me look at mug shots of known leg breakers in the Boston area. There were enough to start a small army.

After about twenty minutes and maybe a quarter of the way through the stack, I found the goon from Fenway. Salvatore, Sal the Scuzz, Scuzzarelli. Appropriate. 5'10", 212 lbs., 28 years old. There was a list of indictments for assault with one eighteen-month stint at Deer Island from October 1983 to May 1985.

I pushed the card across the desk to Stan Janski. He glanced at it as he munched his ham and American cheese submarine sandwich, dripping with chopped onions, pickles, and olive oil.

"Sal Scuzzarelli. Well named. A real scuzz ball. But no one to mess with. He's a piece of shit but mean. We're talking *real* mean, Nick. You remember Joe Baron? This guy's trying to fill the void."

Stan Janski picked up a sweating can of diet Pepsi from his desk and sipped. He took another bite from his sandwich and chewed while he regarded me thoughtfully.

"Nick, I know you're being closemouthed about this and I respect it, but a guy comes in here and wants to know who Sal Scuzz is, I gotta wonder. You into him for something?"

I smiled.

"I mean you're involved with Sal, I gotta tell you, you're involved with someone else. Some pretty heavy hitters. The heaviest. Sal's from Revere but his connection is Prince Street in Boston."

I nodded. Mob headquarters.

"Yeah, that's right. Sal used to free lance but last couple of years he works strictly for Carmen Buono."

Carmen Buono controlled all of New England. Even Providence took orders from him. I wondered how deep I was in.

"That help you any, Nick."

"It's revealing."

"Look, I know I don't have to tell you but then again maybe I do. This is a little different from what we deal with in the MPs. The Sal Scuzz's of the world have a real advantage. They don't care about consequences. They can bust you up or kill you and if all that happens is they're suspected or indicted or even if they're *convicted*, they're not worried about their reputation or their family or their career like someone in the military probably is."

Stan took another big bite from his sandwich. I let him chew for a few moments and then said, "Who does Sal work with?"

"What do you mean?"

"I mean in tandem. Who would he work with?"

"Usually he's alone. If someone was with him, I'd guess Willie, the Pig, Cardani. Vinnie Tamasi. Maybe Charles Rizzo."

"You have shots of them?"

Stan searched and dealt me three cards. I studied the faces a moment and handed the cards back.

"Nice guys, huh? You'd love your daughter to come home with one," Stan said as he put the pictures back.

"I'm going to push my pain in the ass index up another notch, Stan, but could you find out if any of these guys drives a Trans Am?"

Stan nodded. "That registration number you had me look up was to a Trans Am. I was wondering if there was a connection. I hope you're being careful, Nick. Swede Knudson with you on this?"

I nodded.

"I know Swede is a tough sonofabitch, and one-on-one with someone like Sal Scuzz, bare hands or knives or that other jungle shit, there'd be no problem, but remember for these guys, there's no rules."

Stan took a pad from his pocket and wrote a note. "I'll see what I can do. And I'm still looking into that Ritchie guy's involvement in the Combat Zone that you asked about. So far no luck."

Stan eyed me hard. "He's what, the third stiff you're

involved with? The two broads, this Ritchie guy. Throw in Sal Scuzz and Carmen Buono. Sounds awful interesting and kind of scary. Remember, they don't call Carmen Buono 'the Shark' for nothing.''

My second break came at five o'clock with a phone call from Moira.

"Guess what?" she said.

"I give up."

"I got a call from Dr. Lohnes late this morning before I left for classes."

"And?"

"He bit."

"I'll be over in twenty minutes."

Moira greeted me at her door looking very pleased with herself.

"Come in. I'll tell you all about it," she said. We went to the kitchen.

"I was just about to leave for school when I got a phone call from Dr. Lohnes's office. It was his secretary and she told me the doctor would like me to come back in to talk with me. When I asked what about she supposed it was about my exam. When I hesitated, she put the doctor himself on and he said he'd like me to come back in to discuss further what we had discussed yesterday about my 'career.' He said that he had an idea that might interest me."

Moira spoke more rapidly than she usually did, more like an excited teenager than a professor of Celtic literature.

"I told him I didn't have much time and he said he'd see me right away. Said it wouldn't take long to explain what he had in mind."

My face must have clouded because Moira said, "What's the matter?"

"I thought you were going to use an alias."

"I did."

"But he—his office—called you on the phone."

"I left my phone number."

"Did it occur to you that he might check the alias against the phone number?"

"Yes it did. I'm not that dumb. I went to college, you know. I told him that the name I gave him *was* my alias."

"But then wouldn't you have a separate phone number for hooking?"

"Maybe not."

"You would."

"Not necessarily." She sounded defensive.

"It's a mistake. You left yourself open."

"Aw, probably his secretary called without even checking."

"Hmm. Well, anyway?"

"Anyway, I got ushered into his office, not an examination cubby. The desk. The degrees. All very impressive. He said he got thinking about what I said yesterday about getting out of hooking and that he had an alternative that might interest me. He wouldn't come right out and say what he had in mind. Kept asking questions first, really beating around the bush."

"What kind of questions?"

"About my private life. Who I lived with. Who I saw a lot of. Did I work free lance or did I have a pimp? How much did I really want out? Then he began to encourage me to get out, fed my fears that I had expressed to him about AIDS. Said the risk was very high.

"Then he came out with his proposition. Asked if I'd

ever been pregnant and said there was a very strong market for healthy babies, especially one that I might produce. I can quote him. 'To be frank,' he said, 'your ethnic background is excellent. White Anglo-Saxon—Protestant doesn't matter—is desirable.'

"I played being stunned and not understanding what he was driving at. He said it as simple as that. I'd get pregnant and agree to give up the baby at birth for a handsome compensation."

"How handsome?"

"Wait a minute. I'll get to that. 'Who will father the child?' I asked. 'No problem,' he said. He'd inseminate me himself, he said. Artificially, of course. Anonymous donor with good genes, also ethnically desirable and certified AIDS-free.

"As a matter of fact, the good doctor handles the whole thing from conception to prenatal to delivery. All very professional, all very first-rate."

"Jesus," I said, "do you believe this?"

"I know. It's something, isn't it?"

"Okay," I said. "Money. What kind of dough?"

"I guess that's negotiable. He wanted to know what I earn now. I hedged. I told him I did very well. When he pressed, I said I got about three hundred a night, probably four nights a week."

"Good girl. Don't let him think you come cheap."

Moira laughed. "You know, I could probably get that. Not a bad way to make a buck."

I took in her face and figure. She'd get that easily.

"He told me to think over the deal and get back to him. That he was confident we could come up with a money figure that was mutually agreeable."

"And that's how it stands?"

"That's how it stands."

I tapped the table and thought. About connections among an improbable cast: Kristin Williams and Darlene Abbott and Lieutenant Brian Connolly and Dan Ritchie and Lloyd Markham and Dr. Eric Lohnes and Carmen Buono. And Nicholas Toland.

I wondered how to follow up on what Moira had uncovered. One thing was sure: Her involvement was over.

She seemed to read my mind. "I think I should lead him on to find out more. Short of insemination, naturally."

"Look, you've done enough, but that's it."

"There must be more we could learn. I'd simply ask questions as I ostensibly tried to make up my mind."

"Like what?"

"Like how do I get paid? Cash, check, up front or installments? I don't suppose we could right out ask who's behind this but maybe we could think of questions that would lead us to that."

"Too many questions will make him suspicious. It's too dangerous. I'm worried as it is that he'll do a check on you and that your connection to me will be found out."

I took off my jacket and draped it over the back of my chair.

"What's that? You never carry a gun when you're not on duty."

"I just want to be prepared. This whole thing is so backward. First, an attempt to make me look suspicious, then an attempt on my life followed by warnings and inducements to butt out."

Moira straightened up in her chair. "I'm in this far. Let me lead Dr. Lohnes on a little more."

"No."

"I don't need your permission."

"Then why ask? We've been through this. Let's drop it."

"O-h-h, you make me angry sometimes. It's okay for you to mess around and carry guns and have excitement."

"It's my problem, remember?"

I stood. "Come on. I feel like Chinese food."

"You expect me to go with you while you're carrying a gun?"

"Yes. I do expect that. Let's go. I need to eat and I need to think. I can do both together. And I can look at you and realize what a lucky guy I am to have a woman who'd get three bills a night."

The next day when I came into the BMW dealership the sales rep gave me a respectful nod and didn't even sneer at the Fairmont. I walked past him to Swede's office.

For over an hour, we theorized and conjectured and in the end we had a plan of sorts. "It's the only way, Nick. Anything else and we're farting in the wind."

I had to digest this. I sat back and tapped my pen on the desk for a minute or so. Swede leaned back, his big hands behind his head. For a few minutes, we didn't speak. I became conscious of the background music, an FM station that played soft numbers suitable to the tastes of BMW owners.

"I know how you feel," Swede said, "but she'll be okay. We'll be close by all the way."

"Hmmm."

"You gotta go for the weak link or the known enemy. You know that, Nick. In this case it's one and the same. Perfect."

More silence. An orchestral version of "Yesterday" played.

"Aw," Swede said, "we've got a grace period anyway. In

the meantime, maybe something will break or we'll think of something better. Or we can back off. You call it."

He referred to phase one of the plan, which was to do nothing until Nicky finished school and I could scoot him out West to my sister's. We felt there was nothing to lose in waiting a bit longer and I didn't want to pull Nicky out before his final exams.

A grace period. I might as well enjoy it because I knew there was no backing out. Events have a momentum and these were beginning to career toward an inevitable crash. I could stand in the way and wait for ruination of one sort or the other or I could try to steer the events. That could lead to ruination, too.

The next three and a half weeks while I waited for Nicky to finish school were played in slow motion. To appease any operatives Carmen Buono might have tailing me, I became the model of the chastened person who has been scolded and is grateful to his betters that he has been spared further punishment. At least I did that as far as it was possible. I strove for a public face filled with penitence. No trips to the Combat Zone, no digging or sniffing around. I was even careful about what I said on the phone, although I doubted the tentacles were stretched that cleverly at me.

Barbara had to be prepared for Nicky's trip to my sister's. One afternoon, I visited her for that purpose. When I told her of Nicky's going to Colorado, she was, naturally, apprehensive, but I think she was pleased that he'd no longer be staying with Swede. I *know* she was pleased.

We sat in the backyard. It was a delightful day, mid-eighties, low humidity. From a postcard blue sky, the sun constructed short shadows.

Barbara had on shorts and a filmy blouse. We sipped lemonade.

As we talked, as I tried to convince her that nothing about the situation had changed or worsened and that Nicky's visit was just a simple precaution coupled with a chance for him to see the West, I played with emotional dynamite. We were alone in the yard and the house was empty. Gary was at work and Nicky at Swede's. What would be the harm in taking Barbara by the hand and leading her to the bedroom? I wondered whether she'd go and that was part of the fascination. But mainly she was the fascination. The memories of the way it had been. The physical part.

The sun and the breeze fondled her hair, ruffling it and making it glow. Already, she was nicely tanned.

I wondered whether she would ever put a pool in the yard. We had often talked of it. Gary would be a pool person, part of the pool culture, a devotee of antiseptic, waveless, climate-controlled water. I could picture her and Gary sitting around it, dipping in it at night, laughing, touching, and gliding to an end out of sight of Nicky's window. I winced.

"How long will he be gone?" she asked.

I shrugged. "A couple of weeks. Three maybe." Once he was in Colorado, I could stretch it through the summer if necessary.

"I don't know," she said.

We talked some more. She balked but finally agreed.

It was time for me to leave.

But I lingered. I drained my glass of lemonade and watched a bluejay upbraid the world in the locust tree near the fence in the rear of the yard. I had planted the tree ten years ago. It was now a tall, graceful thing, almost tropical looking, its lacy leaves shedding a delicate shade.

I complimented Barbara on how nice the yard looked. The grass was neatly cut, the shrubs trimmed. She had a lawn service come in, she said. That used to be my job and I had liked it. I could picture Gary riding a mower, not pushing one.

I complimented her on how nice she looked. I knew who serviced her. Too easily, I could picture Gary riding her.

I stood and then sat again. I felt my pulse tick in the hollow in my throat. The thing to do was pack it up and leave, get the hell out of here. I had accomplished what I had come for. Don't entangle things by making a fool of yourself, a voice warned. Rejection or acceptance, both led to trouble.

"Would you like some more lemonade?" Barbara asked. I tried to read a message in that question.

I shook my head. "I should be going." Did she want me to go?

She nodded.

But then, "Don't go."

Could she see my pulse tick? I cleared my throat. I didn't trust my voice but I managed a normal sounding, "Well, all right. I'll have some more lemonade."

"I'll get it."

Did her voice sound normal?

"I'll come with you."

"It's just in the house . . . in the kitchen."

"I know."

We stood awkwardly by the refrigerator for a moment, absurdly sipping freshly poured lemonade.

"Do you want to go back outside?" she asked. Her eyes were wide, the way I remembered them when we first met and she appraised me. Some memories are like photographs.

"No."

I set my glass of lemonade on the counter. Then I took hers from her hand and set it beside mine.

My hand came back to hers. Hands cold from lemonade glasses, touching, warming.

"Nick, I think you should go."

"Do you want me to go?" My voice was husky and I couldn't control it.

She seemed flustered. "This isn't easy, Nick. Don't make it more difficult."

Our hands still touched, still cold, but still warming.

"I want to kiss you, Barbara."

At first tentative, the kiss became kisses remembered, soft and warm and then greedy. A prelude to what we couldn't stop.

Quickly, almost, it seemed, without transition or passage, we were in the bedroom, our bedroom, our bed, everything familiar, everything right.

If the first time was a frantic rush to culmination, the second was patient and tender. It had been like this when I came off active duty, a tumultuous celebration of life, of the flesh, verification that we were still as remembered. We touched old responses, rediscovering old joys and ecstasies.

Finally, we lay on cool sheets, inevitably staring at the ceiling, not speaking, the room bright with June afternoon sunshine. I wondered how long it would take for me to crash.

We didn't speak the whole time it took me to dress. We didn't speak when I looked at Barbara still naked on the sheets. I didn't look closely at her eyes.

I let myself out, not knowing what I felt.

*   *   *

Arrangements were made and plans finalized to send Nicky to Colorado. Katherine, my sister, lived in a town that looked like something from a John Denver television special. Aspen and streams and snow-capped mountains. Twice, I had visited her and I wished I could this time with my son. Nicky and I on horseback, riding across sun-dappled meadows, close to nature and each other.

Over the years, Katherine had extended an open invitation to me to stay with her and her family during the summer. This time, I said, I'd take her up on the offer but I was hung up with some college business and could Nicky come out first? I'd join them later if that was no problem. It wasn't, and I vowed to myself that I really would.

The day Nicky was to leave, I picked him up at noon so that we'd have some time together before his four o'clock flight.

Barbara let me in and we passed an awkward moment at the foot of the stairs waiting for Nicky to come down.

We made fumbling conversation filled with forced smiles and fleeting eye contact. In the nearly two weeks since we made love, I hadn't crashed. I wondered whether she had and then dismissed that notion as egoism.

I fought the messages that her perfume and her closeness sent to me. Despite the awkwardness, in a way it seemed so natural to be standing here in what had been my home with the woman who had been my wife. It was as if I were leaving for work. Or coming back to share a midday moment of love and intimacy.

Barbara and I would never get back together but it was easy now to imagine furtive snatches of lovemaking. That was an emotional trap I knew I would yield to if Barbara allowed.

But not today. Nicky came clamoring down the stairs, a suitcase jouncing mutely on the carpet. The three of us walked out to my car.

I put the suitcase in the trunk and Nicky kissed his mother good-bye. I touched Barbara's shoulder, half expecting her to flinch or harden, but she didn't. I assured her everything would be fine and Nicky and I drove to Boston.

In Quincy Market, we had pizza at Regina's and ice cream at Steve's. We walked up to Washington Street and visited a large book store. For the flight and for Colorado, Nicky bought a sports magazine, a car magazine, and a Stephen King paperback.

When we left the book store, we walked up to Tremont Street and sat in the sun by the edge of the Common. Although we had never formally broached the reason for Nicky's going to Colorado, he knew. But we talked of other things. Of Red Sox hopes, of Celtics fulfillments, of what he would do in Colorado. Of cousins he hadn't seen since he was a little boy.

We watched the people: the shoppers, the lawyers and bankers, the loafers. The tourists with garlands of cameras gawking at old churches and burial grounds, at cow path streets where Adamses, Reveres, and Franklins perhaps had walked.

At three o'clock, we drove to Logan Airport and watched the planes take off and land. There is, to me, something bittersweet about airports. About arrivals and departures, reunions and separations. To Nicky it was excitement, a touch-point with speed and distant places.

At three-fifty, Nicky boarded. We shook hands and then hugged, patting shoulders. My eyes stung.

"Be careful, Dad," he said.

I stayed and watched his plane, silver and blue, taxi slowly out to the runway, lights blinking, and then gather itself for the sudden rush, quickly airborne, hurtling skyward at an improbable angle, trailing thick, black plumes, then bending to the west, and finally lost in the afternoon sun.

CHAPTER

14

Stan Janski called me at home the morning of the day that Moira was to see Dr. Lohnes for part one of her role in the scheme Swede and I had concocted.

"Nick. Got something for you. Joanne Lewis, the broad in the Trans Am you had me look up. It seems Joanne Lewis is owner of Pan's Flute, a joint in the Combat Zone."

"What kind of joint?" Mythological allusion. Better than Snatch a View.

"Mainly peep show, but also some alleged whoring goes

on there as it does in most of those places. Or at least it's a conduit to whores if the peeper can work up the courage to face the real thing."

I recalled the place from my recent trips to the Combat Zone.

"Joanne Lewis bought Pan's Flute from a D and L Associates Realty Trust in 1981 for a nominal fee.

"Uh huh."

"D and L Associates stands for Daniels and Lloyd."

Bull's-eye, I thought.

"D and L in turn bought Pan's Flute in 1977, probably for the profit it could generate in its own right but also, no doubt, as a shrewd investment against the day that the urban renewer's ball smashes all the Zone to dust and modern high rises replace it, which isn't too far off, I guess."

Stan paused a moment and then said with a trace of drama, "Now, here's the part you're gonna like. The Daniels part of the realty trust is your expired colleague, Daniel Ritchie. At least he's the signatory of the transfer. I don't know who Lloyd is."

"I do."

Stan Janski gave me a moment to explain and when I didn't he said, "I dug around, talked with a buddy at the Registry of Deeds and voilà or eureka, as you educators would say, he came up with this."

"You say the fee was nominal. How nominal?"

"Twenty K."

I wondered why they would sell. Maybe just a case of cold feet over having their names associated with a den of iniquity. The twenty thousand was enough to build a case that their heart was in the sale, but suggested they could still control the place and reap the profits. They might even have funded Joanne Lewis the money to buy.

And now Lloyd Markham was the sole recipient of those profits unless Dan Ritchie and Lloyd Markham were the straws for someone else to begin with. Possibly someone like Carmen Buono.

I thanked Stan effusively, hung up, and got ready to meet Moira at Cityside at two-thirty after her appointment with Eric Lohnes.

Eric Lohnes, M.D., friend of Joanne Lewis, owner of Pan's Flute. What had his connection to Dan Ritchie been? Maybe Dan and Lloyd Markham had been straws for Eric Lohnes. But was it likely for a doctor to own such a place? Why not? It was money. He'd just be careful to cover his name.

I snapped the .25 in place under my loose-fitting shirt as I left for Boston. I was worried about Moira. I hoped I wasn't leading her in over her head.

I sat, nursing my second Dos Equis beer at an outdoor table at Cityside, worrying and wondering and trying to quell my misgivings. They can paralyze.

The late afternoon sun was still hot and high. Light dazzled from glass buildings. My shirt stuck to my back and I checked to be sure the .25 wasn't showing.

Pigeons patrolled around patrons' feet and under tables. People strolled by, gawking and licking ice creams. Food smells and city noises filled the air but I was only remotely attuned to any of this. I checked my watch and calculated times, those Moira spent with Dr. Lohnes, being in traffic, finding a place to park, and walking to meet me. They were probable but I wasn't reassured.

My waiter came by and asked if I was ready to order. I

reminded him that I was waiting for someone but to assuage him I swilled the Dos Equis and ordered another. I'm easy that way. Dos Equis is Mexican and excellent, although I sometimes wonder about the water it's made from.

I stared at the throngs some more, looking for Moira, and fidgeted. A pigeon pecked at something near my feet and I kicked halfheartedly at him. He ruffled his feathers indignantly but otherwise ignored me. Bold bastard.

Then I saw Moira coming toward me. She was wearing white slacks and a black sleeveless blouse open at the throat. Her pale skin was flawless and her dark hair shone. As always, she drew stares.

I stood and pushed out a chair for her. From her expression, I could tell she was pleased with how things had gone.

"Well?" I said. My tension and the relief from it was compacted into the one syllable.

"Be patient," she said. "In due course." She looked about. "I'm starved. Did you order?"

"Just this." I tapped my bottle of Dos Equis and signaled the waiter. He came and we ordered roast beef sandwiches, *au jus*, and more beer.

"We won't get Montezuma's revenge from drinking that Mex stuff, will we?" Moira asked.

"Enough chitchat. What the hell happened?"

"I might change jobs. He'll pay me fifty thousand for a healthy baby that I might carry. That's after we negotiated. At first it was twenty-five thousand, but he eventually doubled that when I was adamant, as you told me to be. Can you imagine this? What's he get for himself, I wonder."

I shrugged. "What's he have to do but invest a little time?"

"What kind of woman could do this? Carry a child and then give it up? It's so calculating."

Our waiter returned with two bottles of Dos Equis.

"How did he seem?" I asked when the waiter left.

"Businesslike."

"Nervous at all?"

"No."

"Hmmm." I would have preferred a "yes." It would more likely indicate that our theory was correct, that Dr. Lohnes was doing a little sneaking on the side, breaking away from the aegis of the mob on this one, a step that would make any intelligent man nervous.

"But he didn't balk at fifty grand. Did you get the feeling he'd go higher?"

"No. Definitely not. My feeling was that he had a preset a somewhat lower figure. Forty, I'd guess, but reluctantly yielded when I insisted."

"That's good. Shows he thinks you're genuine." That was part of the plan. To set a high price to test his acceptance of Moira.

"So what's next? When do you go back?"

"I'm going to keep a record of my temperature for a month. We discussed my menstrual cycle. He mentioned something about blood tests and even ultrasound to predict fertility time. He could give me something-or-other citrate to regulate ovulation. He said it might take more than one attempt but that he had a very high success rate with artificial insemination. As far as the mechanics of it are concerned, he said there was practically nothing to it. A real quickie, I guess."

"Well, we aren't going to wait any month," I said.

"Course, we don't have to. We'll give it a few days, a week at the outside, before we swing into part two."

"He does the insemination at his home, by the way, in the evening. Apparently, he has all the facilities there."

I didn't like that. Moira would be more vulnerable at the secluded private residence than at the busy office.

"Well, you don't actually have to go there. You can present him with your idea at his office."

"I don't know. He gave me a phone number and told me from now on to call him between eight and eleven if I had any questions."

Our waiter returned with our sandwiches. As we ate quietly for a few moments, I watched Moira. She was obviously caught up in the gamelike aspect of her scam with Dr. Lohnes. For some reason, I was reminded of Tom Austin, a hayseed from Nebraska, a virtual stereotype replete with freckles, sandy hair, gangling body, and boyish grin. His big disappointment was that he ended up in Germany in the MPs rather than in Vietnam in the infantry.

But, ironically, he ended up making the supreme sacrifice anyway. He was shot one evening on the streets of Stuttgart by an unknown assailant, probably someone just simply anti-American. It took him fifteen minutes to die and I was with him the whole time. The ambulance didn't make it on time.

I drove the recollection from my mind.

After we ate, we browsed through some of the shops at North and South Markets and then strolled hand in hand to the waterfront.

The late afternoon and early evening were lovely but I couldn't shake my disquiet and the image of Tom Austin.

I had held his hand for the fifteen minutes it took him to die.

                              *   *   *

I got home around ten and came into the house to my
ringing phone. It was Norm Eigner.

"Haven't seen you since school got out, Nick. Just
checking on things. You know, the Kristin Williams thing,
mainly, I guess. Anything new?"

The less said the better. "No, not really, Norm."

"Oh. Uh, you still working on it?"

"Well, to tell you the truth, I've been pretty busy with
Reserve business. After all, that's what I get paid to do."

"Right. I was just wondering. I'm sitting here reading
some material for the summer course I'm going to teach
and talking to Iago, seeing if I can teach him something
by Yeats, maybe 'Leda and the Swan.' What the hell, I
can't teach it to my students."

We made small talk for a few minutes and when I hung
up I wondered whether it was just my imagination or did
Norm really sound something like the guy who had
phoned me threatening Nicky?

Early the next morning, I drove to Boynton University
just outside Hartford. I remembered that Dan Ritchie got
his Ph.D. at Boynton and I wanted to look at his dissertation. I had called ahead to see whether they would let me
examine it. Some universities allow that, others don't.
Boynton did.

During the night, it had rained heavily, and minarets of
ominous clouds were just now breaking. The road still
glistened and sheets of steam rose at intervals from it, but
when I pulled into Boynton around eleven, the sun was
fully out and the red dirt beside the highway, peculiar to
that part of Connecticut, had dried out.

Boynton's about a hundred years old, I guess, and is

rather small like Colton, but not nearly as quaint and cozy.

In the faculty library, I introduced myself to the librarian and we spent a few moments shaking heads and bemoaning the tragic fate of Dan Ritchie. I told him Dan had been a friend of mine as well as a colleague and that while we had often discussed our respective disciplines, I never really knew his specific expertise. I wanted to look at Dan's doctoral thesis more as a tribute to a friend than to satisfy curiosity. I hoped that didn't sound too corny.

The librarian, a fussy guy about sixty who I'd bet was gay, directed me to a table by a window and told me to make myself comfortable while he got Dan's dissertation.

Sullen gusts of heavy air blew in on me while I waited. In less than five minutes he was back with the bound copy. We exchanged comments about the heat and he left.

As I read, my excitement grew. I was beginning to get a sense of what Dan's experiments that Rick Le Brun alluded to might have been. After about an hour-and-a-half, I perused the bibliography. At one item, I did the classic double take, read again and copied.

I returned the book to the librarian and thanked him. He smiled and said, "You're very welcome. No one ever looks at these things. I'm sure Dan would be pleased. Was it informative?"

"Very," I said. "Dan had depths I never realized. Quite a guy."

I drove back up to the Mass Pike, which I followed directly into Boston. It was midafternoon and I hadn't eaten since breakfast. My stomach, accustomed to immediate gratification, grumbled a protest but it would have to wait. I wanted to see Rick Le Brun. I lucked out and got a spot on Commonwealth Avenue not far from *Hub* magazine headquarters and lucked out again when I found Rick in.

We sat in his tiny cubicle. He seemed wary and I couldn't blame him. Since the last time we had talked about Kristin Williams and Dan Ritchie, Dan had been murdered.

I got to the point.

"Mr. Le Brun, I'd like to ask a small favor. I wonder whether you could dig up a copy of the October tenth, 1971, *Oracle* for me."

He shrugged. "Probably. But you could dig it up easily enough yourself. Just go to their office and ask. They moved to Bay Village, you know, about a year ago. I think they're going to do an all-gay paper pretty soon."

"Yeah, I could, but there's something else. A couple of things, actually. First, I may be getting close to a story. A good one."

There's nothing like a reporter on your side. For a moment, Rick Le Brun looked like a kid on Christmas morning, but then he slipped into nonchalance. "Okay. What else? You said a couple of things."

"Do you remember when I talked with you before, you alluded to 'experiments' that Dan Ritchie might have been involved in?"

"Did I use that word?"

"I believe you did. Can you tell me any more?"

"What's the deal? I tell you something, maybe provide the link you've been looking for and you give me a story? I assume the *Oracle*—what was the date?—has something to do with it."

"October tenth. Seventy-one. And it might."

Rick Le Brun jotted down the date. "There were just

192

rumors. You know, you hear things. I'm surprised you never did. I mean, you worked with the guy."

Rick Le Brun reached behind him to a Mr. Coffee on a small cabinet. "You want a coffee?"

I nodded and he poured a couple of cups. He pushed a package of sugar cubes and a jar of powdered creamer at me. I didn't want the coffee but it might be an avenue to further conversation.

"I didn't know Dan Ritchie that well. Besides, I imagine he'd be careful to keep his underground doings separate from the academic." I thought of Lloyd Markham. Dan didn't keep them that separate.

Rick Le Brun blew on his coffee and sipped.

"How close are you to a story?" he asked.

"Actually, I already have one. But there's a question of proof and I don't have the whole of it yet."

"And it involves, I imagine, the Williams girl. The one doing a paper on black-market adoptions. Is that the story? It's a good one and to tell the truth I've been playing with it in the back of my mind since you talked with me. Dan Ritchie's involved too, huh? Or was."

I plopped a sugar cube into my coffee and a spoonful of phony creamer. I hate the stuff. Full of chemicals and coconut fat.

"Well, I'm afraid I don't have an awful lot I can tell you. If I did, I'd write the damn story myself. Put the pieces together and have myself a scoop."

"Maybe I can save you a lot of legwork."

"Well, it's like this." Rick Le Brun laughed. "I heard Dan Ritchie was involved in crazy ideas about utopian societies and that the key to their success lay in sexual perfection."

"Sexual perfection?"

193

"Yeah. Look, I'm just telling you what I heard. Sounds like bullshit, I know. I mean, you'd be more likely to find sexual perversion than perfection in the Combat Zone."

"Did you ever hear of Dan being involved in sadism?"

"You mean as in sexual sadism? S and M, et cetera?"

"Yes."

"There were rumors."

I took an obligatory sip at my coffee. My stomach rumbled for something solid and I coughed to cover the noise.

"From what I heard," Rick Le Brun said, "Dan felt that pain was the key to sexual perfection. Penance, purgation, that sort of thing. Pain and pleasure are fundamentally related. Nothing terribly original about it all, is there?"

It struck me that Rick Le Brun had heard a lot. He seemed to sense my reaction.

He said, "Look, I'm surmising an awful lot. Really, that's the extent of what I know and am guessing at from what little I've heard."

I nodded and put my cup on the edge of his desk. "That's interesting. About the utopian societies, I mean. You've heard specific mention of Dan's interest there?"

"Well, not in those terms. Street talk from which you surmise. Things like, 'Dan thinks a good whipping will make you like those book people he's always talking about.'"

I said, "I wonder which utopian societies Dan had in mind. Which ones were into pain?"

"Maybe they were utopian only in Dan's mind."

I nodded, thinking of the article I had read by Dan about the minister and his women. He had been sadistic with them to make them pure and suitable for his seed.

I stood. "You've been helpful, Mr. Le Brun. Look, why

don't I just go myself to the *Oracle*? No need to bother you."

"It's no bother. I'm intrigued. I'll go today. Can you drop by tomorrow? For that matter, I'll be coming back and will be here til' about seven this evening."

"One or the other," I said. "This evening or tomorrow."

We shook hands. Conspirators. "I appreciate it," I said. My stomach grumbled all the way to my car.

I crossed the Charles to Cambridge and stopped on Mass Ave at a burger place for two cheeseburgers and a milk shake. I threw the trash on the floor of the Fairmont and drove to Swede's dealership. It was late afternoon, but still hot and sticky, and the city air was heavy with haze and traffic noise. Cambridge may be MIT, Harvard, brick, and ivy, but parts of Massachusetts Avenue are out and out tacky.

The sales associate and I exchanged respectful nods as I found my way to Swede's office. He was on the phone but gestured me to sit. The announcer on the soft-music station was reciting the news. In a modulated voice, he announced that the United States had detonated a nuclear device underground in Nevada with a yield from ten to fifteen times that of the Hiroshima bomb. Traffic was tied up on Route 128 north in Lexington where a truck had jackknifed, the Dow Jones was down 18.25 points, the Red Sox and Oakland As were tied 2–2 going into the last of the ninth, and the forecast was for continued hot, sticky weather.

Music resumed with a stringed version of "Morning Has Broken" by Cat Stevens.

Swede was nodding and mumbling, "uh-huh," into the

phone. He looked at me and raised a finger that said, be just a minute.

After two or three, he continued to say, "uh-huh," but began to make faces and silently mouth obscenities into the phone. When he put the mouthpiece to his buttocks, I walked out to avoid laughing aloud but had to go back in when the sales associate looked at me strangely as I stood by myself shaking with mirth.

"Yes, sir, Mr. Merryman. First thing next week." Swede hung up. "What a pain in the ass. What's up, Nick? How'd it go with Moira?"

"A lot's up. I guess it went well." I told him what Moira told me.

"I don't like it, Swede," I said when I finished. "Especially I don't like the thought of her going out to his place on the Jamaicaway at night. And to keep the plan credible, I think she'll have to."

"Call it off, then. Really. Just call it off. Maybe we've got enough to go to the cops with now."

"What do we have? Moira's word against his. As for the rest of it—them—we have nothing. We've got theories. Circumstantial, suggestive vapor. I don't know who killed Kristin Williams or Darlene Abbott or Dan Ritchie. Did Eric Lohnes? Lloyd Markham? The Mob?"

"Okay, take it easy. You said a lot's up. Like what?"

"Like I'm back to being a nosy bastard. Jesus, I hope they don't know where Nicky is."

"Nick, let me go after this Sal the Scuzz you were telling me about. I guarantee you I'll find out who's behind all this."

"He doesn't know. I mean he knows who gives him orders but we already know that."

"Then I'll take him out of circulation."

I thought of Sal Scuzz, a hydrant at 5'10", 212, an animal who didn't care about consequences. Swede would dismember him in about a minute and a half. I wondered sometimes whether Swede cared about consequences, whether the Green Beret and Vietnam would ever be shaken out of him.

"Swede, I appreciate it, but there's a hundred Sal Scuzz's to do Carmen Buono's dirty work. You can't stamp them all out."

"Yeah, but it'd be a whole lot of fun trying. By the way, speaking of Sal Scuzz, Stan Janski called. Said he tried to get a hold of you but couldn't. Said you wanted to know what kind of cars Sal and his rat shit friends drove. Said Sal drives an eighty-seven 'Vette and, let's see, he named two or three other guys you talked about but none drives a Trans Am, which is what I figure you wanted to know. Which leads us right back to the Lewis broad."

I thought of something else that I wondered whether Stan Janski could get me: the results of the post mortem on Kristin Williams to see if she was pregnant. The Metro cops weren't investigating her murder but still Stan could probably get that information.

"Anyway," Swede said, lighting a cigar, "you still haven't told me how you're being a nosy bastard, which is what I suppose you came by to tell me about."

I told him of my trip to Boynton U., of Dan Ritchie's doctoral paper, and my conversation with Rick Le Brun. I didn't tell him about the *Oracle* article. It bothered me. It made me worry further about Moira. But, until I read it, I wasn't sure of its implications.

"Dan had some weird ideas, Swede, but I'm not sure what it all adds up to."

"Yeah, but I don't see what studying sex habits and customs has to do with illegal adoptions."

"Well, I don't think that's all that was or is going on. I think there may be something really strange here and that the adoption black market is just part of it."

"Like what?"

"Maybe I'll know tonight. Rick Le Brun is going to get me an old copy of the *Oracle*. Dan used it among his sources for his dissertation."

"That rag?" Swede blew a stream of smoke toward the ceiling. "Doesn't sound like a reputable source for a doctoral paper."

"Especially if the article is as weird as it sounds. Of course, dangerous ideas can be couched in innocuous terms. But this scares me. The writer sounds like a wacko."

"Yeah. But who the hell?"

"Our buddy. Eric Lohnes, M.D."

I was back at *Hub* magazine at six-twenty. The building was closed and I had to wait about five minutes while a security guard checked with Rick Le Brun.

Upstairs was brightly lit, but only Rick and another guy in his own cubicle manned the place. Woodward and Bernstein. Rick smiled and waved a copy of the *Oracle* at me. He was working on a bucket of fried chicken.

"Want a piece? Go ahead, grab a piece. Check it out. Not franchise stuff, you know. Guy I know on Tremont Street just started up. Gives you twelve pieces of chicken for five bucks, cooked in vegetable oil, not lard.

"Got your copy of the *Oracle*. I didn't think they were going to be able to find one. Good thing I went instead of you 'cause they really had to dig for it and probably wouldn't have for you. No reflection on you, it's just they don't know you and they know me."

I took a piece of chicken. I wanted the *Oracle* but Rick Le Brun was still clutching it.

"Take another. Good, huh? Guy'll make a bundle. Good product, a lot of it, and the price is right . . .

"Oh, here, this is what you came by for. I didn't get a chance to look at it myself." He handed me the *Oracle*. Rick Le Brun had become gregarious. Maybe he had had a drink or two. Maybe he had accepted me. Most likely, he was horny for a story.

I wiped polyunsaturated chicken-batter grease from my fingers with my handkerchief and carefully turned the yellowing, brittle pages of the *Oracle*.

"Looks like something out of the Civil War, huh? Well, not that old but older than seventy-one. Guess they haven't gone to microfilm yet. I'm glad I got the hell out of there, working for them I mean, especially now that they're going gay, not that I've got anything against gays; you know, to each his own, as long as they leave me alone. But to them—gays—the only issues are gay issues. AIDS, things like that. Find what you want?"

I had.

For a few moments, I skimmed the article entitled "Does Pain Equal Pleasure?" by Eric Lohnes, M.D., and detected a carefully phrased and disguised perversion. Even though Dr. Lohnes had protected himself through euphemism and equivocation, no respectable journal would have published such an article. But maybe *I* wasn't being objective. I wondered how much flak, if any, he had received over the article. Still, doctors are notorious for protecting their own.

"Is there a photocopy machine here? I'd like to copy this."

"Sure. What pages?"

"Here to here. Pages three and four, continued on nine and ten, and then fourteen through sixteen."

"Be right back. Have another hunk of chicken."

I did. It was good. And it made me hungry. All in all, I hadn't eaten much today. I was tempted to snitch another piece from the bucket but there were only three pieces left. Too countable. Maybe I'd pick up a bucket and drop in on Moira with it. We could pop them into the microwave and have chicken and beer.

Microwaves and copiers. What a long way we'd come. But babies were sold, men (and women) killed. Ph.D.'s and M.D.'s crawled in the gutter. And I was a philosopher, with a strong hold on the banal.

"Here you go," he said, handing me the photocopied sheets. "How's this connect to Dan Ritchie and illegal adoptions?"

"I'm not sure it does. I want to read it carefully."

"But you think there's a story?"

"I know there's a story."

He nodded and pulled another piece of chicken from the bucket.

"If we go on this," he said, "I'll write it for the *Chronicle*. I have a by-line with them. They own *Hub*, you know."

I hadn't. The *Chronicle* was one of Boston's three dailies.

"That would be for the immediate impact," Rick Le Brun said. "Then, depending, I'd do an in-depth article for *Hub* later on. But, obviously, we'd have to be sure of our facts."

"Naturally."

He glanced at the copy of the *Oracle* he was holding. "'Does Pain Equal Pleasure?' by Eric Lohnes, M.D. I've heard of him. Big name, good rep. What the hell's he doing writing something for the *Oracle* instead of the *New England Journal of Medicine*?"

"What indeed?" I said.

Rick Le Brun tapped the side of his head. "Eric Lohnes, Eric Lohnes. Now what the hell do I remember about him? Seems to me I remember reading something or other about him."

"It wouldn't have anything to do with this article, would it?"

"I don't think so." He took another piece of chicken and chewed meditatively. "He's from Germany originally. I know that. Maybe that's what I remember."

"How old is he? Do you have any idea?"

"I don't know. Course, I never went to him, him being an ob-gyn. But I've seen his picture. I'd have to say he's between fifty-five and sixty.

"Jesus, don't tell me Eric Lohnes is involved in black-market adoptions." Rick Le Brun's eyes glowed with anticipation. Visions of a Pulitzer Prize probably danced in his head.

"I won't tell you. Because I don't know." I wanted to play this close to the vest, although we both knew it was pretty obvious.

Rick Le Brun ripped a piece of paper off a pad on his desk and wrote on it. "Here's a couple of numbers where you can get me. The top one's here, good even when we're closed, and the bottom one is my home. There's an answering machine, which I realize is a pain to a lot of people but this is starting to sound big. You wouldn't care to spell out what you have now, would you, or think you have?"

"Not yet."

"I can appreciate that, but I mean are we talking murder, you know, the Williams girl *and* Dan Ritchie, as well as illegal adoptions in connection with Eric Lohnes?"

"I don't know."

"Yeah, well, you ought to write it all down or something and put it in a safety deposit box and let someone know where, in case . . ."

"Like in the movies? And the someone should be you?"

"Well, you don't want to take a chance."

He had a point. "I'll keep in touch, believe me, Mr. Le Brun."

"Please. Call me Rick. And you're Nick, right? I'll walk you out."

He walked me to the sidewalk, past the security guard reading a magazine that wasn't *Hub*. Outside, it was still bright and still very warm. Ah, summer. We shook hands.

"By the way," I said as I started to my car, "where did you say that chicken place is?"

CHAPTER

15

Early morning in summer is special. Often I run before it's light and then come home and shower and sit in the yard with the paper and coffee. This morning I sat with coffee and photocopied sheets of the October 10, 1971, *Oracle*. I read "Does Pain Equal Pleasure?" by Eric Lohnes, M.D., twice very carefully.

When I finished, I went inside, had another coffee, some orange juice, and an English muffin. Then I drained the last of the coffee from the Mr. Coffee and went back outside with the *Globe*. But I couldn't concentrate on the paper. Mainly because last night over the bucket of chicken and beer I had persuaded Moira to call Dr. Lohnes at the Jamaicaway number and tell him she wanted to see him tonight. Not that she needed any persuasion. Part two of plan. He agreed and I was nervous.

The other reason I couldn't concentrate on the *Globe* was that I was still trying to assess the significance of the article in the *Oracle*. While I hadn't expected it to give me a concrete incriminating connection of Eric Lohnes to illicit adoptions (which it didn't), it convinced me that Eric Lohnes was potentially dangerous. Not the kind of person in whose unattended presence I wanted Moira to be for any length of time. He and Dan Ritchie had been of the same ilk, birds of a feather, carefully disguised sadists.

When I got home last night, I called Swede. He and I would keep surveillance over the Jamaicaway address while Moira was there. After, we'd follow her car a couple of miles to make sure we were the only tail. Then I'd drive with her to Swede's condo in Belmont to debrief. All reasonably planned, all reasonably risky.

I finished my coffee and went back inside. I wanted to call Nicky but it was too early, especially too early in Colorado.

I needed to kill a couple of hours. I had nothing to read. Television was useless so I drove to Masterson's gym and did some sets of presses and squats, sat in the sauna, and then took another shower. If nothing else, I would have clean pores today.

Back home, I called my sister's number in Colorado, but there was no answer. I let the phone ring ten times before I hung up. It was nine o'clock in Colorado. My sister didn't work. Probably shopping. Maybe they were all horseback riding. Maybe they were fishing or climbing a mountain or at a sing-along with John Denver.

Maybe Sal Scuzz was in Colorado.

I'd call back later.

I made a BLT on Wonder bread and washed it down with two glasses of milk. Then I rewarded myself with a dish of Steve's chocolate ice cream from a quart I had in the freezer.

I watched the noon news, listened to the anchors chitchat and segue themselves through tragedy, weather, and sports.

After the news, I called Colorado again. My sister answered. Everything was just fine and when was I coming out? We talked for a few minutes and she put Nicky on. He said he was having a ball but that he missed home and his friends. And me. We talked for a few more minutes, comparing weather and discussing the Red Sox. He, too, wanted to know when I could come out to Colorado.

I told him soon, that things were moving along and before he knew it, I'd be out there and then we'd be home and going to ball games.

When I hung up, I realized I very much wanted things resolved and to be with my son fishing in a Colorado stream or sitting in the bleachers at Fenway Park.

I sat in a two-year-old BMW, courtesy of Swede's car lot of preowned yuppie wagons, parked between a couple of huge trees on the Jamaicaway. Dr. Lohnes's home was about one hundred yards up the road on my left and Swede was parked about another hundred yards beyond that. Two BMWs on stakeout.

Moira had pulled into Dr. Lohnes's long driveway about a half hour ago, about the limit of the time I had estimated she'd be there, and I was getting edgy.

It was dusk and a windshift to the northwest had blown away the humidity and dropped the temperature ten degrees. Black clouds that had threatened rain were now just long strips of purple and pink.

Light traffic sped by. A pretty young thing jogged past me on the sidewalk with a German shepherd on a leash. Two minutes later a runner zipped past, a guy with a fluorescent-orange running vest. I watched the reflectors on his heels bounce up and down.

It was just about dark now. I started the BMW, pulled down the road and parked opposite Dr. Lohnes's driveway, which made a circle by the front door. Moira's Volvo was parked facing out.

The house, three stories of brick—a mansion, actually— was set back about one hundred feet from the road. A fence of wrought iron spikes in a low brick wall barricaded the house from the street. A double gate at the driveway was pushed open. Lights glowed in a front room downstairs and in one upstairs.

For a few moments, my mind tormented itself with images of Moira strapped to a table with a gloating, fiendish Dr. Lohnes brandishing scalpels at her.

I let ten minutes pass and was considering doing something, although I wasn't sure what. Maybe walking up to Swede's car for a conference. Lights switched on and after a few minutes switched off in another room upstairs.

I was still considering when the Trans Am pulled off the Jamaicaway and into the driveway. It looped around the circle and stopped behind Moira's Volvo. I checked the .25 clipped to my belt.

It was dark and over one hundred feet away but I could tell that whoever got out of the Trans Am wasn't Joanne Lewis. It was a man. He stood under the lamp by the front door and rang the bell but his back was toward me.

I was out of the BMW now and waiting to cross traffic

when Dr. Lohnes's front door opened and the man went in. I saw my chance and crossed the street. I stood by the fence for a few seconds wondering what to do. Then I saw Swede moving quickly toward me.

"Time for the cavalry to move in, Nick? Who got out of the Trans Am, your pals?"

"I couldn't tell. But there was only one."

Swede pulled a revolver from under his jacket. It was a magnum. "Jesus, Swede, haven't you anything more subtle?"

"Stopping power, shocking power. This hits 'em, they're down."

Good point if you're dealing with a crazed water buffalo.

"We going in?" he asked.

I looked at the house. The same lights were on. No shadows moved against curtains. No screams for help.

"Let's wait a bit."

"Geez, Nick, the doc just brought in muscle. I say we move up and take a look and a listen."

"He wouldn't need muscle if he suspected Moira of anything. He could handle it himself."

"A guy like that? A doctor. He wouldn't soil his hands. Maybe he found the bug on her."

We had given Moira a small recorder, courtesy of the 340th, 94th ARCOM, Reserve Military Police, to put in her handbag.

I said, "I'll go in. You stay here and cover me."

I squelched Swede's rising protest. "This is my show, Swede. You stay here. Come in fast, though, if I need you. You notice any kind of security or surveillance? I didn't."

"It looks clear," Swede said.

I went to the driveway and moved in quickly toward

the room with the lights. Crouched low, I was abreast Moira's car when the front door to the house opened and two men stepped out under the light. I got a fleeting but definitive glimpse before I ducked beside the Volvo. One, distinguished looking, late fifties, I presumed was Eric Lohnes. The other wasn't Sal the Scuzz.

From my position, I could hear them talking but couldn't understand the words. They talked two or three minutes and then I heard the Trans Am start and pull out of the driveway. On hands and knees, I scurried to a position where I could get its license number. I repeated it several times, trying to remember the number of the one registered to Joanne Lewis. I had it written at home and would cross-check them later. But I felt it had to be the same car.

I crawled back beside the hood of the Volvo. The front of the house was skirted with large shrubs. I ran to the lighted window and slid between the foundation and a large, nicely manicured yew, but the window ledge was above eye level.

I grabbed it, pushed up with my running shoes against the foundation, and looked in at a paneled library that was like something out of a magazine. Nicely tooled books. Sumptuous leather chairs. An oriental rug.

But no Moira or Dr. Lohnes.

The window was raised with just the screen obscuring the view. Faintly, I heard the canned laughter to a television show. A hallway ran off the library, dimly lit probably from another room toward the rear of the house.

Suddenly, my appraisal was broken by a black and brown shape that bounded from the hall, across the oriental rug, to stare at me through the screen. The Doberman's teeth were bared and a deep rumble resonating from his chest quickly turned to an alarm-sounding bark.

I dropped from the ledge and started back toward the road, but that way was too illuminated and I knew the dog, if let out the front door, would be on me before I made it.

Quickly, I doubled back and to my left, toward the fence about fifty feet away that separated Lohnes's home from its neighbor.

I was beyond the angle where anyone at the front door could see me, but had a good twenty-five feet to the fence, when I heard a man's voice command, "Get him, Baron!"

The gathering thud of paws and muttering snarl told me I wasn't going to make it.

I spun around, pulled the .25 from my belt, waited until he was close, and fired.

He yelped but still came and I fired again. He moaned, kicked his legs, and lay still. I wondered whether the shots would draw notice. The .25 wasn't loud and in a city such sounds are often ignored or dismissed. Lohnes, if he had gone back inside, might not have heard them. But maybe he did and would be coming to investigate.

I hoisted Baron to my shoulders and ran toward the rear of the house. Poor Baron had been a healthy one. Damn dog must have weighed ninety pounds.

I dropped him near some bushes beside an attached greenhouse and then started cautiously back to the front, staying near the shrubs beside the house.

"Nick, you okay?" Swede was crouched by a bush whispering to me. "I saw the dog come out but whoever let him out went right back in."

"I had to shoot him. You hear the shots?"

"Yeah, but they weren't loud. I doubt they heard them inside. Dog didn't get you? You were lucky to stop him right away with the .25. Nice shooting. And in the dark."

"Frank Buck. That's me." Then I thought, but he brought them back alive.

I started for the back of the house again. "Come on, Moira's still in there."

We skirted around the dead Doberman, past the greenhouse, to the corner of the house, diagonally opposite the library. French doors were open to a patio and inside what appeared to be a study or a den were Moira and the man I assumed was Eric Lohnes. Moira was seated facing away from where Swede and I crouched among shrubs behind the ledge of the raised patio of flagstone in concrete. The man, standing, appeared agitated. He and Moira talked for a few minutes and then he came to the doors and whistled and called to the dog.

Branches obscured our faces, but we could see the man clearly. He was average height, rather slight, and distinctly Prussian looking. He called to the dog again and Moira came and stood near him.

"Probably just kids. There have been some break-ins in the neighborhood. But Baron isn't let out often and he's probably sniffing around the yard. I don't think he'd leave the property but, if you'll excuse me, I'd like to take a look." Polite villain.

"Certainly," Moira said. "It's time I left."

He said, "I'd like you to consider my proposal. Think hard on it. It's relatively painless, certainly a lot less inconvenient than what we've previously discussed, although that's still an option. And, quite obviously, the chance of emotional entanglement, of bonding, is virtually nonexistent. I think we can work out a very profitable mutual arrangement."

Moira said something I couldn't make out.

"I'll show you out," Dr. Lohnes said.

I nudged Swede and pointed to the left. "You go back out that way and I'll go this way."

He slid silently away, a blond Tonto, and I headed to the fence that was to have been my escape route from the Doberman. I scaled it, stepping carefully between the spikes gleaming dully in the moonlight, and dropped to the other side. I sprinted to the street, crossed traffic and got in the BMW just as Moira pulled out of the driveway onto the Jamaicaway. I stayed well behind her for over a mile to determine no one was following her or me, then came up close behind and flashed my lights three times. She pulled over to let me get in front and followed me to Swede's lot in Cambridge, where I dropped off the BMW, and together we drove to Belmont.

"My god, this is incredible. I can't believe it was you the dog was barking at. That you were lurking in the bushes. It's like something from a B movie. And that you shot the damned thing."

"You couldn't hear the shot in the house?"

"No. I'll tell you, you were lucky that wolf didn't get you. He was a vicious-looking thing. Made me nervous slinking around the house while we talked." She did a theatrical shudder.

"Well, I wouldn't have been lurking around except that you were in there longer than I expected. That and the return of the Trans Am. By the way, Swede, you don't have that license number, do you?"

"I might. Let me check."

He went to a rolltop desk and rummaged through some papers. Moira eyed him appreciatively. This was the first time the two had met. He eyed her appreciatively too.

"Here it is. Trans Am. Mass registration eight-seven-two-X-C-N."

"Same car," I said. "The one registered to Joanne Lewis. Moira, did you see who was driving it when he came into the house?"

"I was in the den at the back of the house. Dr. Lohnes left me for a few minutes. I never saw who it was."

"Okay," I said. "What do you have? Let's hear that tape."

She took it from her handbag. The miniature mike was concealed in the loops of the bag strap.

"Do you want to listen first or do you want me to summarize?"

"What was he talking about just before you left? Sounded like a new proposal of his own. And how did he react to your proposal?"

Moira sipped the cup of coffee Swede had made for her. "This whole thing defies belief. Dr. Lohnes, I think, is motivated not just by money. There's something else."

"What do you mean?"

"I'll get to that. First, I had to have a tour of the house. I'm there to talk about getting inseminated and selling my baby and this guy insists I see his house. Beautiful house. Library, den. The best of everything. Lovely, tasteful appointments. Very expensive. And, for a while, I thought he'd try to lure me to bed."

"Why did you think that?"

"Oh, nothing specific. Just that he was being very warm and gracious, you know, showing me every room and then leading me upstairs. But he never made a pass. Just the tour. Showing off."

"No one else there?" Swede asked. "No Mrs. Lohnes?"

"No sign of anyone else. Just the dog. Although I didn't

make it to the third floor. I would say there is no Mrs. Lohnes. The bedroom is set up for just a man. No dressing table or vanity."

"I heard a television playing," I said.

"He was watching TV when I got there. He left the set on. After the tour of the regular house, the last thing he showed me was the—the what? The lab? O.R.? Inseminating room? It's in the basement. Actually, it's like an examination room.

"Then we went to the rear of the house. He continued being my host. Offered me a drink. God, you'd think we were socializing, about to discuss favorite novels or watch the BSO on channel two.

"Then I told him what you said to. That I knew another dozen or so girls on the North Shore like me who might be interested in what he proposed to me and that, instead of my being inseminated, I would line them up with him for a commission, say ten thousand each."

"You worded the whole thing out so that it would be clear on the tape what the two of you were discussing?"

She saluted. "Yes, sir. Just as ordered."

Swede chuckled.

"And his reaction?"

"Very unruffled. He seemed to find it an interesting proposal."

"Did he go for it?"

"Ah, this is the part you're going to like, if you can believe it, that is. His counterproposal. This guy is either a genius or a wacko, or is there a difference? He suggested removing my ova, some of my eggs, to be fertilized and implanted in other women. Surrogate wombs, he called them.

"The man's also a racist. He mentioned that doing that

213

would allow for the best utilization of 'nondesirable types.' It would be the best of both worlds, I think is how he termed it. Multiple desirable gene pool embryos without the discomfort and danger of pregnancy incurred by the donor."

"Wait a minute," I said. "Let me see if I can cut through the jargon and get this straight. He'd remove your eggs, fertilize them artificially, and have other women carry the embryos to term?"

"Yes. The procedure would be done in his laboratory, would be quick, safe, and painless, he assured me."

"Jesus," I said.

"A regular Marcus Welby," Swede said. "Did he lay a kindly hand on your shoulder as he talked?"

"What kind of money?" I said.

"To be negotiated. The advantage to me is that I wouldn't have to go through pregnancy."

"That's what he meant, then, when he said you wouldn't have to worry about bonding with the child. This is a warm man."

Swede said, "How does he see that as a better deal for you than you referring him other women for whose services you'd receive a commission?"

"That's what I meant when I said I think the man's in this for other than just the money. I think he'd *like* to do the implanting. It's like tinkering to him."

I said, "I have a feeling you're right. I wouldn't be surprised if he's done a lot of such tinkering. And other kinds, too. These other women, the 'nondesirable' types, would be blacks or Hispanics?"

"Yes. But he was careful to add they were nondesirable only in terms of the money their children would command. Still, my impression was that he meant they were nondesirable racially."

I switched on the recorder. "Okay. Let's see what we have here."

We listened to the tape. The quality was good. The Army provided its cops with good stuff. After a few minutes of listening to Eric Lohnes glow about his home, I fast-forwarded and found the exchange of proposals made between him and Moira.

"It's beautiful," I said. "Just what we wanted."

"I hate to ask," Moira said, "but what are you going to do?"

"The first thing is what *you* are going to do, my love. You're going to take a little vacation out of harm's way. Maybe the Cape. I know a great spot in Chatham. We'll work the particulars out later.

"In the meantime, Swede and I are going to pay a visit to Dr. Lohnes and our illustrious president, Lloyd Markham. I don't think Eric Lohnes would like the idea of Carmen Buono hearing this tape. Maybe the threat of that will prompt him to do some singing."

"Why not just go to the police with the tape?"

I patted her hand. "In due course. But we want to see who else is in on this besides Eric Lohnes and leaving bodies all over the landscape. Not to mention trying to frame or kill me."

I stood. "There's another reason too. I've got a good one for you folks. I recognized the driver of the Trans Am. It was the cop I went to originally. Lieutenant Brian Connolly."

CHAPTER

16

I stayed at Moira's overnight and in the morning, after I called ahead to confirm a vacancy, I wrote out directions for her to a place in Chatham where Barbara and I had stayed several times.

I assured her that I was convinced things would be cleared up soon and we'd spend some time together at the Cape out from under the figurative clouds that had been darkening my life. This had the potential to be a good summer if I could fulfill all the assurances I had been making: the Cape with Moira, Colorado and Fenway with Nicky. Just a small matter or two stood in the way.

When Moira left, I drove home. I killed the remainder of the morning running and, after lunch, I went to the public library and got half a dozen light novels and spent the afternoon in the yard getting about three-quarters of the way through one of them. Then I took a shower and drove to Swede's condo. On the way, I picked up two six-packs. We phoned out for a couple of delivered pizzas and discussed plans over the pizza and beer.

At 7:30, we drove to the Jamaicaway and stopped for a moment across from Eric Lohnes's home. A Mercedes with MD plates was in the driveway but we wanted to be sure Dr. Lohnes was alone. We drove to a drugstore and I went in to use the phone. I dialed the unlisted number Dr. Lohnes had given Moira and he answered on the fourth ring.

"Are you alone, Doctor?" I said. Silently, I mouthed "Who is this?" in anticipation of his inevitable response.

"Who is this?" he said.

"You don't know me, but I think it is important that I come to talk to you tonight. Listen carefully. I want to discuss illegal adoptions, some rather creative wrinkles on white slavery, and unethical use of artificial insemination, among other things."

"Who the hell is this? What are you talking about?"

"Let's drop the pretenses and the righteous indignation. I can be at your place in five minutes and intend to if you are alone. It is to our mutual advantage if we are alone. Are you?"

He didn't answer and I thought he might be ready to hang up.

"Doctor, don't hang up on me. I have enough concrete evidence so that, at the very least, you'll never practice medicine again. What we're working on now is a possible

217

prison sentence and its length. Now use your head and tell me whether you're alone."

I heard a nervous cough at the end of the line.

"Are you alone, Doctor? I'll also tell you who killed your dog."

"You killed Baron? You bastard."

"I'll be at your place in five minutes. Don't call anyone. I've taken precautions that if anything happens to me you are a ruined man. As it stands now, it's to your advantage to hear me out."

After a pause, Eric Lohnes said, "I'm alone."

"I have the feeling he won't give me the grand tour of the house," I said to Swede when I got back in the car.

We sat in the same den that he and Moira were in last night. Swede stayed in the car as backup. If I didn't come out in twenty minutes, he'd come in. I felt it wouldn't take the twenty minutes because I wanted to keep it short and sweet.

Eric Lohnes was fastidiously neat and clothing-model distinguished, the kind of doctor who'd inspire confidence. Gray hair parted neatly on the left. A blue Ralph Lauren short-sleeve shirt, and tan summer-weight slacks with a razor crease. White tennis sneakers, no socks. The effect was stiff casualness.

A slender, athletic build like a tennis player. Frosty blue eyes, high cheekbones. An authoritative air.

"I'll get right to the point, Doctor. I can document everything that I said on the phone."

"White slavery?"

"I tend to think so. A variation, at least. Perhaps we could quibble over the interpretation of coercion. But what choice did some of these girls have? Being whores or selling their babies."

"What kind of documentation of your allegations are you talking about? Very vague allegations, at that."

I noticed he didn't ask, what girls? I said, "Oh, I'll be more specific. Don't worry about that."

I took a recorder from my pocket and started it. It was set to the exchange of proposals he and Moira had made. We listened for less than thirty seconds.

"You can turn that off." He smiled. "She was such a beautiful thing. It is odd, isn't it, how beauty can blind us to the possibility of duplicity. I assume you have copies."

"Yes." Swede had made them this morning.

"What do you intend to do?"

"I'd like you to come clean about your involvement in a black-market adoption ring. This tape isn't the only evidence I have of your involvement. I don't know whether the name Kristin Williams means anything to you. But I have materials that belonged to her that link your name to such a ring. She, by the way, was murdered."

"Why should I come clean, as you put it, about something that remains to be proven? I can easily claim that tape is doctored. What does it prove? As for this other person, this Kristin Williams, I have no idea what you're talking about. This is ridiculous. Are you trying to blackmail me? Do you take me for a fool? You might besmirch my reputation with that tape, but I assure you that I will fight it. Now get out of my home or I'll call the police."

He went to a phone on a desk near the wall and stood dramatically with his hand on it. It was a pose from dozens of movies.

For a moment, I considered an equally Hollywoodish yanking of the phone cord from the wall.

"How do you think Carmen Buono will take to someone trying to do a little moonlighting on the side? Cutting him out? Come, come, we've all seen enough *Godfather*-type movies to know one doesn't cross the Mob with impunity. I wonder how it would be. Would you be found stuffed in a car trunk somewhere? Or perhaps you'd be found floating in Boston Harbor among the turds."

"What the hell *are* you talking about?"

I was dealing from uncertainty here. He might not know about Carmen Buono. But he didn't pick up the phone.

"Let me throw some names at you, Doctor. Lieutenant Brian Connolly, Boston Police Department. Joanne Lewis. Daniel Ritchie. Lloyd Markham. The aforementioned Kristin Williams. Darlene Abbott. Add in Pan's Flute, a very classy establishment in the Combat Zone. Three murders. You are involved in some heavy-duty shit, Doctor."

I looked at him carefully. He was wiry. Strong-looking arms that might be capable of breaking Kristin Williams's neck but certainly not Dan Ritchie's.

"I'll spell it out," I said. "You tell the police everything you know about the adoption racket, who's involved, or I see to it that Carmen Buono gets a copy of this tape. Now, in the unlikely event that you don't know who Carmen Buono is, I'll tell you. He controls the local underworld. He also happens to be tied into what you've been tied into. That usually happens. If there's a big, illegal buck being made through some clever, organized scheme, the Mob's involved. Either they originate it or they move in on it and there isn't much you can do about it. It's like when hyenas make a kill and a pride of lions takes it away." I can create an image if I work at it.

"Think of the options, Doctor. Carmen Buono, on one hand. Or I could simply give everything I know to a certain reporter so that at the very least you get dragged through the slime, maybe before Carmen Buono puts you out of your misery."

I wondered whether I was being too heavy-handed. I checked my watch. I didn't want Swede to come rushing in.

"On the other hand, I go to the police and things get very ugly. You deny everything but you get dragged into not just unethical and illegal behavior, but murder." I made a giant leap. "Imprisonment."

I paused.

"Prison. Think of prison, Dr. Lohnes. A guy like you in prison. Think of the other inmates. You'd be a prize, a treat. All those *non-Caucasians* would gobble you up. You'd be spread-eagle over a bunk and buggered faster than you can say, 'oh it hurts.' And they wouldn't have a bedside manner worth a shit. It'd be ugly.

"But, you 'fess up, turn evidence, as they say, and you work a deal. Immunity, maybe at worst a short sentence at some country club–type minimum security place." I paused to let that sink in.

"It's all over, Doctor. You can make it hard or easy on yourself. And I want to remind you that if anything happens to me, it's automatically leaked."

For several seconds, Eric Lohnes stood by the phone saying nothing. Then he came back and stood by his chair looking down at me.

"Who the hell are you? Why are you doing this? Why don't you just go to the police if you have so much proof?"

"It doesn't matter who I am." The line was corny but what else could I say? "But I'll do what I say. What does matter is that I'm giving you an option. And, I'll do this too. I'll give you tonight to think about it, unless you're ready to go to the police now."

221

Eric Lohnes smiled. A good-looking man. Looks, money, a physician. Why?

"The woman I spoke to last night. Your friend? Your lover?"

"Would you like to go to the police now? Tonight?"

"My poor deluded friend," he said. "You misguided fool. I intend to do no such thing. If all is as you say, I, one, call this Carmen Buono and simply tell him that I had come up with a marvelous opportunity to increase business. Mine and his. I think he would commend my innovation, my financial acumen. So much for my bullet-riddled body found in a car trunk or floating in Boston Harbor.

"Two, as for your reporter, no publication would risk a lawsuit on the basis of your puny allegations and a tape like that.

"Three, go to the police. Go to hell. What do you have? You have shit."

He walked back to the desk. In a way, I had to hand it to him. He was cool. I didn't know whether he was bluffing or not.

"What I intend to do is what I said. You get the hell out of here or I will call the police."

I watched him intently. Instead of the phone, his hand went to a drawer in the desk. I pulled the automatic from my belt and moved quickly toward him. I pulled open the drawer. A .38 Special lay on the green velvet lining. "How disappointing," I said. "I would have thought a Luger or a Walther."

I took the .38 from the desk and tucked it under my belt.

"Okay, Dr. Lohnes. I also intend to do what I said. I'll give you until tomorrow morning at eight. I'll call you here at that time and you'll either say, 'yes, I will go to the police with you,' or I will follow through as indicated. If you don't answer my call, I will also follow through. I assume you won't be leaving before eight."

I put the automatic back in my pocket.

"You give it lots of thought. Tonight you were being impetuous and I can understand that."

He shook his head slowly and smiled wanly as though he were dealing with a sad case indeed. Then he said, "You bastard. It's too bad Baron didn't rip out your throat."

Swede was parked on a side street in a spot where the car was obscured by trees but from which we could see enough of the Lohnes home and driveway to tell whether anyone came or left.

I told him what happened.

"What do you think?" he said.

"I'm not sure. Obviously, he was edgy to begin with or he wouldn't have let me come to talk with him, but he seemed cool enough toward the end. The fact that he might have shot me says that maybe he doesn't believe it when I say he's a ruined man if anything happens to me. On the other hand, it hasn't had time to sink in."

"So now we wait?" he said.

"Yeah, when it gets dark we'll pull down to get a better view."

We switched seats so that I was behind the wheel. Swede had insisted on staying with me and pulling a watch later so that I could get some sleep.

We talked until it got dark, when I pulled down almost to the corner of the Jamaicaway and a better view.

Swede put his head back on his seat and was asleep in

less than five minutes. I prepared myself for a long, dull night.

I stared across at Eric Lohnes's Mercedes and his brick mansion. I wondered whether another car was in the garage, a Trans Am perhaps. Maybe Lohnes would leave, in which case I'd follow him. That could lead to anything or nothing.

From my position, I could see the side of the house and the den at the left rear where we had talked. At eleven-thirty, the light in it went off and a few seconds later one on the second floor went on. That stayed on until ten minutes to one and then, as far as I could tell, the house was in total darkness.

Traffic was now next to nothing. Swede made small sleep noises, the night was warm, and I started to feel drowsy. Quietly, I got out of the car and walked briskly up and down the sidewalk, about one hundred feet in each direction, several times.

When I got back in the car, I checked my watch. It was incredible how slowly time was passing. Swede had said to wake him at three and he'd take over. That was about an hour and a half away. But I wouldn't wake him. This was my show. I was grateful for all he had done.

Eventually, even before any sign of brightness, the birds began to twitter and quickly were in full tune. Then, imperceptibly, the sky brightened and soon it was quite bright. I looked at my watch. It was just five.

I ran my hand over the stubble on my face. My mouth tasted as fuzzy and shitty as my head felt. I wanted a cup of coffee. A plate of bacon and eggs would be nice too. And then eight hours' sleep.

But I had three hours to go before I called Eric Lohnes. The son of a bitch was probably sleeping like a baby.

At six o'clock, Swede woke up and seemed bewildered about where he was for a few seconds. He stretched elaborately and then shook his finger at me. "You know keeping an all-night watch ain't conducive to an efficient next day."

"Aw, it's just a case of *noblesse oblige*, Swede."

"There you go, pulling that intellectual stuff on me. I'm not even going to ask for a translation. Nothing happened, huh?"

"Nothing."

At six-thirty, Swede took a walk to see if he could rustle us up some coffee and chow to go. At 7:05, he was back with two large coffees and half a dozen doughnuts.

We sipped and munched quietly. The coffee scalded the scum out of my mouth and dissolved the cotton in my head. My stomach juices flowed greedily around the doughnut.

At 7:55, I drove to the drugstore and dialed Eric Lohnes's number.

"Yes," he said.

"Does that mean, hello, or is it your answer?"

After a slight pause, he said, "It's my answer. Yes, I will do as you ask."

Elation displaced my weariness. I started to say something, but he interrupted me. "How do you want to work it? The, uh, details. Will you come here?"

The arrogance, the condescension of last night were gone from the voice. He sounded weary.

"You are prepared to make a statement?"

"Yes."

"It might be best if I came out there to start."

"Naturally, I will have an attorney present. Why don't we say noon. Here."

"That sounds fine."

"You can assure me that Mr. Buono knows nothing of this, nothing of that tape?"

So that was it. Nothing like fear to motivate.

"I assure you."

"Very well. Noon here. Will the police be with you?"

"No. We will go to the police."

"Just one thing. Please. Don't gloat."

He hung up. I wouldn't gloat but already I could see myself at Chatham tonight with Moira making champagne toasts.

We went back to Swede's to shave and shower and grab a light lunch before going back out. Swede insisted on coming back with me.

"Hell, what's the sense of owning a business if you can't phone in and take a day off? It's not like an ice cream store where the help robs you blind if you're not there. I mean, they can't leave the cash register drawer open and sell a BMW and not tell me."

At noon sharp, we were back on the Jamaicaway. Swede parked across from Eric Lohnes's driveway.

"You just gonna go marching in there without any reconnoitering? Could be a trap."

"Could be but I doubt it. It's a chance but what am I going to do? It's broad daylight. I can't go slinking up and peering in the windows. If anyone's there, they'll be hidden until I get in anyway. Besides, you'll be my backup out here."

"Where's the lawyer's car?" Swede said. "What'd he do, come out on a bike?"

The Benz still sat alone in the driveway, shining in the sun.

"Important people are never on time," I said as I got out.

After several unanswered rings and three or four minutes of standing by the front door, I felt the first pangs of disquiet. I wondered if I had been had. I looked back at the car. Swede was leaning against the driver's door, his arms folded across his chest.

Tentatively, I twisted the knob but the door was locked. I walked around the side, past the greenhouse to the French doors by the patio and den. An air conditioner compressor by the foundation beyond the patio hummed.

The patio was shaded by a medium tree, a dogwood I guessed. The French doors were shut. I pressed close to the glass, shielded my eyes, and peered in. It was empty. I rapped on the glass but knew that was useless. When I tried the knob, I was surprised that the door opened and I stepped into the cool of the den.

A Chelsea ship's clock on the mantle was just finishing striking twelve. I was fast or it was slow. When it finished, there was no other sound. No radio, no television. Eric Lohnes was too fastidious a man to leave his home with a door unlocked. I hated to stereotype, but if he was German he was probably punctual.

Something was wrong. Was I being set up? I took the automatic from its holster in my pocket.

The smart thing to do was get the hell out. Go back and wait with Swede for twenty minutes or so and then go give another call later. If there was no answer, maybe call again tonight and, if none then, go ahead with what I told him I'd do. I forced down a bitter disappointment.

I walked from the den into the hallway that I had seen two nights ago from the front window. On the other side, opposite the den, was the kitchen. I looked in. Looked like the set from a TV gourmet show. Baron's food bowl was still in its place. Beyond the kitchen was the entrance to the greenhouse. As I walked back into the hall, the refrigerator kicked in.

Moira was right. The house was beautifully done. Even the hallway, wider than hallways of digs I was accustomed to, was furnished expensively and tastefully. But a crushed cigarette in a piece of Wedgwood on a mahogany lowboy was out of place.

I paused at the stairway, went to the narrow window beside the front door, pulled the curtain aside, and peered out. Swede still leaned against the car across the street.

I looked into both front rooms and then started up the stairs.

A hall ran off the second-floor landing from one side of the house to the other. The bedroom whose lights were on last night was to my right at the end of the hall. Its door was open. One look and then I'd get the hell out of here.

It was a large room, high ceiling, oriental rug. Tipped on the rug was a chair, matching the mahogany desk in the corner.

Crossing the ceiling were boxed beams. In one, over the tipped chair, was screwed a large hook with clothesline tied into it.

I felt as if the wind had been knocked out of me and I almost staggered to the bed. I slumped on it.

I looked up to the large hook screwed into the box beam on that high ceiling. My eyes followed the clothesline down to the body of Eric Lohnes, dangling limp and grotesque, his eyes staring unflinchingly into mine.

CHAPTER

17

I went to the window and looked out. Swede was still in position. No police cruisers pulled into the driveway. If I were being set up, wouldn't the cops be pouring in now?

I talked with Eric Lohnes at eight and it was now shortly after noon. How long had he been dead? I touched his hand. It was cool.

As I went back down the stairs, I ran my handkerchief over the banister. I couldn't remember whether I touched it coming up. I also turned the knob on the French doors with the handkerchief and wiped the outside knob.

As nonchalantly as possible, I walked down the driveway and crossed traffic.

"Let's get the hell out of here," I said to Swede.

As he drove, I told him about Eric Lohnes.

"Jesus, Swede, I'm sorry. I didn't want you dragged into this."

"He committed suicide. How does that involve us? You gotta call the cops. You know that, Nick."

"Let me think for a minute, Swede. Pull over somewhere. I have to think this out. I think the shit's hitting the fan."

We had crossed into Brookline. Swede turned into a shady side street and stopped. Under ordinary circumstances, the only thing to do was call the police. But the circumstances weren't ordinary. I already looked suspicious to at least one Boston cop and another was probably involved in that which I looked suspicious about. And by wiping banisters and door knobs I had tampered with evidence to what I was sure was another murder, for I didn't think Eric Lohnes had committed suicide.

"Okay," I said. "In a way it seems logical that he committed suicide. He faced ruination and disgrace or Carmen Buono. But I don't know. That's a quick change of mind. Less than four hours."

"How long was he dead?"

"I don't know. His hand was cool. But some people have cool hands when they're alive. He didn't seem stiff but I didn't really check. It just seems like an odd way to commit suicide. Too involved. He had to screw a hook in the ceiling beam. I know he couldn't swallow his revolver because I took it but wouldn't a doctor have pills or something easier and less painful?"

"Okay, so someone pulled the plug. Who?"

"Good question. I *know* no one came to the house last night. At least no one *drove* to the house."

"Then they came this morning while we were gone. They knew Lohnes was going to blow the whistle."

I shook my head. "No, no. It's not right. It doesn't add up."

"Why the hell doesn't it?"

"How would they find out?"

"Nick, we're dealing with the Mob here. Maybe they've got his line tapped. They do that shit, I think. Maybe by chance Carmen Buono dropped by this morning for something, the doc got nervous, Buono sensed it, got the truth out of him, and strung him up."

"The Mob doesn't string a guy up to make it look like suicide."

"How do you know that? You done research on it? You're just going by books and movies."

"That's not their m.o. What I don't understand is why didn't they wait for me and get me too. Or else tip the cops so that I'm in the house while Eric Lohnes is swinging from his ceiling. They, whoever the hell 'they' are, have been trying to frame me too."

"So we're back to premise one. He committed suicide."

My sleepless night was catching up to me and my mind was finding it hard to focus.

Then I thought of something from two nights ago.

"I'm a stupid shit. Take me back to your place. I need my car."

"Now what?"

"I want to check something."

"Need company?"

"Thanks, but you've got a car dealership to attend to."

I used Swede's phone to call Chatham. When Moira

didn't answer, I asked the desk to see whether she was at the pool. They did and she wasn't. Chatham was loaded with quaint shops and with the whole of Cape Cod at her disposal, it was unlikely Moira would stick around her room to watch the soaps. I told myself that several times.

"Probably shopping," I said to Swede.

"Uh huh. What are you thinking?"

"I'm thinking I've got to get to Marblehead in a real hurry. I'll probably call you tonight or tomorrow. I've got a feeling things are going to happen fast."

It took me an hour and twenty minutes to get to Moira's via the Fellsway to Route One. For early afternoon, traffic was heavy, but the main problem with trying to get to Marblehead is that it's at the end of the line. No major highway connects to it.

It was ten degrees cooler in Marblehead, as it usually is, but that wasn't the reason I felt a chill when I pulled into Moira's driveway and got out of my car. If I hadn't been looking for it, I wouldn't have noticed the ripped screen on the bedroom window.

I let myself in the front door with the spare key which she had left me. I was sure there would be no one there now, but I had the .25 in my hand anyway.

The desk in the living room had been rifled and, in her bedroom, drawers had been pulled and contents dumped. Of course, it was possible that a petty B and E had occurred, but I was sure the disarray was just a cover.

What I was really interested in was in the kitchen by the phone. And I was sure that it was what interested whoever had broken in.

The memo pad was on a piece of stained pine with a Currier and Ives scene at the top. I took the pad to the window and held it in the light. The directions to Chatham and the name of the motel were etched through from the sheet I had given Moira.

I looked at my watch. Still too early for Moira to be in her room but I picked up the phone and dialed the motel anyway. She wasn't in and wasn't at the pool.

I drove home, phoned again with the same results, fed Boxer, took a shower, and phoned once more.

She answered and I let my breath out in a subdued whistle.

"Listen carefully and just do as I tell you. I'll explain later. Get out of the motel and go to the police station. Tell them some guy's been following you. Make up a story, make up a description. It doesn't matter what. Tell them that your boyfriend's coming down to be with you and can you stay there until he arrives. Believe me, they won't kick you out. Got that?"

"Yes. What's happened, Nick?"

"Later, Moira. How soon can you get out of there?"

"I just changed into my bathing suit. I was going to the pool."

"Change back and get the hell out. Take your things and settle the bill. I'm home. As soon as you get to the police station, call me here and tell me you're there. I'll leave right away."

"Where's the police station?"

"I don't know. Ask at the desk."

When I hung up, I called *Hub* magazine and got through to Rick Le Brun. How late would he be in?

"I'm leaving shortly. What's up, Nick?"

"I'll be swinging through town, probably within an hour. I want you to have an envelope. In it there will be a letter. It's not the whole story yet and a lot of it is still conjecture but I want you to have it." I paused. "In the event.

"Also in the envelope will be a cassette which will be explained in the letter."

"I'll wait. I have some things I can do."

I hung up, found a pad of paper, and started to write. Fifteen minutes later, I finished. I sealed the letter and cassette in a manila envelope and waited for Moira's call.

Through my adrenaline flow, I felt two sensations. Fatigue and hunger. I couldn't do anything about the first yet but I could do a little about the second. In my refrigerator were three yogurts with various fruit which I ate when the closet yuppie in me came out. I selected one with strawberries and banana, practically inhaled it, and started on an apple when Moira called.

"Oh, Nick, thank God you're in. I'm at the Chatham police station. Remember that weirdo who was following me back home? Well, I think he's here. I'm really afraid. When are you coming down?"

It took me a couple of seconds to realize she was acting. Probably there was a desk man at her elbow, listening, pretending to be sympathetic—poor little defenseless thing—while he ogled her.

"I've got to stop in Boston but I should be there . . ." I looked at my watch ". . . by eight. Don't leave the station."

I double parked outside *Hub* while I rushed in to give the envelope to Rick Le Brun. "I've got a lot of specifics there but probably not enough that's provable for you to do anything with it yet," I said as I handed him the envelope. "There's more on the way, though, and I've got the feeling you'll be getting it pretty soon. I'll be in touch."

"By the way," he said, "remember I told you there was something about Eric Lohnes I had heard of but couldn't put my finger on? Well, it came to me. Actually that article he wrote for the *Oracle* that I got you should have tipped me off. Seems Eric Lohnes did a sex study, you know, a Masters and Johnson or Hite Report kind of thing on the role of pain or sadism as an aphrodisiac. He couldn't get it published in anything reputable and for a while his reputation suffered because his premise was so off the wall. The whole thing died down and was forgotten eventually. But I kept thinking about it and it came to me. The papers batted it around for a while."

I tried to file the information in my whirling mind, thanked Rick Le Brun, and left. Outside, I found some phones and dialed Swede at work. He was still there.

"Two things, Swede. One, keep on your toes. Are you carrying?"

"I will be."

"Two. Can you get a copy of the cassette to Stan Janski and tell him I'll explain later. Better also tell him there's a stiff swinging from the ceiling at a certain house on the Jamaicaway. Ask him to say he got an anonymous tip and to give me two days to explain. I know it's asking a lot but I think he'll go along."

"Want me to fill him in on what we know?"

"Thanks, but you play dumb. Better not get yourself any more involved than you have to. He knows you've been with me on this but not to what degree. Course, if I should have a heart attack or happen to run my car into a tree, or commit suicide, let's say by stringing myself up, that's a different matter. But, otherwise, I'll talk with him within forty-eight hours.

"Another thing, tell him—if he agrees to give me forty-eight hours—tell him that if I don't get to see him to contact a Rick Le Brun, a reporter with *Hub* magazine."

"Watch yourself, Nick."

"Oh, don't you worry. I'll be doing that."

Even though he probably had to be at least in his midtwenties, the cop at the desk in Chatham looked about fifteen. He also looked as though he had fallen in love. And he didn't look any too happy to see me, the interloper who was about to take away the object of his love and admiration.

I improvised and added to the tale that Moira had fabricated about a pervert who had been following her. I wondered how many guys about six feet, one-eighty, brown hair, twenty-five to thirty-five years old would be hassled by the Chatham cops.

I followed Moira to Hyannis, where we stopped at a Wendy's to keep body and soul together. Moira did the salad bar and I did a couple of burgers and some fries. The place was busy so we took our food out to her car and ate and talked.

I told her what had happened since she talked with Eric Lohnes two nights ago but didn't tell her of the break-in at her place.

"My god, we pushed him over the edge." She shook her head. "He was probably close to insane anyway."

"Depends on how you define insane," I said, "but that's neither here nor there. Besides, I'm not convinced he committed suicide. As a matter of fact, I'm convinced he didn't."

I explained the reason for my doubts, basically the same I had related to Swede.

236

"Then who?"

"I have a theory but—"

"But that's not why you rushed me out of that motel."

"No. When we leave here, I'll stay behind you for a while to make sure no one's following. Don't go home. Drive to New Hampshire. North Conway. You remember that little place we stopped last winter? I'll call you there tomorrow."

I finished my first burger and unwrapped the second. Moira hadn't made much of a dent in her salad and I doubted she would. She seemed shaken.

Very deliberately, she said, "All right, then, so why the abrupt change of venue for me?"

"The night you were at Dr. Lohnes's, that cop, Lieutenant Connolly, parked right behind you. Now whether Eric Lohnes told him of you, the whys and wherefores of your conversation, a cop sees a strange car in a situation like that, what's he do?"

"He notices the license number."

"He runs a trace, checks on you, finds you teach where I do. It's no great leap from there. I should have thought of it earlier."

I didn't want to frighten her further, but she needed to understand the seriousness of her situation, one which I had gotten her into. I told her of the break-in at her place and what I found.

"Well, at least I didn't have much for them to take."

She ate a forkful of salad.

"So now what? Am I to spend the summer jumping from motel to motel around New England?"

"Give me a couple of days." I took her hand. "I'm sorry about this. I involved you and I shouldn't have."

"I asked for it, remember? I wanted to play adventuress." She rested her salad on her lap. "A couple of days to do what?"

"Don't ask. What really bothers me is that I'm going to have to use Swede. Seems I'm involving everyone with my problem."

"Maybe Swede will tell you to go fry your ass." She said the words matter of factly, without spite.

"That's the thing. He won't. He thrives on danger and excitement. He loved Vietnam. I could never understand why he didn't become a soldier of fortune or CIA spook after the war."

I finished my second burger and bag of French fries. Moira pushed her salad aside.

"Okay," I said, "time to move. Go straight to New Hampshire."

I kissed her and went to my car. I followed her almost to Boston before I lost her in traffic, but I was certain no one was tailing us.

As I drove home, my body tingled with fatigue but my mind scrutinized and evaluated what I planned to do and what I hoped it would accomplish.

That which I didn't tell Moira.

It was pretty uncomplicated, actually. I was simply going to wave a red flag in front of the bull.

The problem was that Swede and I were the red flag.

I slept nine hours and woke rested. I called Moira in New Hampshire. She told me she had been up since five but waited around for my call.

"What the hell am I supposed to do with myself up here? The options are limited, you know."

"Relax. Loll around the pool. Read. Improve your mind."

238

"Oh, sure, I'll be able to relax wondering what's going on, worrying about you."

"It's nice to know you care."

"I do. Nick, just go to the police. Give them the cassette. Dammit, you're a cop. You know that's what you should do."

"Got to pick my cops. Inspector Gallo thinks I'm guilty already. What'll he think if I go waltzing in with a cassette of conversation with a dead man? And how do I know who is or isn't in collusion with Lieutenant Connolly? But not to worry. I have a buddy with the Metro Police I have been and will be talking to and I've seen a reporter."

"Well, if you're going to live dangerously, maybe I will. Maybe I'll climb Mount Washington or go hang gliding."

"See you soon. I'll call tonight or tomorrow morning," I said.

"Be careful. I love you."

I started coffee and took a shower. When I stepped out, the phone was ringing.

It was Barbara.

"Just checking in, Nick. Everything's all right? You know, with . . ."

"That? Yeah, everything's on an even keel."

"Think Nicky can come home soon?"

"Oh, sure. Won't be long now but he'll probably want to stay on a little longer. He's having a ball. I just sent him some more money. And Katherine says he's no bother."

"I'm sure he's not. Nicky gets along with anyone." A pause. Then, "I've been thinking about you, Nick, you know, since . . ."

Jesus, I didn't need this now.

"I was wondering if you might drop by again some morning."

Like this morning?

"I mean, just to talk."

We'll discuss the issues. The deficit. Trade imbalance. Acid rain. That sort of thing.

"That would be nice, Barbara. There's no reason we can't maintain communications. Be friends. I guess a lot of ex's do."

There was another pause.

"God, it's been hot, hasn't it?"

"I want you to know, Barbara, that I've been thinking of you too. It was nice, I mean, that afternoon." *Nice?* What an inadequate, trivial word.

"That part was always good, Nick."

Was this how it would be? We'd maintain "that part," salvage the one thing from our marriage that worked? But we'd each have someone else—she, Gary; I, Moira—for those things that with us didn't work. Like day-to-day civility.

"I never complained," I said.

"I thought I might do a little shopping this morning before it gets too hot, but I'll probably be home by eleven or so."

The sentence dangled, the invitation an enticement.

But the timing was terrible. Not today. Not with Moira in New Hampshire because of me, having just told me she loved me. Not when I was about to try to bring the mess I was in to a conclusion. But I didn't want to hurt Barbara.

"Barbara, can we leave it that maybe I'll swing by if I get a chance? Actually, there is a small matter that I'm trying to deal with concerning the shit I stepped in and I might be tied up."

I hoped she wouldn't press me for specifics.

She said, "I'll be home all day. Gary's usually here by six."

"Uh huh. By the way, any more phone calls?"

"No. Thank God."

"Amen to that. Look, Barbara, I've got to run. I appreciate your calling and that you've been thinking of me."

It was an inane thing to say but better than, "Have a good day."

I dressed in loose chino pants and a green short-sleeve jersey with no alligator, animal, or insignia of any kind. I laced my Nike running shoes and strapped the holstered .25 to my right calf under the chino pants.

I filled Boxer's bowls with water and dry pellets and stepped out to my car and the first phase of today's activity, a visit to Lloyd Markham at Colton. That would allow the afternoon for some running before meeting Swede at six. I had called him last night before hitting the sack and he was raring to go.

Or I could use the afternoon to visit Barbara. I didn't have to decide now.

It was going to be another hot summer's day, with the humidity beginning to rise again. The midmorning traffic was light, and I pulled into the faculty parking lot in no time.

Mrs. Flowers, Lloyd Markham's secretary, smiled at me when I walked into the office. "Why, Dr. Toland, hello. You're certainly a stranger around here in the summer."

I had never taught summer courses and hoped I never would.

"How are you, Mrs. Flowers, on this fine summer's morning? Is Dr. Markham available, by any chance?"

I knew that he was in. I had checked his schedule earlier by phone with the provost.

"Well, I think he's busy, Dr. Toland. Do you have an appointment?"

"I haven't, Mrs. Flowers, but if you'll buzz him and tell him I'm here, I'm sure he'll see me."

Mrs. Flowers leveled a gaze designed to tell me that I was sadly mistaken if I thought just anyone could sail in here, snap his fingers, and have an instant audience with Dr. Lloyd Markham, President of Colton College.

"Dr. Markham's standing orders are that he's not to be disturbed without an appointment unless it's a very urgent matter."

Maybe someday I too could be such an important person to issue those standing orders not to be disturbed by the mundane world while I philosophised and brooded over lofty matters.

I said, "It's very urgent. Extremely urgent, actually."

"Can you tell me what it's about?"

"I'm afraid I can't."

Mrs. Flowers sighed deeply. She seemed quite unhappy.

"Why don't you have a seat, Dr. Toland, and I'll check whether Dr. Markham will be able to see you."

She went into the inner office and was back out within thirty seconds. "Dr. Markham will see you in a moment, Dr. Toland," she said without a smile.

Probably to Mrs. Flower's delight, Lloyd Markham kept me waiting over ten minutes and I was beginning to wonder whether he had skipped out a back way when he opened his door and beckoned to me.

"Well, Nick," he said as I came in, "you look fit. Enjoying your summer? Too bad you didn't take up my offer. You could be visiting Stratford or sailing down the Thames."

I shut the door behind me.

"Lloyd, I didn't come here to banter with you. I think it's time you folded your tent. It's all over."

I paused and allowed him to say, "What's all over? What are you talking about?"

"I never imagined you'd ask those two questions. Do you know Dr. Eric Lohnes, a rather prominent physician at Beacon General? Of course you do but what you might not know is that Dr. Lohnes is recently deceased and I might say that I'm rather surprised that you are still living."

Lloyd Markham sat behind his desk. The jacket to his summer-weight suit was draped over the back of his chair. His sleeves were rolled up. This was his casual but no-nonsense look.

"You see, what happened was I convinced Dr. Lohnes it was to his best interest to tell the police all about his activities in the adoption black market that he—and you— were involved in.

"But you know how it is when you get involved in unsavory schemes and places, you also get involved with unsavory people. Not refined types like us, Lloyd, pedagogues with fine sensibilities and gentle manners, but vicious lowlife types. Lloyd, I'll tell you, you're out of your league. You really are. I'd say right now that you're facing the same things that Eric Lohnes recognized he was facing. Disgrace, ruination, and prison, or—" I paused and shrugged. "They hanged Eric Lohnes. Strung him up. Imagine that?"

I figured I'd not convey my puzzlement over who did that.

"You see, the house is collapsing all around them and they're trying to cover their tracks so they're eliminating all the weak links, pardon the mixed clichés, and you, I'm afraid, are a weak link.

"How'd it start, Lloyd? At Pan's Flute? In some way or other, that was the connecting point, wasn't it? I think I've got it pretty well figured out. What did you do, supply some of the girls? Probably not that. Probably you were a pipe to people with big bucks who'd pay top dollar for a baby and didn't want to wait. Maybe you did both. Probably Eric Lohnes, though, was the main pipe to childless couples with the means to buy a baby, a nice blond-haired, blue-eyed Beech Nut baby. I mean, he must have treated lots of women who couldn't have a child."

Small beads of perspiration dotted Lloyd Markham's upper lip.

"You know, if you were smart, you'd come with me to the police and help me fill in the spots I'm fuzzy on. Want to do that?"

Lloyd Markham's mouth started to work but no sound came out.

"Let me tell you what I know and what I figure, just for the hell of it, Lloyd.

"Kristin Williams, Norm Eigner's and Dan Ritchie's student, in doing research for her journalism course on prostitutes in the Combat Zone, found out from a runaway about a black market for babies of runaways and prostitutes.

"Now, Kristin was an inventive girl. To get close to the story, she became a prostitute. To what degree she actually worked her trade, I don't know. Probably she was clever enough so that she didn't have to. But through other whores she found the way to make contact with the market. She found that it was not just a case of getting knocked up and selling the child on your own. It's a highly organized thing, Mob sanctioned, with a physician who'll inseminate the girl and deliver the baby.

"But, son of a gun, she's turning in notecards about all

244

this to a guy who's involved: Dan Ritchie. Talk about bad luck.

"So, she has to be eliminated. Gets her neck broken and is dumped in the woods. At first, I thought Dan did it. He was a big, strong guy, but when he got his own neck broken that seemed to dash that theory a bit.

"How am I doing, Lloyd? So far pretty obvious, huh?"

Lloyd Markham stood up. The perspiration had spread to his forehead and a couple of half moons were waxing through his shirt under his arms.

"I think you've said enough. You get the hell out of here."

"Aw, c'mon, lighten up, Lloyd. Sit down. There's just a little more. Then you can either come to the cops with me or make your phone calls. But for your own sake, they better be to a travel agent.

"When Kris's friend, Darlene Abbott, comes to me via Norm Eigner all worried about her missing friend and is then herself killed for messing around and probably getting close to the whole sick truth, I, good citizen and semi-cop, go to the police under whose jurisdiction this falls, to the very cop whose name Kris had listed on one of her cards and, it turns out, one of the bad guys. And Kristin knew he was. But I thought she had his name because he worked vice and maybe gave her some information.

"So now Lieutenant Connolly knows I know. You do know him, huh, Lloyd? What to do about me? It's a problem because bumping off a cop, even a part-time MP, can be sticky, especially since another party, Norm Eigner in this case, knows what I've started to look into. Killing me calls further attention to the whole business in a big way and would mean having to kill Norm too. A bit much. Starts to assume Shakespearian dimensions if they do that.

"Not going too fast, am I, with all these names?

"These are nice people. And resourceful. If it's a bit messy to kill me, why not frame me? Get the nosy bastard any way they can. They plant my phone number and drugs on the bodies of the two girls. In Darlene Abbott's case, the phone number was already there. I had given it to her that very day. Whoever killed her didn't want the death to look similar to Kristin Williams's when Kristin's body was eventually discovered, so they stabbed her instead of breaking her neck, searched her, found the number and put it in with a bottle of crack to make the killing look drug-related.

"Later, when I talk to Connolly, it occurs to him that this is a good way to implicate me. He knows about the phone number on Darlene Abbott's body. It's simple to go back to Kristin Williams's body and plant the crack and my phone number on it too.

"What I'm wondering is why was Dan Ritchie killed and who killed him? Probably he was beginning to panic and it looked as if he might give everything away. Can you help me there, Lloyd?

"In the meantime, someone tells Carmen Buono about me, and he tries a little friendly persuasion, but he's some distance removed from all this, and doesn't take me all that seriously. I imagine that's changed or is about to. Even you, Lloyd, get in the act. Try to get me away, let me know that if I butt out I can expect some preferential treatment around here. Was that your own idea?

"I still have a few gaps to fill in but I'm nearly there. Or else the police will fill them in. Like who tried to run me down with a Trans Am? Probably some of Brian Connolly's lowlife companions from the Combat Zone when he—they—started really getting tired of me. This whole thing smacks of committee mentality. But what I'd really like to know, Lloyd, is what the hell goes on at Pan's Flute? Care to fill me in on that?"

Lloyd Markham slouched behind his desk. He stared at a spot between his spread-apart hands lying flat on the glass-top desk. Slowly, he looked up at me and then down again to the desk top.

"Nothing to say, huh? I've got the feeling you'll be doing a lot of talking soon, Lloyd. Then again, maybe absolutely none at all."

I let myself out.

"Going to be a hot one, Mrs. Flowers. A real steamer."

I could be at Barbara's just as she arrived home from shopping. Help her in with the bundles, maybe sip some more lemonade by the kitchen sink and talk for a while, polite as hell to one another, and then crash into the sack.

Not today. Maybe because of Moira. Maybe because I had too much else on my mind. Maybe because I was noble. Or maybe just because I knew I could.

I drove home and dressed for a midday run in the heat of the sun. Just shoes, shorts, and a towel wrapped around a .25 automatic.

I did ten miles and afterward some sit-ups, chin-ups, and push-ups. To hell with the gym.

Then I showered and lay down in the relative cool of my living room, wondering whether Lloyd Markham had made any phone calls.

And thinking about my trip tonight with Swede to Pan's Flute.

I was starting to doze when the phone rang. It was Stan Janski. He didn't sound friendly. "Nick, what the hell are you trying to do to me? I like being a cop. I'm looking forward to a nice retirement. Are you trying to screw all that up?"

"Stan. I asked for two days. I'll have something for you tomorrow. One way or the other."

"You'd better. I went out on a limb. Way out. You don't have something for me, word gets out I sat on any part of this, and they'll have my head."

"Stan, as long as I've committed myself to being a pushy bastard, I'm wondering whether you can tell me a couple of things. You wouldn't have heard about the Williams's girl postmortem, would you, whether or not she was pregnant?"

"Hell, Nick, what gives you the idea that you've been pushy? You're much too hard on yourself." He paused to let his irony sink in. "Of course I checked her p.m. With all the digging around you were doing, what did you think I'd do?"

"And?"

"And, she wasn't pregnant. Also there were no signs of sexual assault." Another pause. "You said a couple of things. What's the other, as much as I hate to ask?"

"The postmortem on Dr. Eric Lohnes?" Stan wouldn't have jurisdiction in that. He would have notified the Boston Police.

"It just so happens."

"What can you tell me?"

He told me.

"That fits, Stan. Yeah, that makes things fall a little more into place."

"How? For chrissake, Nick, open up."

"I'm not sure exactly. Be patient, Stan, huh? By tomorrow. Maybe even tonight."

CHAPTER

18

We parked Swede's BMW under the Common and walked across Tremont and into the Combat Zone.

I had on the same loose-fitting chino pants with the .25 strapped to my calf but changed the shirt to a navy blue. In a way I wished it were winter. Walking around with a handgun strapped to your leg is a definite pain in the ass.

Swede was wearing Levis and a loose-fitting long-sleeve shirt that hung over his belt. The sleeves were rolled and the front was open about a third of the way down. It concealed the short-barreled magnum strapped to his hip.

Even though the Zone wasn't fully cranked up yet, it pulsed with the sights and sounds, the promises and anticipations of sex and drugs, but somehow in the heat of a summer's night all of it seemed to hang in the air like a bad smell.

As we walked past Snatch a View, I wondered about its proprietor, John Desi, and why he had been at Dan Ritchie's funeral. At some point, he had probably been a supplier of girls to Dan.

Pan's Flute was part of a seven-story building and shared the first floor with three bars and strip joints. Inside, Pan's Flute was dimly lit and hotter than outside. The air was stale with various odors, none of them pleasant. It took my eyes a few seconds to adjust to the change of light.

A cashier's booth was directly in front of us. A large black man sat in it. Behind and off each side of the cashier's booth ran two aisles, off which were compartments, each with its own closed door.

"You guys wanna see a show it's one per booth. You wanna play together, go out in the alley."

I smiled. "We look like the type who'd want to go in one of those closets and watch dirty movies? Couple of guys like us?"

"The hell I know what type you are? All types come in here. Goddamn priests come in here and I don't think they're hearing confession. You don't like the action, get y'asses out."

I kept the smile pasted on. "Hey, look, we're down from Concord, New Hampshire. Someone told me back home, you want some really good action go to a place called Pan's Flute. Looks to me like just a bunch of peep show rooms. I didn't come to Boss-Town for that."

"Who told you that?"

"Just a guy I know."

"That right?"

The cashier, about thirty-five, was assessing us carefully. He was mainly fat, but not just that. His hands were big and his shoulders broad. He had a cigarette going on the counter beside him.

"What kind of action he tell you you could get here?"

I laughed. "That's the goddamn thing of it. What it was, he was in his car stopped at a red light and I'm leaning in his window telling him I'm coming to Boston for, you know, a little action and he starts to tell me to be sure to check out Pan's Flute for some really different stuff and then the goddamn light turns green and everyone starts blowing their horns so he has to take off."

I shrugged. "So here we are. We gotta be back tomorrow morning so we thought we'd check out this place first."

The black guy nodded, picked up his cigarette and took a drag.

"Your friend probably meant we got some really good movies you can see in the booths. We got the best around."

I took a chance. Smiling conspiratorily, I leaned close. "Come on. What the hell you got upstairs?"

He shook his head. "Nothin'."

I leaned past his booth and looked down the aisle to a door at the end. "He gave me some names. Christ, he knows everyone down here. Works right here in town, y'know. John Desi. You know him? My friend mentioned his name."

The black guy shrugged. "Hey, bro', you wastin' time."

"I guess John Desi gave him another name. Some

broad. Joanne Lewis. My friend says tell 'em you know Joanne Lewis. Probably I should have said I know Joanne Lewis right off the bat, huh?"

The black guy deadpanned us.

I nudged Swede. "Come on. Let's get the hell out of here."

"Slow down. Fifty bucks each gets you in. That's the cover charge. It's more bread for other stuff but you can pay as you go."

I pealed five twenties from my wallet. He handed me two stubs for a Wakefield Elks TV raffle over a year old. Gesturing toward the door at the end of the aisle, he said, "Two flights up. Knock at the door at the top of the landing and give the dude there the tickets."

At the first landing, Swede touched the magnum under his shirt. "What about these?"

"We keep them," I said. "If they want to search us, we just turn around and back out."

This was once an all-purpose office building. Insurance agents' and dentists' names were still lettered on the doors of suites now empty. The stairs were marble. Crescents were worn on either side.

We started up to the second landing. Swede said, "That was a pretty corny line you fed Black Joe. I didn't think he'd go for it."

"I don't think he did. I think we might be going into the spider web. You want to leave?"

Swede smiled. "We got our stingers with us."

The door at the top of the second landing had HAYDEN, HAYDEN, POTTER, AND WELCH, ATTORNEYS-AT-LAW lettered on its frosted glass. I flicked three quick, hard raps, waited about half a minute, and rapped again. The floor creaked, a shadow loomed behind the glass and the door opened.

252

He was built like a basketball guard, six-four or five, hair shaved close, head shiny black, white baggy cotton pants, white sleeveless shirt. His arms were long and heavily corded.

I handed him the stubs. He looked at them, looked at us and said, "I'm Sam. Follow me."

We went through two doors, into another corridor running perpendicular to the first, and followed it to the end of the building.

We took a stairway up one flight. Faintly, I heard sensuous, mystical music, like something from an Arabian Nights movie.

Sam led us to the end of the hall. The floor here was carpeted in an oriental design and the walls were painted off-white.

We stopped at black doors with crescent moons and stars in silver. The words "Pandora's Box," in script designed to look Turkish or Arabian, were above the doors. Sam unlocked the left door and pushed it open.

"You gents just gonna watch the show or you want some company?"

I said, "Why don't we just start with the show. That okay?"

"Sure, work up an appetite. Show time in 'bout five minutes."

He went back out shutting the door behind him.

Inside Pandora's Box was like a set from a 1940s Errol Flynn movie. It appeared to occupy most of the floor, all of the partitions between offices having been torn away. Supporting columns were made to look like something from the Colosseum. Or maybe from what Dan Ritchie had imagined utopia to look like or perhaps what he thought his audiences might imagine it, people who had never read or heard of Thomas More.

But the motifs were mixed as if Dan had wished to cover all bases. Mosques and minarets were outlined on the walls. Lighting was dim and indirect. The air was cool from air-conditioning.

Sideless, backless divans were arranged in a rough circle around the edge of Pandora's Box near the walls. The center was cluttered with stage props: fake palm trees, movable Doric columns, a couple more divans. In the midst of all this was a bedroom set: bed, chest of drawers, etc.

Most of the divans near the walls were occupied, as far as I could tell, by men at least middle-aged. They lolled like so many Neros in designer jeans and shirts. Many had girls dressed as though they belonged in a Roman court. I counted twenty-two divans. Five were empty. Swede and I grabbed two side-by-side.

The tempo of the music increased, snake charmer's music. The lights dimmed even more, except over the props, where a spotlight illuminated the bedroom set.

A girl in a nightgown came from somewhere to my left, rolled the bed covers down and sat in the bed propped by the pillows. She was blond, young, and pretty.

For a minute or two, she read from a paperback book, making theatrical expressions of absorption at what she read.

Then a man came into the bedroom, stripped down to his shorts, and got on the bed beside her. We went through a few moments of his impatiently watching her read. He placed his hand on her thigh. She continued to read. The music was now soft and liltingly sensual.

The man's hand became busy, stroking the woman's thigh. He rolled over to her, nuzzled into her neck, and blew into her ear. She ignored him and turned the page of her book.

"She's got a headache," someone yelled from one of the divans.

"This looks familiar," someone else said. "She's been watching my wife."

The man's efforts at seduction became more urgent but were met with continued indifference. He rolled her so that she was facing him and tried to smother her with kisses but she turned her face, held the book high and continued to read. He rolled away and fumed for a bit and then lit a cigarette.

Suddenly, the bedroom door flung open and a Zorro clone with mask, whip, and cape posed dramatically in the spotlight that highlighted him. He gestured a command to the man on the bed to move out smartly and punctuated it with a lash of the whip. The poor, rebuffed lover slunk like a beaten cur into the darkness.

The audience howled. Swede and I groaned.

The heroine on the bed put down her book and stared in fascination. Who is this masked man? He now stood at the foot of her bed. Dramatically, he ran the whip through his hand. She ran her tongue over her lips. A murmur of expectation buzzed from the divans.

I yawned.

Zorro lashed the whip two sharp cracks beside the bed. Actually, it was obvious the cracks were sound effects supplied from backstage as the whip itself was nothing more than a soft prop. How else to effect the flagellation that was sure to come?

She dropped her paperback to the floor and lay flat in supplication. I'm yours. But first the dual themes of purification and pleasure through pain had to be played out. And these poor, dumb clucks in the audience thought this was just a sadistic whipping coming up. They didn't appreciate Dan Ritchie's depths. The poor man went to his grave with his artistry misunderstood.

"We paid fifty bucks for this?" Swede said. "Dan Ritchie deserved to have his neck broken."

The whipping began. Zorro laid it on and the girl twisted in ecstasy and purgation. This went on for a few more minutes until they finally got to what the audience was waiting for, a pretty standard porno show, about as interesting and inspiring as a dollar-fifty video except this was in 3-D.

We endured the show for the ten minutes or so that it ran. Zorro kept his cape and mask on the whole time. When it was over, he and his maiden left, probably to attend a cast party and worry about reviews. Some of the divans emptied too; the performance, if nothing else, having been an aphrodisiac.

I stifled a yawn and wondered what the hell I was doing here. Much more of this and I'd leave it all to Rick Le Brun and Stan Janski. This was far beyond the call of duty.

"Rescue me, Nick," Swede said. "Get me the hell out of here."

I was considering it when I was joined on my divan. The dim light flattered her.

"You fellas getting lonely or thirsty?" She smiled. "Or anything else?"

"How about bored," I said.

"We can always do something about that. Whyn't I send a couple of girls to keep you company? You can stay and watch the show for a while or go upstairs."

"That sounds real hospitable." I nearly said, "ma'am." "We'll be right here just a sittin' and a waitin'."

She winked at us and slithered away.

"You figure maybe this is the setup, Nick?"

"I sure hope so. I can't take another of these."

When the girls arrived, the next show was just starting. This time the girl was chained to a rack to be stretched and whipped both.

"Who writes this stuff?" I said to my new companion. She and Swede's friend were dressed like a couple of Cleopatras.

"Good, huh?"

"Creative."

She nudged into me, pulled me down on the divan, and massaged my neck and shoulders.

In a breathy, seductive voice, she said, "Why don't we go upstairs to our own private party and then come back down later? These shows go on all night. You won't really miss anything."

"It'll be an irrevocable loss, but you're worth it."

She led me by the hand out the door Sam had brought us in and up a set of stairs. Swede and his companion followed.

At the top of the stairs, we turned left into a corridor. The girl stopped at the third door on the right, coquettishly removed a key from her cleavage, and unlocked the door.

When Swede's girl started to lead him to another room, he said, "Why don't we just have a nice foursome party?"

The door snapped open and a man stepped out covering Swede and me with an old .45 automatic, like what I used on duty.

He said, "Why don't we just stop the bullshit?"

He was about thirty, about six-foot-two, very black and very powerful. Body by Nautilus and steroids. Sculpted, bulked musculature rippled under light summer clothing.

With a shake of his head, he signaled the girls to leave. To Swede and me, he said, "Get in the room."

He kicked the door shut behind him. There were two beds, a couple of chairs, a clothes rack, and a sink. Lighting was from a single lamp overhead. But at least the bulb wasn't bare. A touch of class. And there were two end tables, each with an unlit lamp.

"You—blondie—you sit over there on that bed," he said to Swede. "And you sit here on this one."

He stood to the side of the beds, covering us both.

"I know you're both carrying. Blondie, first you. Very slowly, with your left hand, take it out and put it on the floor."

Swede did.

"What you plan to shoot with that, an elephant? You watch too many Dirty Harry movies."

He looked at me. "Now you." When I pulled up my pant leg at the cuff and removed the .25, he said, "Shee-it, now I know you guys watch too many movies. Let's see the other leg.

He looked back at Swede. "Roll up your pants. Both legs."

Then, one at a time, he made us lean against the wall and patted us down. Satisfied, he told us to sit on the beds again. He sat between us, about five feet from the ends of the beds, the arm with the .45 resting on the back of the turned around chair.

"Now we wait." He looked at me. "You have been one pain in the ass, let me tell you."

He didn't elaborate and we sat in silence except for faint music below. The poor girl on the rack was probably in the throes of pleasure pain.

I said, "Just to make conversation, by any chance you ever try to run me down with a Trans Am?"

A smile slowly split his face and then slowly faded. "You are a nosy bastard, aren't you?"

Was this the same voice that had called me a nosy bastard on the phone? It hadn't sounded black then but I wasn't sure and was I stereotyping? Jesus, this was no time to worry about stereotyping. Mr. Liberal to the end. But I really wasn't sure.

"What are we waiting *for*?" I asked.

"Oh, you'll see. You *will* see."

We sat in silence for another minute. Exotic music still played below, punctuated by whip lashes.

"That's Dan Ritchie's crap, huh?" I said. "That's what he'd write when he knew he didn't have to be careful and sound scholarly.

"Even when he *was* being scholarly, he was sick, you know that? Only he covered it."

I leaned forward a little and the .45 flipped up. If fired, it would remove my head and neck.

"You know what he did his Ph.D. thesis on? Sadism in various cultures throughout history and in the literature of those cultures. But what came through, if you knew what you were looking for, was that Dan *believed* in it. Sadism, I mean. He liked it. I bet when he was a little kid he got his jollies from pulling the wings off flies. Probably graduated to kicking kittens."

I checked this guy's eyes. He was listening to me, which was more than I could say about many of my students during a lecture. With his left hand he pulled a pack of Camels, the filterless kind, from his pocket and lit up.

"You ever get a chance to work the whips down there?" I said. "I mean, Dan Ritchie was a sick, cruel man and probably associated with people as sick as he was. Of course poor old Dan is dead, but his ideas live on, proudly presented six nights a week at Pan's Flute."

259

Our captor stared at me, expressionless.

"I don't think he wants to talk about it," Swede said. "He just wants to do it."

"You suckers do all the talking you want. You think you're gonna use some kind of reverse psychology on me, go right ahead and have your little fun."

I leaned back and wondered how far to push this guy. Probably, there was no harm talking. If he were going to waste us, he'd have done it by now. He was waiting for orders. I wondered whose.

Joanne Lewis?

Brian Connolly?

Lloyd Markham?

Carmen Buono?

I could have kicked myself for walking into a trap, especially since I had anticipated there would be one.

But there was still an angle. This guy was a gofer, an orders taker, and as such he'd be mainly concerned with his own skin. If he felt the ship was going down, he might jump overboard first.

I said, "And, of course, Dan's buddy, Dr. Eric Lohnes, was the same way. Just as sick. But worse because he was a doctor. You knew Dr. Lohnes, didn't you?"

I thought his eyes flickered.

"You must have."

He took a drag on his Camel and blew the smoke at my face. No manners, no class.

As I looked at the Camel an image popped into my mind. Of a crushed cigarette in a piece of Wedgwood. Before I went up the stairs and found Eric Lohnes swinging from his bedroom ceiling, I had seen a crushed filterless cigarette in a piece of Wedgwood. The Wedgwood was not an ashtray but a guy like this might think it was. At the time the cigarette in the Wedgwood seemed out of place to me but I had forgotten it in the shock of discovering Eric Lohnes's body. Some detective.

A hypothesis started to shape in my mind and I decided to push it, to test it.

"Yeah, you knew Eric Lohnes, all right. You killed him. You broke his neck."

"What the christ you talkin' 'bout?"

"Eric Lohnes. You broke his neck. Just like you broke Kristin Williams's and Dan Ritchie's. But you were told to break *their* necks. Did you stab Darlene Abbott too?"

"Man, you do run off at the mouth but I advise you to shut it. Like right now."

"No one told you to break Eric Lohnes's neck so you covered it up by stringing him up afterward."

"Shut it."

It made some kind of sense although there was much I was guessing at. The filterless cigarette crushed in Wedgwood—someone had put it there and it wouldn't have been Eric Lohnes even if he smoked. What Stan Janski had told me this afternoon on the phone. This guy's physique, which exuded a strength capable of breaking necks rather easily.

But why would he kill Eric Lohnes? I didn't know nor did I really know that he did but the only chance Swede and I had was to provoke him.

"Yeah, I don't imagine that certain people will take kindly to your having wiped out Dr. Lohnes. And you know something, I'll be able to tell them some things that'll convince them you did."

He took another drag on his Camel. "My, my," he said, "you are just scaring me to death."

Beneath the bravado, I thought I detected some uncertainty. "But why would you do it?" Push this guy, I thought. "You didn't have a thing for Dr. Lohnes, did you? Did you two have a lovers' quarrel? I mean, he wasn't a bad-looking guy and you're quite a good-looking stud yourself. I bet that was it. You probably came over to see the doctor, had yourselves a little spat, and before you knew it, big brute that you are, you broke his neck. Tch, tch, we've got ourselves a fruit here. Who'd believe it?"

He kicked the chair out from under him and lunged forward, his hand swinging in a sideways arc to pistol-whip me, but I anticipated it and ducked away as Swede grabbed him from behind.

I moved in quickly. It was no time for the niceties of fair play. As Swede struggled to hold him, I neutralized him with a strategically placed right knee.

He groaned and dropped the .45. I picked it up and jammed the barrel into his mouth. Swede had him in a full Nelson. I said, "Okay, real quick, who are we waiting for and how soon are they coming? When I take this out of your mouth, start talking." Swede was bending back his index finger. I held the .45 at face level.

He stared at me mutely. With enough time, we'd have this guy talking, but I felt as though I had it pretty well figured out and while we were trying to loosen him up, we were leaving ourselves open to whomever we were waiting for.

"Forget it, Swede. I'll cover him and you secure him."

Within five minutes, Swede had him hog-tied, gagged, and lying on the floor beside the bed closest to the wall. A slat from one of the beds ran from neck to tailbone; arms and legs were tightly trussed with lamp cord and a torn pillow case was stuffed in his mouth. I put the .25 back on my calf and tucked the .45 in my belt. Swede had retrieved his magnum. I put my ear to the door and listened but could hear nothing.

I opened the door and leaned into the corridor. Nothing.

Motioning for Swede to come to the door and cover me, I walked down the corridor to the door of the next room, put my ear to it and listened. No screams, bleats of ecstasy, or heavy breathing. No whips being lashed, no bed springs creaking.

Before turning the knob, I tossed the .45 back to Swede. If I interrupted anyone, I'd play the stumblebum, say they told me to come up to this room and wait for a girl. Sorry, got the wrong room.

I turned the knob and found the switch. The room was empty.

I went back to Swede, took the .45, and handed him a card from my wallet with a phone number. I gave him hurried instructions and watched him disappear down the stairs.

Then I went back into the room with my trussed-up friend, shut the door and waited.

CHAPTER

19

After a half hour I began to worry. Swede should have been back.

I worried about whether he made it to a phone.

Whether he got through to Inspector Gallo and Stan Janski.

Whether they'd come out here.

Whether, if they did, they'd get here before Brian Connolly.

Whether Brian Connolly was even the one my prisoner had been waiting for.

Whether I had things figured right.

Whether I was being a fool.

A lot of whethers.

I gave it another five minutes, checked the gag and tie job Swede had done, and left the room. There was no point in being the tethered goat without the big guns next door.

I started to check the corridor for another way out and then said the hell with that. There were four other closed doors and sounds of occupants behind each.

I went back to the room. I recognized a bad symptom. I was getting jumpy, indecisive, and careless.

Sitting on the bed, I looked down at my prisoner. I should have tried to get more information out of him. Swede could have. I knew I couldn't. I could ungag him and stick the .45 in his mouth again but I knew he'd see that as a bluff.

I untied his feet, told him to get up, and shoved the .45 against his back. I walked him into the next room and retied his feet. I would have liked him further removed but I didn't want to run the risk of going up another flight.

I was at the door when I heard voices near the top of the stairs. A man's and a woman's. I closed the door nearly tight. Dammit, probably coming in here for a night's debauchery. I could say my prisoner and I were into gay bondage.

Then I recognized the man's voice.

It was Brian Connolly's.

They went into the room I had just left. Through the wall, Brian Connolly's voice was agitated and although I couldn't make out what he was saying, I could guess. Would he look in here?

I had been looking for the classic B-movie decoy, Brian Connolly coming after me and saying incriminating things while Inspector Gallo and Stan Janski listened in concealment. It had been a shot but its failure now made it seem naïve. But it wasn't the end of the road.

In less than three minutes, they were back out and headed down the stairs. I figured the woman to be Joanne Lewis.

I waited two minutes and followed, the .45 in my hand at my side.

It was time to find Swede and get out of here. Time to put all I knew in front of Inspector Gallo and, for good measure and because I said I would, Stan Janski. Time to let Rick Le Brun do what he could. Maybe that would be nothing.

Maybe Lloyd Markham was at this moment blabbing to the police. Maybe Eric Lohnes *had* committed suicide. Maybe they all would.

I was near the top of the next flight when the door below opened and Brian Connolly started up, followed by Sam, who let Swede and me into Pandora's Box.

Down the corridor, to my right, the door to Pandora's Box opened too and a man and a woman came out. He was about sixty, she about twenty. He was pawing her already as she led him by the hand.

Holding the .45 close to my hip and out of sight, I darted toward the door before it shut and locked. They paid me no attention and I slipped in. I held the door open a crack and peered out.

They stopped at the top of the stairs. Brian Connolly said something to Sam, who came my way, while he continued up the other flight of stairs.

I let the door shut and looked for someplace to go. No one paid me any attention. I couldn't tell what the scenario on stage was this time and didn't care. Brian Connolly was sure to find my prisoner and the two of them would be down soon to help Sam.

Quickly, I skirted the wall behind the divans, trying to look as nonchalant as possible and keeping the .45 at my side.

A girl dressed like Aphrodite walked toward me and I took her hand and slid onto an empty divan, putting her between me and the door. I slid the .45 under a pillow.

"Hi, beautiful," I said. "Will you keep me company?"

The door opened and Sam stepped in, surveying the area carefully. It would take a moment for his eyes to adjust to the dim light.

"Gee, honey," the girl said, "I'd love to stay but I'm already with a guy. I can send someone else over, though."

I held onto her hand. I had to be careful not to antagonize her and have her raise her voice.

"Just my luck," I said, smiling. "I think I've fallen in love."

She patted my hand. "Sure you have. And I love you but I gotta go."

"Geez. What could have been, huh?" I said.

Over her shoulder, I watched Sam peering about, scrutinizing the divans. His eyes would swing this way anytime.

"Can you tell me just one thing before you go?" I said, not having the slightest idea what the one thing was that I would ask about as I phrased the question. I just wanted her to stay with me as camouflage. "Tell me . . ." I groped for a question. "Tell me, is getting whipped really what it's cracked up to be?" I doubted she'd get the pun.

She laughed. "Try it sometime."

Sam was walking close to the wall but the other way. Maybe he had spotted the guy by himself that the girl was going to. If he talked to her, he'd be back to me in a hurry. But I couldn't hold her any longer. She was starting to get off the divan.

"Okay, I'll let you go," I said to the girl.

"I'll send someone," she said as she left.

I smiled and got off the divan, keeping my eye on Sam. I was trying to decide whether to go back out the way I came in or to look for another exit. But the only other one had to be from where the performers entered, a screened-off chute about twenty feet from me. Maybe when I got out of here, I'd get them on a fire-law violation.

My decision was settled when the door opened again and Brian Connolly and my former prisoner stepped in.

I stepped to the chute, hoping to get there before their eyes adjusted or Sam looked my way.

Behind the screened chute was a prop and costume area that was still actually part of the main room. Three men and two women lolled on cots. They were passing a joint around.

"Hey, Ace, what happened, you get lost?" one of the men said. "No one back here. Get your ass back out."

"Sorry," I said. I was sidling, trying to keep the .45 out of sight. Beyond them was a door. I looked at it, trying to decide.

Suddenly, I became aware of the music from the stage area. It was jungle drums this time.

I moved toward the door and when the three men came at me, I raised the .45.

"Just stay there," I said.

I pushed the door open and, instead of finding a corridor or staircase, I was in the control room for music and lighting. A wizened man, who looked like a lecherous grandfather, was peering through slits at the stage, his hands on a bank of knobs and switches.

He turned and peered at me and then focused on the .45.

I looked behind me, through the door. The three men were staring at me but one of the women was moving quickly away. Brian Connolly and his henchmen would be here in seconds.

"Can you control all the lights from here?" I said.

The man nodded dumbly, his eyes transfixed on the .45.

"Kill them all."

He continued to stare dumbly. His mouth worked a little, as if he were eating something distasteful. Or getting ready to yell.

I gestured with the .45.

"Kill all the lights. Every one." I moved toward him.

"Goddammit, do what I tell you. Kill every light on this floor."

His hands moved toward the switches. I pressed the .45 into his side and grabbed the back of his shirt high, just below the collar.

My mouth was close to his ear. His shirt smelled of stale perspiration. "Turn the music up as loud as it will go."

His hands made a couple of quick motions and I pulled him by the shirt outside the control room and shut the door.

We were in complete darkness and my ears throbbed from the amplifiers reverberating jungle drums and the confused yellings and screamings of many voices. The decibel level was extremely high.

Holding onto his shirt tightly, I pushed the frightened

old man ahead of me. I didn't want him going back and turning the lights on and I could use him as a buffer between me and obstacles.

It was as dark as a child's nightmare. No exit signs glowed. I really had them on fire-law violations.

I pushed in the direction I had come in, gauging distances.

Someone bumped into me and then bounced away. I pushed the old man's back hard, but not too hard. I didn't want him to stumble.

We had to be near the divans now. The drums were incredibly loud. It was a powerful sound system.

Bodies pressed in on me from both sides. I pushed harder and we slithered through.

I found the wall to my right and let go of the man's shirt. I put the .45 in my left hand and with my right hand against the wall, I moved toward the door. I estimated I had twenty feet to go.

I took my finger from the trigger. A bump or a stumble and the gun could fire. I was lucky it hadn't already happened.

The lights went on blindingly bright just as I was wondering whether someone would make it to the control room. The drums banged away unabated. High noon in the jungle.

The door was just ahead but as I went for it something slammed into my side and then knocked the .45 from my hand.

Spinning around, I faced Sam. He lunged at me but the move was unsophisticated and I ducked under his arms and drove my knee up. As his head came down, my right hand caught him under the nose. With a grunt, he crumpled to the floor, perhaps seriously hurt.

My ex-prisoner was rushing toward me now and would be at me before I could reach the door or get at the .25 on my calf. I waited until he was almost on me, making his move, before I parried.

Right away I knew I was in trouble. He had some training and, while I did too, I was no *summa cum laude* at the martial arts. In addition, he had an enormous size, strength, and age advantage.

Quickly, we were in a tangle, which was bad for me. He was moving for my head and a move that would break my neck. Our faces were close and I remembered an adage of training: Do what works. It doesn't have to be smooth, pretty, fair, or even masculine.

I spit hard in his eye.

It was a reflex which loosened his grip and I slithered away. But he was quick as a cat and at me again. I drove an elbow into the side of his chin, followed by a good right into his gut which nearly broke my hand, because it wasn't a gut as much as a slab of oak.

When he tried to close, I was able to get in a quick succession of blows with my feet and hands but they had no noticeable effect.

He forced me back. I hit a divan and rolled over it, obliquely aware of the heavy pulse of drums and voices.

I found my feet and sprang back. I had to get at the .25. It was my only chance but he was coming too quickly for me to reach it.

I was at the stage now, amid an oasis of plastic palm trees.

From my front, my attacker was almost on me and to my left I saw Brian Connolly leveling a revolver. Behind one of the palms, a woman screamed and irrelevantly I noticed she was blond, pretty, and nude.

When the man plowed into me, I went for the eyes, nose, throat, and groin. We crashed into the palm tree and rolled on top of the girl. She was beneath us both, her eyes showing a lot of white.

I slammed fists and fingers into what should have been vulnerable places, with what seemed little effect. All the time, he was pummeling me and I thought I was going to black out.

When he raised his head, I drove my right fist into his windpipe. He clutched his throat and I kicked him away.

We rose to our feet, stepping on soft flesh. Screaming, the girl twisted and rolled away.

Peripherally, I saw Brian Connolly coming in close, and then he was backing away, the revolver at his side.

I felt a strong hand on my arm. It was Swede.

Behind him were Inspector Gallo, Stan Janski, and four uniformed police officers spreading through the crowd.

Swede was saying something but I couldn't understand him.

Jungle drums beat against my ears.

CHAPTER

20

We sat—Moira, Swede, and I—in a friendly little restaurant in Marblehead, all oak and hanging plants. We had finished eating and were talking, the three of us nursing beers.

Last night, when he left me at Pan's Flute, Swede was unable to get Inspector Gallo at first and didn't know whether to continue trying or to come back. Now, I was glad he had waited.

"Between records Eric Lohnes kept, names from Kristin Williams's list, some of whom will talk, your tape, Moira, and Gerald Mason's testimony, there should be enough to wrap everything up," I said.

"Gerald Mason?" Moira said.

"That's the guy I was tangling with when Swede showed up. His name was on one of Kristin Williams's note cards. A real sweetheart. He killed Kristin, Darlene Abbott, Dan Ritchie, and Eric Lohnes. And nearly me. Stan Janski says Mason's willing to work a deal to save his skin. He'll talk, which means it sure looks as though the Boston Police Department will need a new lieutenant and Colton College will need a new President. Maybe I'll apply."

"Just what *was* Lieutenant Connolly's and Lloyd Markham's connection?" Moira asked. "What the hell was what?"

"I'm not sure who originated the idea for the adoption scheme, but there's an obvious market out there. Not only do you have women who can't conceive, but there are plenty who don't *want* to. They have their careers. They've waited until they're in their late thirties, early forties, and suddenly decide they want a family without the fuss and bother of a pregnancy. They can afford to pay.

"Probably it started with Brian Connolly because he would need the others and would have sought them more than they'd need him.

"As a vice cop, he had contact with prostitutes and runaways and probably started on a small scale with them, maybe originally not even dealing with particularly affluent markets.

"Obviously, it was his being a vice cop that allowed him to make connection with Dan Ritchie and Lloyd Markham and their supply of girls at Pan's Flute. Joanne

Lewis might actually have been one of the original child-bearers and I wouldn't be surprised if she was also Brian Connolly's girlfriend.

"Dan Ritchie was the link to Eric Lohnes. I'm sure they met as a result of Dan's research. Dan had used the article by Eric Lohnes in the *Oracle* as part of his bibliography. It's easy to imagine them refining the deal that already existed between Dan and Brian Connolly. Maybe the link to Lohnes was Joanne Lewis. Perhaps he was her gynecologist."

I sipped my beer. It was O'Keefe's this time.

"What I don't get," Swede said, "is why this Mason guy would kill Dr. Lohnes."

I said, "That one's easier. At least now that I've talked with Stan Janski about what Mason told him. Last night I was just guessing and trying to push him into doing something. Luckily, it turned out all right. Anyway, Mason had gone out to Dr. Lohnes's home about one of the girls he had pimped for whom Lohnes was giving prenatal care to. Actually, the girl was Mason's honey and she was bent out of shape over Lohnes's bedside manner.

"I imagine Mason's going out to the Jamaicaway must have set the good doctor off. Superfly among the Chippendales and Queen Annes. Mason said Lohnes tried to kick him out. Told him the show was over. So, through fear or anger, Mason broke his neck."

"Yeah, but why would Mason try to make it look like suicide? Why wouldn't he just take credit for saving the day, saving everyone's necks? And then wait for you. Lohnes must have told him it was you coming out to bring him to the cops. It was his chance to finally get you."

"Well, for one thing, he couldn't prove that Eric Lohnes

was going to blow the whistle. He had just killed the really important contributor to the whole scheme, and killed him in a manner that was his trademark, a broken neck. Stan Janski told me the results of the postmortem on Eric Lohnes showed his neck was already broken before he was hanged and in a manner not consistent with a drop on a rope.

"Mason knew full well whom he was dealing with in Carmen Buono and didn't want to end up buried in cement if Buono didn't believe him. Maybe he didn't wait for me because he didn't know who the hell I'd be coming out with. Maybe he just wasn't thinking straight."

"Why on earth would Eric Lohnes keep records on an illicit operation?" Moira asked.

I shrugged. "I'm sure Lohnes felt he'd have time to destroy them if he had to."

"Will the Mob come tumbling down as a result of this?" she said.

"Don't hold your breath," Swede said.

"Their connection was strictly that they took a cut and allowed the operation to continue," I said. "They controlled the girls and the joints so that anyone taking girls out of commission for nine months had to have a good explanation and a way to more than compensate for the revenue lost. Eric Lohnes got greedy when you went to him with your proposition. He figured he had a high-class independent suburban hooker not working under the auspices of the Mob. So that anything you and he worked out, he thought, was between the two of you. Money under the table for him. When I threatened to let Carmen Buono hear that tape, that's what really motivated the doctor to cooperate. More than threats of my going to the police or the press."

I took another sip of O'Keefe's. "No, there's no way you could trace the connection. Carmen Buono will be mightily pissed but hardly hurt."

I thought of Sal the Scuzz.

"Now what?" Moira said.

"Colorado. Want to come?"

My hand was damp against the phone. I had told Barbara that everything was now okay and that I'd be going out to spend some time with Nicky before bringing him home. I didn't tell her that Moira was coming with me.

The morning sun was bright in my window and Boxer lay curled on the rug, catching some rays.

"Will you have a chance to come by and see me, Nick? You know, before you go?"

What had happened that afternoon between us I now knew couldn't happen again. It wasn't worth the risk of pain to Barbara or me. Most of all, it wasn't worth the risk of losing what I had with Moira. "I don't think so, Barbara." The words were blunt and I tried to soften them. "That afternoon we had together will remain very special to me. Why don't we leave it like that?"

There was a pause, a moment's absorption and assessment.

"Give Nicky a kiss from his mom."

I checked the address in the Revere phone book and drove out and waited. I was surprised he was in the book. Cocky bastard. I got there about five in the afternoon and saw him drive in about six. Waterfront property. Ocean and sky seemed one hazy blue entity in the late afternoon sun.

At seven, he was back out, got in his Corvette, and drove off, I guessed to watch the dogs race at Wonderland. He even had the car I wanted, but a new one, not a '77 with low, one-owner miles.

As I followed, I thought of what Stan Janski had said about how people like Sal Scuzz don't worry about consequences. How people like me are bound by them.

When he stopped at a stop sign, I came up behind him and let the front of the Fairmont kiss his rear end at about three miles an hour. There was a sea wall to our right.

He pulled over and got out, anger further darkening his swarthy face.

I pulled over behind him and also got out.

I could tell he didn't recognize me. Probably intimidated so many people and broke so many limbs that the world had become one big, anonymous wimp to him.

Now, he'd get the license and registration of the asshole who dared hit his Corvette, a symbol of his own prowess, and scare the shit out of him to boot.

I crouched between the two cars, peering nervously back and forth from one to the other as if trying to assess any damage I had caused.

When he loomed over me, muttering about my low IQ and my ancestry, I stood abruptly with the .25 in my hand and pressed it into the soft spot in his throat.

"Back up," I said. "To the wall."

I checked around. No traffic was coming but that wouldn't last. At the wall, I told him to jump over and I followed. It was about six feet down to the sand. A guy and his girl lying on a blanket about seventy feet to our left took one look at us, the .25 in my hand, got up and quickly moved away.

Surprise and the .25 in my hand were my only chance against a guy like Sal Scuzz. I would like to think that I could fairly and squarely work him over and beat him to a pulp. But guys like him don't play fair either so such considerations didn't bother me about what I planned to do.

His back was to the wall and the .25 was close to his face. His eyes were focused on it and with my left hand I slammed his head against the wall.

He grunted, and as he started to collapse, I hit him hard twice in the belly. It wasn't the piece of oak Gerald Mason's had been.

I propped him up. "Look at me," I said. "Do you remember me? Fenway Park. You and one of your baboon friends put the squeeze on me. Took my son out to the bridge over the Mass Pike and told me you'd drop him over. Remember that?" His eyes couldn't seem to focus. His head must have hit the wall harder than I thought. Good. I slapped his face twice. I could smell his cologne.

"Do you remember?"

He muttered something.

"What was that?"

He nodded. "I remember."

"I know to you it was just a job. But spilling my son over the wall would have been no harder for you than swatting a fly. You think the world's one big asshole, don't you, and you're going to ream it.

"Now get this," I said. "If anything ever happened to you, a lot of people, people like cops, for instance, wouldn't give two shits. Matter of fact, they'd be goddamn happy.

"You ever come near me or my son again, I'll do my best to make them happy."

I let go of him and stood back. What I was doing probably wasn't very smart but I was in this far so I might as well punctuate it effectively for whatever satisfaction and results I hoped it would bring.

I kicked his feet out from under him and he toppled over. I reached down, grabbed his hair, and pushed his face into the sand, holding it there. Twisting.

"You better go home and take another shower," I said.

I jumped back up over the wall and got in my car. I drove past Sal Scuzz's idling Corvette to Marblehead to be with Moira.

We'd sleep well tonight and tomorrow we'd fly to Colorado.